The
Playground

Michelle Lee

This is a work of fiction. Names, characters, incidences, and places either are the product of the author's imagination or are used fictitiously.

ISBN (Print): 978-1-54399-521-3
ISBN (eBook): 978-1-54399-522-0

For Roc,

My rock.

Prologue

There are two ways to cross a moral line: Either slowly, so slowly it seems like you're standing still; or by diving over, speeding toward water without thought as to what's beneath the plunge.

Those who creep up to the line go with the flow, make decisions slowly, or don't make decisions at all. They follow. Those who dive over the line are risk-takers, money-makers, leaders.

I was never a follower.

The first time I crossed the line was when I punched Charlie Butters in the sixth grade.

For weeks, Charlie had been vying for my attention. At first, he passed me little notes: *Will you go out with me? Check Yes or No.* But I wasn't interested in the half-grown boys of Coral Cliffs Elementary School. I was saving my romantic energy for Adam Peck, who was already in eighth grade. Besides, if I were interested in such boys, it certainly would not be a tawdry, little punk like Charlie. I ignored the notes.

After my blatant snubbing, Charlie promoted attention-seeking to poking. He poked me as I walked by in the hallways or as I searched for a book in the library. I would scowl at him, "Grow up, Charlie." And he would sneer, as if the gibe had no relevance.

All of that, I could handle. Weasels like Charlie weren't going to ruin my day with notes and pokes. But Charlie really screwed up when he messed with my family.

"Where's your hat, Bran?" I asked my younger brother, as we walked toward the bus to take us home.

"Dunno," he replied diffidently.

"How do you not know?" I asked impatiently.

"Charlie took it," Robert, our other brother, chimed in.

I stopped walking and turned Bran around to face me. "Charlie took your hat?"

His lip started trembling, but not as much as my temper did.

"Stay here. Don't get on that bus," I commanded Bran and Robert.

I walked to Bus 315, lined up two buses behind ours, filed in, and made my way to the back where Charlie was turned around talking loudly to other kids. He was wearing Bran's hat.

I plucked it off his head. "You're a jerk, Charlie! Don't mess with my brothers ever again!" I shouted with as much bluster as I could conjure.

Charlie smirked with his hands up in surrender. "Okay, sorry, Anna." The boys next to him all joined the commotion with smug laughter.

I could have inched back from crossing the line then and walked away. But I didn't.

"Another thing, Charlie. The next time you want to ask me out with those stupid little notes, make sure you spell girlfriend correctly. Friend is 'i-e,' not 'e-i,' you moron."

Charlie's face turned prickly pear red and he stood up to rush me, but I punched him square in the nose before he could. Blood gushed down his face and I stammered back with a still-clenched fist; it was throbbing, but I couldn't feel the pain.

The bus driver thrust back, and the next thing I knew, I was sitting in the principal's office with my two younger brothers waiting for our parents to pick us up.

But at least Bran was wearing his hat again.

This time, the moral line I crossed felt as expansive as the Great Salt Lake. Bile rose in my throat as I sat in my office holding what I now knew was a duffel bag stuffed with cocaine.

How did I get here? I castigated myself, exhaling forcefully.

But the bag didn't find me. I replayed the steps that led me to this bag, backtracking the last seven years to when I met the man who would change the course of my life on a snowy Philadelphia day. *Yes;* it had all started then.

And I wouldn't change a minute of it.

Chapter One

I always knew my life in Utah was temporary, though I had nothing to complain about my childhood there.

I spent my days running barefoot in the red desert hills of St. George, chasing lizards and catching pollywogs in the creeks between the mountains where we would go to escape the 120^0F summer days. Then, my three closest friends and I—two sisters and an awkward girl named Mickey—would drag our dirty bodies home, where we'd separate to scavenge for loose change between couch cushions, car floors, and drawer bottoms. When, among the four of us, we had gathered 50 cents ($1 on a good day), we'd walk the mile to the Market to buy as much penny candy as we could manage with our couch finds.

One day, as we played M.A.S.H. under the shade of a trampoline, the girls giggled as my fortune resolved that "when I grew up" I would live in an apartment in a city, work as a dog walker, marry Matt Tines, and birth 100 children.

"Ew, Matt Tines?!" Rebecca threw her head back with a gag.

Angie frowned. "At least if you had to marry Matt, you'd be lucky enough to live on the beach!"

"Or live in a mansion," Mickey added.

But I didn't feel sad about my fortune because it contained what was paramount to my future: Living in a city. Since our school project on skyscrapers, I had become obsessed with a whole new world full of concrete and steel, crowded streets, and people who seemingly had purpose.

I itched for city life: Bigger, faster, and full of opportunities.

I made it as far as Salt Lake City after college. And though I was still inside the walls of Utah, Salt Lake seemed like a metropolis compared with the desert hills of St. George. I landed a job at a global bank working in a niche department for special clients. It was here that I would overhear the 14 words that would finally offer the way out.

"How am I going to find someone to move to Philadelphia in six weeks?" a senior vice president mumbled as he walked past my cubicle one October morning.

"I will!" I blurted.

He pivoted. "Anna, right?"

"Yes, sir," I replied.

"You don't know what the job entails. But you're willing to go, just like that?"

"Yes, sir."

I didn't jump at this opportunity; I plunged.

Chapter Two

I stepped onto Chestnut Street and was instantly immersed in the sounds and smells of Philadelphia: Taxis honking their horns; the weighty footsteps of horse-drawn carriages clopping tourists through cobbled streets; and the smell of soft pretzels, cheesesteaks, and coffee wafting from vending trucks. I could hear the street lights changing colors and feel the surge of energy that followed with accelerating cars and people rushing across the street. *People with purpose,* I thought.

I was headed to my interview with Kahn & Hague, a client my bank had been servicing for a decade. My body buzzed with excitement to be standing on the same streets as Benjamin Franklin and George Washington.

I continued to observe the city as I walked to the Kahn & Hague building, curious about the people fulfilling their morning routines. There was a man in a dirty jacket sitting on the marble steps of an old stone building, throwing crumbs from a paper bag to a flock of pigeons. I wondered if he considered these pigeons his friends: The interaction appeared ritualistic.

A woman with oversized sunglasses walked her baby in an

aerodynamic contraption of a stroller. She didn't have the dewy new-mother look I was accustomed to seeing in Utah. She seemed rushed and miserable, and in pursuit of strong coffee.

And my eye caught on a man wearing a leather jacket standing precariously between adjacent brick buildings. He was short, almost boy-short, though he was clearly not a boy. As he lit a cigarette, he shuffled his feet as though he were standing on something hot. The conversation with a tall man whose back was to me ended abruptly, and the boy-man ducked off in the opposite direction.

I thought contentedly: *City Life.*

Standing in the birthplace of America's freedom, I couldn't help but feel that perhaps Philadelphia also would become the birthplace of mine.

My meeting was with Benoit Massenet.

Benoit was a key director from the Paris office. He reported to Kahn & Hague's acting CEO, so surely had a name to make for himself. Which meant he'd be looking for something specific during this interview.

I had prepared for the interview with research and readiness to address an international corporate superstar. The former didn't concern me: I excelled at my job, although I was still somewhat junior. But the latter did: I had been prepped for the interview with guidance that Benoit was "very European." I didn't know what being *very European* meant. My cultural experiences were limited growing up in a small desert town. We had an Indian girl join our school in ninth grade: On occasions that she dressed in a full saree, we would pet her as she walked by like she was an exotic peacock.

As I waited on the top floor of the Kahn & Hague building, a drab eyesore of aluminum lattice and concrete—nothing like the skyscrapers of my dreams—I tapped my foot on the leg of the veneered conference table and ran numbers over in my head.

The door opened and Bob Linden walked in. Bob was in Procurement and worked for Benoit two management layers down. Bob was nondescript, like the extra in a movie who was cast as a stand-in for any average white male actor in his mid-forties. He was medium everything.

"You must be Anna!" Bob said, jovially.

"Hi, Bob. Thank you for meeting with me today." For small talk, I added as sincerely as I could muster, "This building is remarkable."

"This building is obnoxious," Bob sneered. His smile also was medium, but genuine. I liked him immediately. "Benoit will be here shortly. How do you like Philadelphia?"

"This is my first time here. I haven't had much time to explore, but I like what I've seen so far."

"Have you had a cheesesteak yet?" he asked.

As I started to respond, the door swung open and in swept a tall, attractive man with brown manicured hair and a beautifully tailored gray suit. An inaudible gasp caught in my throat as he closed the door behind him and nodded to Bob, whose demeanor markedly changed. An imperceptible pause swept over Benoit's face before he extended his bronzed hand out to me, the peek of his French cuff revealing a fleur-de-lis cufflink. "You must be Anna."

I shook his hand. "It's a pleasure to meet you." Benoit was much more magnetizing in person than he was in his corporate photo; it was hard not to be instantly sucked into his presence.

"Thank you for coming to Philadelphia from…Utah, I believe?" Benoit asked. "I understand you are here about the prospect of consulting on our cash management practices. Forgive me for being curt, but since you're already privy to some of Kahn & Hague's payables data, tell me what value you could bring to us by being dedicated to our account here in Philadelphia."

"Mr. Massenet…" I began.

"Call me Benoit."

"Benoit." I caught a trifling of an upward curl in his lips.

"Kahn & Hague has been a customer for nine years," I continued, "with a rebate basis point of .65 in your commercial card spend, which equivocates to roughly $300,000 per quarter back to your business as a rebate. As I dove into your actual spend, however, I realized we only are capturing your *travel* spend. If you were to reallocate your purchasing spend—specifically, the raw materials—it would be four times as much as travel, thereby giving you an extra $1.2 million in rebate per quarter.

"And this is only one area of spend. I have identified three others, which add another $2.1 million in rebates. If given a chance to analyze your full payables, I am confident I could find a significant amount more."

Benoit's expression stayed the same. I could tell I got his attention, but it wasn't enough. What was he looking for?

"And once you've identified these areas of savings and rebates, how do you execute the plan?" He did not change his position or tone.

"My first step would be to work directly with Accounts Payable to strategize on payment terms. One large area of interest that often gets overlooked is the use of credit cards for everyday payables, ones you would typically issue a check for. It can extend your payment terms by 30, sometimes up to 90, days. The interest made on the money for the extended payment terms could be quite significant. Not to mention the rebates you'll earn on the card spend. Second, I'd work with Treasury to analyze your debt terms. I'm only aware of the debt you hold with our bank. But if you'd allow me to, under full nondisclosure of course, I can look at the terms across the board and determine where it might make sense to consolidate or shift your debt. Debt management, again, in my opinion, is often a game that needs delicate handling. After that, we'd move on to managing terms in contracts and investing cash flow appropriately."

Benoit's eyes narrowed the slightest bit, as if amused. "I have a treasury team, a very large one, that is supposed to be doing all of this."

"True. Most companies do. But in my experience, even the departments meant to have a wide reach typically end up working in silos. The advantage to bringing in someone from the outside is that I have no loyalty to any one department. My only loyalty lies in making and saving you money, which in turn, of course, makes my bank money," I smiled tenuously.

"And how will I know if you're succeeding?" Benoit probed.

"I'll provide you with weekly and monthly reports, and to Bob of course," I added, remembering that Bob was in the room. "I'll prepare a quarterly presentation. Whatever you need to see the measure of my success. I'll give you a report each day if you'd like."

He remained in the same position in which he started the

conversation, with the same facial expression and tone, staring as if we were in a Western fast-draw.

"Why are you interested in this?" Benoit asked. "What are you gaining by coming here?"

"Opportunity," I said matter-of-factly.

"Opportunity?" he smiled briefly. "I'm not convinced that you understand how much work this will be if you achieve all that you've laid out to me today. The groups here can be slow to take to change, and even slower to helping it along once they've taken to it. I'm not an extraordinarily patient man, so I'd expect results quickly, especially with the fee required to get you here."

I blinked quickly. I knew this move would mean a promotion, but we hadn't finalized my new salary. I was glad to have the knowledge now that the bank was charging a substantial fee for my services: I'd surely use that to negotiate.

"So, does this still sound like an opportunity to you, Anna?"

I smiled confidently. "Opportunity is missed by most people because it is dressed in overalls and looks like work."

I saw for the first time a hint of warmth in Benoit's eyes. "I'm not sure I follow."

"Thomas Edison said that," I recited, then remembered Benoit was French. "The American inventor. I'm sure you know that. I just mean that I find the reward far greater if it took hard work to obtain."

His eyes narrowed into a smirk. "Thomas Edison. He invented the lightbulb?"

I nodded, embarrassed. *Why had I brought up Thomas Edison?*

"He met with Gustave Eiffel during the construction of the Eiffel Tower, if I recall French history correctly," he added.

I countered, surprised. "He did. In his secret apartment."

We exchanged a look that could have been confused as flirting. And perhaps it was: Benoit clearly had read my resume, and was playing off my minor in American History.

Benoit stood up from the table and we followed. "I must run to another meeting, but I think this will be a good fit for you, Anna. Can you be here before the holidays?"

"Absolutely. Thank you. I really look forward to working with you."

Benoit nodded to Bob, then turned to shake my hand. "Me, too." Before letting go, he glanced at my left hand, then left.

"Well, if that wasn't the fastest interview I've ever witnessed!" Bob chaffed.

As we gathered our belongings, a mixture of relief and excitement hummed through my belly. There was another sensation I tried to temper with professionalism and reason; the nuisance of a flutter.

Benoit had looked at my left hand for a wedding ring. I was sure of it.

Chapter Three

Six weeks later as autumn fleeted and winter loomed, I packed up my life in Utah, including my Lab-sized mutt, Polo, and moved it into an apartment in Philadelphia's Old City district, one mile from the Kahn & Hague building.

"You sure you'll be okay?" I had asked my parents as I sat on the couch with them before leaving. My mother shared the same tired expression she had for as long as I could remember, though since Dad's accident, the lines ran deeper. Her hands had the gnarled wear of one who works three jobs.

My dad reached his thin hand out and I squeezed it tenderly. "Of course we'll be okay," he said in a sure voice. My mother's languid nod concurred.

"I can't wait for you to come visit," I said. But we all knew they wouldn't be visiting any time soon, if ever. One consolation was that my move to Philadelphia came with a two-level promotion and a substantial pay increase, which meant I could send money home to help with some expenses. I'd love to help Mom quit that waitressing job.

It was just before Christmas, and I had three free days between my last working day in Utah and my first working day in Philadelphia. I put off unpacking, and instead took Polo out to explore the city. The city was laced with lit snowflakes, bustling patrons, and plumes of sugar and cinnamon.

I routed my walk to the Kahn & Hague building, timing how long it would take and which streets to avoid. I noted the coffee shops along the route and took pleasure trying each barista's version of soy chai latte before choosing the one that would become my regular. I found a little grocery store and stocked up on a few essential items.

My first evening in Philadelphia, I met Kam. A tall, shiny-skinned black man sat smoking a cigarette on the patio I shared with my upstairs neighbors as I arrived back at my apartment with Polo. With a wide grin, he exclaimed, "You must be our new neighbor!" He held the gate open while I walked in.

"Yes, I'm Anna."

"I am Kam!" he exclaimed with a loud, deep, smooth, accented voice that I couldn't place.

"Pleasure to meet you, Kam. You live upstairs?"

"Yes, me and Angelique," he said, staccato-like. "You will meet her. You will love her. As long as you're not offended by loud, temperamental Lithuanian women, that is." He laughed at his comment, clapping his hands together loudly before taking an elegant drag of his cigarette. I couldn't stop staring at how beautiful his skin was.

"Who is this, then?" he asked, holding his hands out to Polo.

Polo lurched eagerly for Kam to scratch his ears. Polo playfully growled and jumped up on Kam, who took his front paws and bear-hugged him.

"This is Polo," I laughed.

"You must come for dinner. Both of you," he said. "Thursday night. It is my night off. We are having some friends over. It will be a welcome to the neighborhood party, although none of our neighbors will be there. I can't say Angelique and I win on being social. Not here at least."

I knew the feeling. I worked too much to be social. "I look forward to it."

I said goodnight, and Polo said goodbye with a lick to Kam's hand. I couldn't help but feel like an astronaut who just found life on another planet: I had made a friend in a foreign place, and it made me feel as high as the moon.

My first day at Kahn & Hague arrived. Bob Linden walked me to my desk.

"Hope you're adjusting to Philadelphia?" Bob asked nervously as we strolled past cubicles in the center of the floor; large offices lined the perimeter. He stopped in front of a small office on one of the inner walls. "This is you."

I hid my surprise at being granted an office, a real office with a name plaque outside the door. It was windowless and had paint the color of gravy, but it was an office, and it was mine.

"It's perfect."

"Great, well, uh, if you need anything, Cyndi can order you supplies or whatnot." He pointed to a woman typing at a cubicle.

"I think I can manage. I had most of my stuff shipped. Is it here?"

I looked around, then noticed my two boxes sitting on the floor beside my desk.

"Okay then, I'll let you be. IT should be sending someone to set up your passwords and all that. Oh, and I almost forgot: I asked a colleague, Kelly, to show you around Philly today. Like a little tour, I guess," Bob shrugged.

"That sounds great. Thanks Bob."

Bob left. I picked up one of the boxes and started taking out items, putting them in their new spots. A young man with piercings came to set up my networks, and I spent the day settling in.

Kelly Malan poked her head into my office around 1 pm. She was my age, mid-20s, attractive, with short, white-blonde hair and blue eyes. She was wearing a black lace top with a black skirt and red heels. "Hey. I'm Kelly. You're Anna?" she asked as she stood in my doorway.

"Yeah, I'm Anna. Nice to meet you, Kelly. Bob tells me you got the shit job of taking the new girl around town?"

"Shit job? No! This got me out of a meeting that made me want to stick a steak knife in my eye. Ready?" Kelly tapped the side of the door.

I laughed as I grabbed my coat and purse.

Kelly and I took the elevator to the B2 floor, which required a special badge to access, two stories underground. A parking attendant met us off the elevator. Kelly gave him a white card and he disappeared around the corner. Moments later, screeching tires echoed off the walls and the headlights of a small white minivan with a Kahn & Hague door logo appeared and slowed to a park in front of us.

Kelly snorted. "I haven't driven in three years and they give me a minivan? This will be fun."

We got into the minivan and exited the parking lot to a cold, but sunny Philadelphia day.

"You haven't driven in three years?" I asked. "Is it because you just don't like driving?" In Utah, if you didn't drive, usually it was because you lost your license for a reason that you were not proud of.

"Nah, my fiancé and I have lived in the city for four years. Three years ago, our car broke down and we didn't bother getting a new one. Haven't missed it. Everything we need is a walk or train ride away. By the way, that's the department store they filmed *Mannequin* in," Kelly said while pointing to a beautiful white building with a grand entrance. "The other big white building ahead is City Hall."

"Who's that statue on top of City Hall?" I asked.

"I actually don't know. I'm from Pittsburgh and I hate history. I'm seriously the worst person to give you a tour. But Bob insisted, saying I was the only person at Kahn & Hague who was close to your age. The people there are fucking dinosaurs."

I laughed as she rounded the turn next to City Hall. I knew the statue was William Penn, founder of Philadelphia, but I wasn't about to reveal that, or that I loved history and read historical biographies for fun. I was hoping to make my second friend in Philadelphia and being a straight-A new kid didn't seem likely to win people over.

"Where do you and your fiancé live?" I asked.

"In the Art Museum District. We'll drive by. Are you living down-town? Or somewhere else?"

"I have an apartment on Front and Callowhill." I shrugged my shoulders as if to say *I don't know if that's bad or good?*

"Oh, in Old City. I like Old City. Great bar down there called Mission Fig. They have good live music—not novice crap—good acoustic artists. The bartender is good there, too, Jason. And he's beautiful. Like Johnny Depp-beautiful."

"I'll keep that in mind," I smiled.

"The men in this city are going to love you." She scanned my body indifferently. "You don't look like a typical Philadelphian." *Whatever that meant.* "That's not a bad thing, by the way," she continued. "You just have more of an exotic look. That's not your real hair color, right?"

I grabbed at a strand of my hair. "No, I highlight it."

Something about Kelly made me feel instantly comfortable; her vibe was warm and genuine. She seemed the type who wasn't interested in frivolous gossip or weekend friends. I was somewhat of a loner in Utah by design and even the friends I had were not great friends. They were boring and prudish and mostly married.

"What does that mean anyway, Old City? Is that a good part of the city to live in?" I asked.

"Oh yeah. Old City is a little more artsy. Less commercial. It's the more historic part of Philadelphia, where all the old history people lived, like the lady who made the flag." *Betsy Ross*, I said in my head.

"Then there's Center City," she rambled, "which is where all the yuppies live among the skyscrapers. Center City, especially the Rittenhouse area, is where you'll find all your bankers, lawyers, and CEOs. So if that's what you're into, go there for drinks. You'll get to know the different neighborhoods as you learn the city."

I was eager to be as educated about these neighborhoods as Kelly was. I wanted to know this city intimately and be *from somewhere.*

"Thing about Philly," she said, "is that it's not a city that screams, 'Welcome, I'm Philadelphia and I'm here to embrace you!' It's more of a town that you have to get to know. It's like playing a board game with no directions or rules. You have to figure it out, but once you do, it's your favorite game."

I appreciated the insight. I also appreciated the challenge: Philadelphia playing hard to get? I loved this game.

Chapter Four

I spent my first six weeks in Philadelphia with my head in the books, or more accurately, my laptop, which I worked on for about 12 hours a day.

The other four waking hours I spent eating and exploring the city with Polo. I took advantage of every invite, though scarce, that I received to socialize. I went to dinner at Kam and Angelique's on the Thursday night I was invited, and twice again. I learned that Kam, short for Klenam, was from Ghana, and he met Angelique in Atlantic City; he as a blackjack dealer, she as a dancer. I didn't pry into what kind of dancer, but later learned an exotic one. Most of their friends were Lithuanian or Russian, and every Thursday night, Angelique cooked authentic Lithuanian dishes. Fried breads, beetroot soup, potato pancakes, and other strong smells of spices and vegetables later wafted into my apartment.

I enjoyed Kam and Angelique and was grateful for my first glimpse into Eastern European culture. But I quickly realized I would not be an every-Thursday guest, as I limited the flow of conversation when everyone had to stop to translate to English for me. Kam and Angelique also had a volatile relationship. At least once a week, I would hear them screaming at each other, loud banging of objects hitting walls and floors, or sometimes thrown out of the window to the shared patio. The fights usually ended with Kam storming out, lighting a cigarette after slamming the door, and walking off saying loudly, "These fucking Lithuanian women! They breathe fire like dragons!" A couple of hours later, soft footsteps up the stairs, followed shortly by the hard banging of the headboard and loud moans of make-up lovemaking.

A more promising relationship was budding with Kelly. Kelly was in Logistics and hated her job and her boss. She got easily overwhelmed and would send me an instant message: *Coffee?* At least two to three times per day. At Kahn & Hague, there were no rules about lunches or breaks, or how often, or how long you could take them. I was a contractor, and not bound to Kahn & Hague's rules anyway; and working 12 hours a day, I allowed myself the indulgent coffee breaks.

Kelly and I built a good rapport during those coffee breaks. She asked me daily if I had gotten laid yet; and liked to joke that someone as pretty as me shouldn't get out of practice.

"It's just not a good look," Kelly advised. "Men know when women aren't getting laid and they stay away from things other men don't want. It's like having a really nice steak sitting on the counter that everyone is walking past: It could be the best steak, but if everyone's walking past it, you aren't going to be the douchebag to try it."

I laughed Kelly off, but knew she was right. The longer I went without nurturing the part of my soul that needed intimacy, the less I'd need it. And I didn't come all this way to live the same life in a different place.

I sat at my desk pounding my frozen thighs as if they were thawing chicken breasts from the one-mile walk in the coldest weather I had ever endured. While defrosting, I received a meeting notification on my Kahn & Hague calendar from Benoit Massenet. A wave of excitement and anxiety rolled through me.

The subject read, "Review of Progress & Q1 Plan" and was scheduled for the following day. I scrolled to see the invitees and was surprised that Bob was not invited, nor anyone else. I hadn't seen Benoit since my initial interview, which wasn't abnormal, considering I mostly reported to Bob, and Bob reported to Jeff, who quasi-reported to Suzanne, who reported to Benoit. That, and the fact that Benoit had been in Paris, or somewhere overseas, for the majority of the time that I had been at Kahn & Hague.

It was evident that Benoit was back in Philadelphia. People's desks were cleared of old coffee mugs and scattered papers. The women wore more blush and sat up straighter. The men seemed to talk louder and walk faster, with purpose. For once, I felt like I wasn't the only person in the building who worked 12 hours a day and actually gave a shit about my job.

But I was a bit nervous for a couple of reasons. First, it had taken me weeks to get the data I needed; every person I requested reports from treated my request as optional, with no relative urgency. I requested access to Kahn & Hague's accounting system, which took 12 days to get, and ran most of the reports myself. The time lost put me back on my plan by two weeks, and I had worked furiously to make it up.

Second, the invite was for 4:00 p.m. End-of-day meetings were usually reserved for items of little importance, such as planning a holiday party or handing out bonuses. The other obvious reason to schedule an end-of-day meeting was to fire someone. It was always after a 4:00 p.m. meeting that someone came out of the conference room, escorted by a manager, to pack up his desk. My stomach flipped at the thought.

I accepted the invitation and began strategizing on how to present my progress to Benoit. My fingers worked nimbly between keyboard and mouse as I organized the data. Three hours later, I had a completed presentation that I sent to the local print shop for five bound copies to be picked up at 8:00 a.m. the next morning—plenty of time for rework, if needed. I realized it was past lunchtime, but I didn't feel hungry, so I sent an IM to Kelly for a coffee break.

We headed out into the frigid winter streets toward Lore's Coffee Shop, walking slowly to avoid patches of ice on the sidewalks beneath underpasses where sunlight doesn't reach.

"I have a meeting with Benoit tomorrow," I said.

"With Benoit? It must be an important meeting if Benoit is attending."

"Actually, Benoit scheduled the meeting."

"Who's going to be there?" Kelly asked.

"From the looks of it, just me and him. It's in his office. I printed extra copies of the presentation in case other people show up."

Kelly stopped walking and turned to me. "Wait a minute. It's just you and Benoit?"

"From what I can tell, yes. I didn't see any other attendees in the invitation." I could feel my palms getting hot. "What, Kelly? You're making me nervous."

"I just don't get why he would schedule it with just you two. Maybe you're getting fired. Have you made any progress since being here?"

Her statement confirmed my fears. "Of course I've made progress. I mean, we haven't implemented any of my suggestions, but they knew that my first six weeks were going to be exploratory. I have to crunch numbers before I can formulate a plan of action. I gave Bob my plan when I started!"

"Calm down. Worrying might give you a wrinkle. Then what would you do?"

"Seriously, Kelly. I don't know why he called the meeting. Maybe I should have been updating him more since I started. I just figured Bob was sending him the updates I was providing…." I was in unfamiliar territory of feeling unprepared, or even worse, perceived as being useless.

"Nah. I'm sure it's exactly what it seems – a progress meeting. Maybe he needs to forecast some Q1 numbers. Everyone is doing that right now. Just wear your black skirt with the zipper and everything will be fine."

I laughed perplexedly. "I hardly see how that's relevant to this conversation."

"It's very relevant. He'll be so distracted by your skirt that it won't matter what you say," she said matter-of-factly.

"Jesus, Kelly."

"What?" She grinned. "You really should know better by now than to ask for my advice."

Chapter Five

Ten minutes before our meeting, I took a deep breath, scooped up the presentations, and walked across the rows of cubicles to the perimeter wall of offices with a view. Benoit's door was closed, so I took a seat in one of the waiting chairs outside his office.

Minutes passed as I tapped my foot impatiently in the air, admiring the rock studs on my new heels, which, in keeping with Kelly's ridiculous logic, went perfectly with my black skirt with the gold zipper.

Finally, the door slung open and a man in a brown suit walked backward as he said goodbye to Benoit, who was following him out.

"I'll see you this weekend, then," Brown-suit said as he turned and shot me an inattentive glance. Then, as if he saw something surprising, he quickly looked back at me with both eyebrows raised. Realizing the need to compensate for his double-take: "It's sure cold in Philly today, huh?"

I winced at his awkward cover-up. "It's cold, yes."

I caught him smiling broadly at Benoit out of the corner of my eye as he walked away and thought I couldn't see him.

Benoit stood in the doorway with both hands in the pockets of his perfectly tailored navy suit. A flutter pulsed through me. Nerves, I told myself. But if it wasn't nerves, it was because Benoit looked like he crawled out of a *GQ* magazine and walked straight onto the cover of *Forbes.*

"Benoit, it's a pleasure to see you again."

He didn't move as he stared at me with a calm and poised half-smile. His eyes were remarkably blue against the white winter sky that illuminated through his broadly windowed office.

I wasn't sure if his nonresponsiveness was a ploy to intimidate me, or if he was deep in thought. Regardless, it irritated me. "Shall we start?" I gestured toward his office.

"Are you thirsty?" he asked in the same glib way someone might ask *do you know what time it is?*

I stuttered at the unexpected question. "Uh, no, thanks, I'm fine."

"I just flew into Philly last night and have been in meetings all day. I'm thirsty and would like to get out of here early," he said casually. "Join me for a drink."

My mouth parted slightly. *Is he kidding me?* I prepared tirelessly on this presentation, sweating over the intentions of this meeting, wondering if it would be my last day consulting for Kahn & Hague, and he wanted to get a cocktail? I didn't know if I should be relieved or offended, or maybe flattered? I allayed the latter thought with a gulp.

"Uh," I stammered. "I'm sorry, but I thought we were having a meeting to..." I was losing my train of thought. "...to go over progress and Q1 projections."

"We can still discuss all of that over drinks. A happy hour meeting, if that's okay with you, of course." A hint of amusement wrinkled the corners of his eyes.

Benoit's invitation confused me: It was a professional invite that seemed less than professional. Happy hour meetings were common practice in banking, but they usually were meant to build relationships in an informal setting, not to go over detailed presentations. Perhaps I misinterpreted the invitation, both of them. Either way, as he stood in the doorway with his confident smirk and glowing eyes, I couldn't find a reason not to go to a happy hour meeting with Benoit.

"I could use a drink, I suppose," I said warily.

The second full smile I'd seen spread across his face. "I'll grab my coat; let's go now."

"I'll need a minute to gather my things," I said. "I'll meet you in the lobby in 10 minutes?"

He swiveled around. "I can wait for you up here; I don't mind. I can meet you at your office."

Meet me at my office? A colleague would meet me in the lobby. A date would meet me at my door. Don't be ridiculous, I assured myself. This was a happy hour meeting.

"I'll meet you in the lobby in 10."

The elevator door opened with hesitation, as if mimicking its passenger.

Benoit stood waiting with one hand in his pocket, the other hand holding a briefcase, looking nearly regal.

"So, where to?" I asked.

"We'll go two blocks south, Fourth and Chestnut." He drew his scarf tight around his chin. "You're okay to walk in those heels?"

"I could walk to Ohio in these heels."

He smiled approvingly and put his hand out to gesture I lead the way.

The sky was starting to shade with the early winter sunset. Street lights created shadows on the icy pavement as we walked. Cars whirred past with the occasional thud of a tire hitting a pothole. The air was still; the stillness that preceded snow when the weather froze in time while the clouds brewed.

"Right in here." He motioned toward a low-lit restaurant with a large window facing the street. The sign was made of old wood, and the paint had faded over the raised letters: La Castagne.

Benoit opened the door for me, and a wave of warmth welcomed us into a small dining room with no more than a dozen tables. A thin, aged man with wiry hair rushed over to greet us. Upon seeing Benoit: "Ah, Benoit! Ciao! Where have you been for so long?"

"Hello Alfonso," Benoit said in a comfortable tone. "I just got back. This is Anna." He gestured toward me.

I smiled genially, confused by the familiarity of their interaction.

"Welcome, Anna!" Alfonso pronounced in a thick, Italian accent as he raised his hands, grabbed both my shoulders, and kissed one cheek, then the other. "What a beauty you are!" He looked sideways at Benoit and lifted both eyebrows. "Come, I have your table ready!"

Alfonso showed us to a table with a lit votive candle and a single red rose. "Will you have your usual wine, Benoit?"

"Anna, would you care to join me?" Benoit asked. "It's a Bordeaux that Alfonso keeps for me. It is happy hour, after all," he added.

"Uh, sure, I'll do the same," I said.

I raised one eyebrow. "I take it you've been here before?"

"I stay at the hotel across the street when I'm in Philadelphia," he said casually. "Alfonso takes care of me when I'm in town."

Alfonso returned with a bottle of wine, two glasses, and a menu, although the latter wasn't necessary. "Alfonso, bring us some plates to share, whatever you choose is fine," said Benoit confidently.

Then he toasted: "To your first Philadelphia winter, Anna. May you fare better in the snow than actual Philadelphians do."

I smiled confidently. "Of all things to hold me up, it will not be a little snow, I assure you." We clinked our glasses gently and took a sip of wine. The wine was delicious; ripe, both sweet and bitter, and velvety. I let it sit on my tongue for a long moment before swallowing.

I still couldn't gauge where to take the conversation. It was becoming increasingly obvious that Benoit wasn't interested in talking about business, but I was eager to make sense of his intentions of bringing me to this not-so-happy-hour spot.

"Benoit, I've prepared a detailed presentation of the things I've been working on to share with you today, if you're interested in that now? Or is another time better?" I paused politely while he took another sip of wine.

"I am interested, eventually." he answered in a relaxed, controlled way. "But I'm enjoying this glass of wine and your company for now." He looked at his two-color gradient Rolex. "Just for an hour or so?"

I swallowed down a knot of surprise that had lodged in my throat. "Of course." My face was surely a mixture of just-saw-a-ghost and holy-shit-my-thighs-are-getting-hot. I took another sip of wine to compose myself.

"So, you're originally from Paris?" I asked, then added, "I don't hear much of an accent."

"Yes, I'm originally from Paris, but my mother is American. She's from upstate New York, near Lake George. We spent a lot of summers at the lake with my grandparents. My Dad is, you can probably guess, French, but we only spoke English in the home. I also went to Oxford. I guess a combination of those things helped with my English."

I was intrigued and wanted to know more. As we enjoyed the small feast Alfonso had laid out, Benoit told me about his mother, who home-schooled him and his sister, Eloise. His father was an architect, although according to Benoit, not a very good one. Conversation flowed as easily as the wine, and the need for clear direction of the night was lessening by the glassful.

"Your mom must be an amazing woman to have home-schooled you into Oxford," I marveled.

Melancholy swept over his face. He reached for his wine and took a long draw. "Indeed, as a woman and as a teacher. But my mother died two days before I received my acceptance letter," he said while distracting himself with a bite.

My stomach lurched; I knew exactly how it felt to say something so poignant in a frivolous way, as though it happens to everyone. When my dad got into his accident the summer before I was supposed to go to college, I waved off the sympathetic smiles when I announced I was going to an in-state college, instead of a big-city one.

"I am so sorry," I said, and I meant it. "And your sister, Eloise? And your father?" I asked, knowing the domino effect such things had on a family.

"My father took it the hardest. He started drinking, a lot. I took over the rest of my sister's schooling, enough for her to pass the tests for her basic education, after which point, she decided to go to culinary school."

"And did Eloise finish culinary school?" I asked, warmly picturing Benoit home-schooling his younger sister.

"Yes, she did. She runs a little patisserie in Paris." The way he said "patisserie" made my legs surge with heat. I reached for my glass of wine, which was almost empty. Benoit grabbed the bottle to fill it and we watched with disappointment as the wine fell to a slow drip, leaving it short of a proper pour. "Another bottle?"

We already had loosened up from sharing the first bottle; our movements had become relaxed, our words spilled easily. I had noticed his tanned forearms and the peek of his chest through his shirt, and I knew that another bottle of wine would lead me to become more brazen. *What the hell*, I reasoned boldly, as I stared at Benoit's chiseled jaw line.

"Absolutely," I said. "Just for the sake that poor Alfonso doesn't keep French wine in his Italian restaurant in vain."

Benoit laughed; his entire face yielding a blue warmth as reassuring as a blanket on a cold night. I wanted to hear him laugh again.

As if Alfonso was listening from the other room, he appeared with another bottle of wine. Benoit and I stared at each other as Alfonso removed the cork with a brief hiss, then filled our glasses. A hundred questions hung in the air between us.

"Your turn to make the toast." Benoit lifted his glass. We had both leaned over the table, our elbows resting gently.

I gave a congenial nod. Though Benoit seemed reluctant to state his intentions of the evening, I had decided to subtly state mine. I paused and glanced down at his shirt, picturing unbuttoning just a couple of buttons. "To getting to know each other," I said. "Better."

His eyes didn't blink as an aroused smile unfurled, then he clinked my glass and we both sipped the fumy new wine, our gaze remaining unbroken.

"Anna, I—" he started to say, but Alfonso appeared with dessert, and a distracted look out the window.

"The snow is starting to fall now, you see?" Alfonso pointed.

Benoit and I looked out to see large, fluffy flakes floating down, the kind I caught on my tongue as a little girl. I had a moment of panic. What time was it? Polo – I needed to walk him, and feed him. And how was I going to walk home in my heels in this snow?

"Are you okay?" Benoit sensed my panic.

"I didn't realize how late it was getting," I exasperated, fumbling with my napkin as if looking for car keys. "I have to let my dog out. I didn't bring boots to get home, which is no big deal, I'll grab a cab, but—"

He stopped me mid-sentence, reached over the table, and grabbed my hand. "No worries. We'll go take care of your dog." He turned to Alfonso. "Can you make the dessert 'to go' please?"

"Ah, molto bene!" Alfonso said as he hurried toward the curtain.

We'll go take care of your dog? Did I hear him correctly? *We?* In a million years, I couldn't have seen today ending with Benoit and I walking Polo. And dessert 'to go'? It was time for me to make sense of this meeting, or date, or whatever this was.

"Benoit, I don't want this to sound…" I hesitated, "like I haven't had a wonderful time tonight, because I have," I smiled. "But I'm wondering why exactly did you ask me here tonight?"

He stared at me seriously; I could see words forming behind his eyes, but I couldn't read them. He reached his other hand over the table and took both my hands in his. A lusty sigh escaped me.

"I asked you here tonight because you are the first woman who has literally taken my breath away."

I gasped.

"When I first saw you at the interview, I just…." He stopped. "I couldn't stop noticing how beautiful you were. And then you spoke, and you were smart, too. Very smart."

I bit my lip to temper the thrum in my chest.

"I thought about you when I left for Paris," he said. "I wanted to see you again when I got back to Philadelphia. I know I should've just asked you to dinner, but I didn't know if that would seem too forward. And honestly," he shifted uncomfortably, "I didn't know if I would feel the same way seeing you again. But when I walked out of my office today and saw you standing there," he said nervously, "asking you for a drink was the only thing I could think to do."

He thought about me in Paris? I stared at his face, so sincere and serious. A gamut of emotions were stuck somewhere in a panty inhale.

"Let's get out of here." I said.

Benoit smiled, surprised, "Yes?"

"Yeah."

Benoit signed the check, grabbed my hand, and led me swiftly toward the door. When we stepped onto the sidewalk, my heels sank in the snow, coldness spilling into the bare of my feet. I gasped, and without thought, Benoit scooped me up.

I squealed between gusty laughs. He was laughing, too, as he stared at me in his arms. We went quiet, the glittery snowflakes falling like powdered sugar. I leaned in close to his face, stopping just before our lips touched, our heady breath smoking in the cold air between us. He closed the gap to kiss me longingly. The kiss was as sincere and honest as he was, and we were lost in the heat of it. We finally broke away, smiling at each other.

"Let's get a cab. To your place? To take care of your dog, of course," he said in a low voice, staring at my lips.

I sealed his suggestion with another kiss.

Chapter Six

F ive minutes later, the cab pulled up to my apartment.

I could hear Polo inside the door, his collar jingling to the rhythm of his wagging tail. I grabbed the lapels of Benoit's jacket and pulled him close. He wrapped his arms around my waist, and we looked at each other breathlessly before diving into another kiss, which started slowly, but hurriedly turned feverish. His lips crawled down my neck and into my chest as my head drew back with a groan. Suddenly, Polo barked and scared us both into a laughing fit.

"Hi, old boy!" Benoit crouched down to pet Polo, who was swirling, enjoying the rubs from this side, then the other. I shook my head and shrugged, "Meet Polo."

I closed the door behind us, strategizing how to balance my domestic dog-mom duties with the desire to take Benoit straight to my bedroom. "I'm going to put on some boots to let Polo out; you stay here. Do you know how to make a fire?" I asked.

Benoit tipped his head with an *are you serious?* smirk. He started toward the fireplace in the living room, but I stopped him before he reached it. "Not that one."

He looked at me, confused. "The one upstairs," I said. He grinned and nodded in understanding.

I pulled on my rain boots, the nearest gear to grab, with a wink. Benoit stared at me, dressed in my high rain boots, hair a soggy mess, skirt, blouse, with an open coat.

"You are beautiful," he said pensively.

How many times could he take my breath away?

I took Polo out and once inside again, filled his puzzle ball with a treat to keep him busy. I grabbed a bottle of champagne from the fridge, one my boss sent me when I moved to Philadelphia, and two whiskey glasses because *who has flutes?* Before heading upstairs, I took a quick glance at my phone. Four missed calls from Kelly and at least a dozen text messages:

Where are you?

I'm worried.

Call me please.

You better call me or I'm going to call the police.

I don't dare call the police, but I will kill you when I see you. CALLLLLL ME.

Anna, where the fuck are you?

And so on. I pictured Kelly's cycle of rage and worry, and I grinned. I sent a quick reply:

Sorry, I'm fine. Long story. I'll call you in the morning.

I turned off my phone so I wouldn't hear her reply, then went upstairs, champagne and glasses in hand.

Benoit was sitting on the floor next to a roaring fire when I entered my bedroom. His shirt was unbuttoned at the top; he looked casual, less polished, and God, so sexy. The amber light of the fire illuminated his profile as he looked over at me. He rose to help me with the champagne. He put the bottle and glasses on the dresser and turned to me.

"Well, you certainly know how to light a fire," I said, and he grabbed me around the waist and pulled me close with urgency. An aroused whimper escaped me. We grasped at each other's face, shoulders, neck; our lips wandering, then finding each other's again. I unbuttoned the rest of his shirt slowly. He lifted my blouse with a gentle peel. We were ravenous, but we were taking our time; unwrapping each other slowly, as one does of a delicate truffle. His body was smooth and softly muscular. I removed his pants, threw them aside. He turned me around authoritatively, seized both sides of my hips, and swiveled me with a gentle force. A wave of arousal swept over me and I held onto my dresser, surrendering the removal of my skirt. He ran a hand firmly up my spine toward my neck, then down toward the long zipper of my skirt. He grabbed the gold tab and slowly unzipped. My breath was shallow with every inch it moved down, and when it finally reached the end, we both let out a lusty sigh. He turned me back around. We looked at each other with fiery desire. He lifted me and laid me onto the bed, where we made love like animals who found an oasis in a desert; a swell of water from deep beneath the earth, emerging to quench a thirst.

Afterward, when the fire had waned to a muted glow and the tangle of sheets bound us for the night, we drank champagne and ate chocolate cake and tiramisu in bed.

I woke the next day to a bluish-gray light seeping through the shades of the window. I looked at the clock: 7:00 a.m.

Fuck, we're late for work. I couldn't remember the last time I arrived at work after 7:00 a.m. Fortunately, it was Friday, and things tended to be even more laid back than the already informal atmosphere I'd come to realize at Kahn & Hague.

I quietly got out of bed, grabbed a robe, and tiptoed toward the bathroom, careful not to disturb Benoit, sleeping peacefully under a cloud-like duvet. I shook my head and wondered if we would share the awkward morning-after conversation and politeness that came when the morning sun shone a light on the inhibitions that were covered by darkness and wine the night before. I hoped not.

I brushed my teeth quickly, then grabbed a long coat and my high rain boots before leading Polo outside. I opened the door and gasped. Past the landing of my doorstep, snow was at least a foot deep, likely more. The wind was howling, sending drifts of snow through the air that landed somewhere other than where they originally fell. Not a single car was on the street, nor a single person outside. And the snow was still rapidly falling. Of course, I had seen snow, a lot of snow: Salt Lake City hosted the goddamn Winter Olympics. But I had never seen this much snow at one time, piling untouched, obstructing an entire city.

Polo and I had no choice but to step out, though it didn't come without a groan from him. When we trudged back in, Polo shook off the snow, though knots of it stuck to his belly and sides. My high boots barely kept the snow out and my knees were red with wet welts. I grabbed my laptop and turned on the TV to watch the local news; it reported a State of Emergency for Philadelphia. An email from Kahn & Hague Human Resources advised that the office building would be closed. All employees were asked to work remotely, if possible.

A snow day? I scoffed at the notion.

I went to the kitchen and grabbed the French press, still baffled by a so-called State of Emergency. I filled the teapot and slung it onto the stove to boil. I had given up trying to make a soy chai latte at home that rivaled my favorite barista's. I had found the next best thing was a dark roast French press cup of coffee. The percolated machines, even the touted European ones, just didn't have the same effect as my old, stained French press. I whirred the coffee grounds in the grinder, then scooped them into the bottom of the press. The teapot whistled, and I filled the press, watching the grounds swim around the murky water. I placed the top of the press on lightly, the needle standing tall, and waited.

I didn't hear Benoit approach, so I jumped when he hugged me from behind and kissed my shoulder.

"Good morning," he smiled.

"Oh my God, you scared me," I said with a startled laughter. I turned around and put my hands around his neck. His hair was tousled, but his blue eyes were bright. He looked as sexy in the morning as he looked any other time of day, or night. He wore just his underwear and a blanket that was wrapped around his shoulders, which now partly enveloped me.

"We're snowed in," I said.

"I can see that." He gently kissed me. His breath was minty; he must have noticed the extra toothbrush I laid out for him.

"The office is closed," I muffled into his neck. The heady scent of his body was making it difficult to let go, but I pushed back. "You won't believe it. The snow is up to here." I exaggeratedly put my hand sideways against my chest.

He raised both eyebrows. "Looks like we're not going anywhere then. I smell coffee. Do you have flour, let's see, eggs, sugar, and… milk?"

I did. Of course, I did.

"You're in for a treat then. A Frenchman in underwear is going to make you breakfast."

I laughed aloud. "And I don't even have to pay for this show?"

"I accept many forms of payment." He demonstrated with another kiss, this one a little longer than the last. I didn't know why we were going to waste time on breakfast when we could go back into that bed. Benoit released me from his blanket cocoon and walked to the fridge, where he pulled out eggs and milk. I sulkily fetched the sugar and flour, among other things he began rattling off: a flat pan and vanilla. He found a bowl and began adding ingredients. I poured us two cups of coffee, cream and sugar for me, black for him.

"As much as I like a Frenchman in underwear, I wish I could offer you something else to wear," I said.

"Don't worry about me. Joel will bring me some clothes. Whisk?"

I looked for a whisk, contemplating his casual mention of Joel, as if everyone knew who *Joel* was.

"Joel? Is Joel, like, your genie?" I was incredulous. There was not a soul outside and the snow was still coming down in heavy sheets.

"No, Joel's not a genie." He swirled a pat of butter in the pan, and the butter quickly liquefied and bubbled. "But he's resourceful; he'll find a way here."

"He's…a friend, then?" I asked curiously.

He shrugged and smirked, as if wanting to laugh at the notion. "Eh, kind of. I've known him a long time. He just helps me with things."

I resisted the urge to ask more about Joel. I wasn't Benoit's mother, or his wife, or his girlfriend, or maybe even his friend. I didn't know what the hell I was, but I was not somebody who could ask more about Joel.

"Where can I find a Joel?" I teased.

"What do you want? I'll get it for you." I couldn't tell if he was joking as he ladled a runny scoop of batter into the pan.

"Hmmm, well, if it's that easy…" I tapped my finger on my chin and looked him up and down. "I'll just stick with a Frenchman in his underwear making me breakfast for now. But I reserve the right to come back to your question."

He smiled a sideways glance at me as he flipped what I now realized was a crepe. After preparing a small folded stack of them and topping it with sliced strawberries, he went back to the stove and cracked two eggs into a bowl, whisked, and poured the mixture into a pan.

"Scrambled eggs, too?"

"Omelet. I can't join you for the crepes." He sprinkled some cheese and carefully folded over the omelet.

"You went to all that trouble not to join me?"

"No trouble at all. I love making crepes and I haven't had a kitchen for a long time."

I watched him confusedly as he picked up both our plates and walk toward the couch. I followed him with our coffees. "But if you love cooking crepes so much, why aren't you eating them?"

"I can't. I'm diabetic."

"Oh," I said, then alarmingly, "but all that cake last night…."

"Last night was fine, but I don't have enough insulin with me for today."

My eyes widened.

"Don't worry, love," he chuckled. "Joel will bring some, but until then, no crepes."

I nodded, but I was not convinced and wondered what to expect if Joel didn't show up with insulin. Meanwhile, it wasn't lost on me that he called me *love*.

He grabbed a blanket from the couch and wrapped it around my shoulders. "Bon Appetit!" he wished in perfect French, raising his coffee mug. I raised my mug.

"This is very good coffee," he said. "Do you always use a French press?"

"I have a thing about coffee," I said as I prepared my first bite of crepe. "I'm more of a tea drinker, but I can't resist a French pressed cup of coffee. But only French press."

He watched as I closed my eyes at the pillowy bite of crepe. How did the French just know how to make a crepe?

"How did I do?" Benoit asked with beaming anticipation.

"Fucking amazing," I replied with a straight face, mouth half-full.

He laughed, clearly pleased. "Tell me more about your family," he said. "I talked so much about myself last night, I didn't get to learn as much about you. What is your mother like? Is she as beautiful as you? Did you get your green eyes from her?"

I blushed. "My mom is lovely, and yes, she's beautiful."

"And your father?"

"He's not as beautiful as me," I quipped.

"I figured that much. But what does he do?"

"My dad got into an accident a while back. It was pretty serious. He was in a coma for six months. When he woke up, he was never the same. He can walk, but not well. His motor skills are, well, not good."

"I'm so sorry. How long ago?"

"Right before college. That's why I ended up at an in-state college," I shrugged.

"Because of the accident?"

I nodded as I felt emotions bubble up, which I swallowed with a swig of coffee. "You know how it is. I have two younger brothers, and my mom had to get multiple jobs to cover expenses. Out-of-state tuition was out of the question, and I wanted to stay local to help out my mom."

He nodded morosely. "Is that why you wanted to come to Philadelphia? Because you didn't get to leave Utah when you were younger?"

"Yes, partly. Mostly. This may sound strange, but I always knew that I was meant to leave Utah. I knew that staying there would leave me…," I searched for the words, "Stuck."

Benoit looked surprised. "Stuck? Stuck, how?"

"It was probably different for you growing up in Paris, but I came from a much smaller world. There's a predictability where I grew up of a life that often involved getting married young, having babies quickly, then repeating that pattern generation after generation. It works for a lot of people. But it always left me feeling...stuck."

I pictured my mother, and my grandmother, and her mother, all having married young, no college, no career goals, leaving them reliant on their husbands for a paycheck. After my dad's accident, I watched as my mom corralled all her strength to work one tireless job after another just to make ends meet. It was admirable. But it always bothered me that my mom seemed stuck; stuck with no real opportunity to change her life.

I had resolved never to be stuck.

"So, you wanted to be in a bigger world?" he asked.

"I guess I just wanted the option. I worked hard in college, and again as I moved north and started my career, to have the opportunity to do something else, go somewhere else. To be different," I said humbly.

Benoit looked at me affectionately. "Different you are, Anna. You are very different."

Chapter Seven

We were back lying in bed. I could hear the clink of a fork hitting the plate as Polo lapped up the remnants of our breakfast. I didn't care. I was absorbed in this moment, wrapped in Benoit's arms, the fire hissing and popping again. Through the window, snow continued to fall against the gray sky, creating an almost purple hue in the room, cut by the orange light of the fire.

I didn't want to change the mood by asking what we were doing, or how things might be when we weren't snowed in, or what these last 24 hours meant to Benoit. I knew what these hours had meant to me. I liked Benoit, and I wanted more of him. I started to feel myself move from "whatever happens, happens" to "I'll be very sad if it doesn't continue to happen."

As if he could hear my thoughts, Benoit said softly, "Anna?"

He propped up a pillow behind him. I settled with my head and chest cradling a pillow to look at him, our legs still tangled. "I have this charity event coming up. Would you like to come with me?"

There was my answer: He wanted to continue things between us, as well. I couldn't help smiling.

"I would love to. When is it?"

"Two weeks, I think. Maybe three. I'll check the invitation and let you know."

"Well, I have an extraordinarily busy social calendar, so," I raised my eyebrows teasingly, "the sooner the better."

"Do you?" He narrowed his eyes, warily. "What if I promise to make it worth your while?" He inched his fingers along the sheets between us and walked them up my arm. I giggled. When he realized he was approaching a ticklish spot, he looked at me expectantly.

"Don't you dare," I smiled seriously.

He raised his eyebrows amusedly and stopped finger-climbing for a moment, contemplating my threat. He continued along my chest, up my neck, then cupped behind my head and pulled me to him. We were both giggling as he pulled me in for a long kiss.

Buzz. Bzzz-bzzzz-bzzzz. My gate buzzer cut sharply through our kiss. Polo barked wildly. I sat up, alarmed.

"That's Joel," Benoit said.

"Right, of course." I got out of bed and pulled on a pair of sweatpants and a T-shirt. Benoit grabbed his blanket and wrapped it around himself again.

"I'll go out to meet him," he said, searching for his clothes, strewn about the room.

I looked at Benoit. There was over a foot of snow outside and besides his underwear and a blanket, he only had a suit and dress shoes to trudge outside in.

Bzzz-bzzzz-bzzzz. Joel was buzzing again.

"You are not going out like that!" You'll freeze. And ruin your shoes, which are very nice, by the way."

He had fetched his shirt and was looking for his pants.

"I will go out and meet him," I said. "You stay put."

"No, no, I insist, please, let me go. I can handle a little snow." He seemed a little panicked. "Besides, I have my blanket." He proudly donned his signature blanket look.

"It really is a good look on you. But I don't mind. I have boots. And I have Polo. I'll be fine." Polo was by the front door now, barking incessantly and wagging his tail.

"That's not it—" But I had already started down the stairs and had reached my high rain boots before he trailed after me, shirt and pants in hand, to finish. "It's just that Joel's expecting me. He's not used to, uh, other people."

I put on a heavy coat, pulling the hood up loosely around my post-coital hair. "Surely, Joel doesn't bite?"

Benoit shrugged apprehensively. "No, but…," he sighed. "I guess, just be quick. He should only have a couple bags to give you."

I looked outside. "I'm pretty sure quick is all you can be in this weather. When I get back in, you and I are taking a long, hot shower." He raised his eyebrows and smiled, though a troubled look remained on his face.

Bzzz-bzzzz-bzzzz. Jesus, Joel, *okay,* I thought as I opened the door.

Polo ran out ahead of me, barking loudly as he labored through the snow toward the gate.

Joel jumped back. "Shit!"

"Hi! He's alright, he won't hurt you!" I hollered as I dragged along, each step sinking deeply in the snow. Cold drips ran down my calves as snow spilled into the top of my boots. Polo stood at the gate barking.

He was wagging his tail excitedly, yet the fur at the nape of his neck stood up as if he couldn't decide how to feel about Joel.

I reached the gate, panting a little. I grabbed Polo by the collar and looked up at Joel with a smile. My smile waned as I recognized him, though I couldn't place him.

"Uh, hi, Miss," Joel said, keeping a cautious gaze on Polo. "I'm Joel. I'm here for Benoit? I brought him some stuff." He held two bags up on either side of him. Beside him a snow shovel leaned against the wall.

"Yes, hi. I'm Anna." He watched Polo gently buck against my hold.

Joel was smaller than I pictured for an assistant-type, and not wearing a cheap, skinny tie. Joel was short; really short. He had the worn look of a heavy drinker, his skin gray and dry, making him look older than he probably was. Scars laced across his buzzed scalp and forehead as though he fell and hit the edge of a bar far too many times. When he smiled though, his impossibly white teeth gave an almost-friendly vibe and his eyes crinkled warmly. I felt about him the way Polo must: Joel wasn't a guy I'd run away from, but he wasn't someone I'd run toward, either.

"Benoit's inside. He, uh, didn't have the right shoes to, um, come outside and meet you." I thought of Benoit wrapped in a blanket with nothing on underneath.

"Yeh," he said nervously. "Okay. I brought him shoes. Boots. I brought him boots. And wine. And a toothbrush. And some other stuff. Shit, is he gonna bite me?" he nodded toward Polo.

I looked at Polo, who wouldn't eat a fly if it landed on his lip. "Nah, he'll be alright."

"Yeh, but his hair is all standing up like he's mad," he said in a gruff Philly accent. "Are you sure?"

It was true. Polo seemed uncharacteristically agitated, which surprised me, but he'd never hurt anyone before. He probably was just being protective.

"Polo will be fine as long as I'm fine." I unlocked the gate for Joel and Polo lunged toward him with a nervous growl. Joel jumped back straight as a board and fell into the snow like a snow angel, the bags landed on both sides of him with a dull thump.

"Oh my God, Joel! I'm sorry!" I reached to pull him up. Polo pranced around him wildly like a dog who had found a bone. "He was just playing with you. Look at him." I nodded toward Polo, but for the first time, I wasn't confident that Polo's lunge was entirely innocent, and I worked to hold him at a distance.

"Are you okay?" I asked with concern. I grabbed one of the bags that had fallen into the snow beside him. Joel brushed the snow off his pants and the sleeves of his leather jacket.

"Oh, yeh, no, it's okay," he gave an abating laugh, as though it was nothing, but I could tell he was rattled. I shooed Polo away and he reluctantly wandered off to sniff around in the deep snow.

"Joel, do you want to come inside? I really am sorry." I bit my lip and looked at him apologetically. I had no intentions of inviting Joel in before Polo scared the shit out of him, but now I felt the need to assuage the situation.

"Oh, no, thanks. I'm just delivering these things for Benoit." He picked up the other bag and handed it to me.

"Thank you for bringing these. I'm sure he'll appreciate them greatly." I thought about the much-needed insulin in one of the bags.

"Yeh, sure," he said.

"Be careful out here." I looked past him at the streets. Still no cars on the road. Not even ploughs. "How did you get here anyway?"

"I walked," he said. He *walked*? From where, I wondered. How did he get these supplies? I was intrigued; but also, I was cold.

"Right. Well, it was a pleasure to meet you. Thanks again. I hope we meet again under better circumstances."

I called for Polo, who pulled his nose out of a deep burrow in the snow and came leaping toward us. Polo snorted sharply at Joel as he passed him. Joel flinched.

I winced apologetically. "'Bye then, Joel." I turned to close the gate and walk toward my door.

"Oh, uh, Miss?"

I turned around. It was then, as I saw Joel from a distance, shuffling his feet, that I realized how I knew him. Joel was the man standing between the buildings on the day of my Kahn & Hague interview. He was talking earnestly with a tall man in a gray suit. My stomach lurched. Could it possibly have been the same tall man who was wrapped up in a blanket in my apartment? *No*, I muddled.

"Ma'am?" Joel repeated.

I snapped back to focus. "Sorry. Did you need something, Joel?"

"I brought a shovel. To shovel your walkway. If that's okay with you?" He looked past me at Polo, watching carefully that he was not going to charge him.

"That's really nice of you. You're a lifesaver."

He shifted uncomfortably again. "No problem."

Benoit was standing next to the window when I walked in; he had clearly watched our interaction. There was a disconcerting scowl on his face.

"You could have told me that Joel doesn't like dogs," I smirked.

"I didn't know until just now," he said.

"I've never seen someone just fall over like that, like he got zapped into paralysis," I laughed. I couldn't help it; people falling was funny. Benoit's face finally softened and he snickered.

"Did you know he's shoveling my walkway?" I asked.

"Yes, I told him to bring a shovel."

"Does Joel do anything you ask him to do?"

Benoit took the bags and set them down on the floor to help me out of my coat. I pulled off my boots, which sloshed off with a suction-cup sound. My cheeks felt hot with a cold flush.

"Joel's happy to help out," he answered indifferently, same as before.

"I have good friends, but none that would trudge through this storm to bring me underwear and wine." That was a lie, the good friends part. I only had one real friend in Philadelphia; anywhere really. But I was more curious about Joel now than I was before.

"Joel doesn't have much else going on." He grabbed me around the waist and pulled me in. "Now, about that shower-" he kissed beneath my frozen ear.

I giggled. "Yes, about that shower…."

Chapter Eight

"I still can't believe you're dating Benoit Mass-uh-whatever. How do you even say his fucking name?" Kelly asked as we walked to get coffee.

It was Tuesday, about two weeks after the snow storm that held me and Benoit hostage. Kelly had been pulled into a temporary group project, which meant our liberal coffee breaks were much less liberal the past two weeks. Fortunately, the project was over, and I was happy to see her "*Coffee?*" IM come through today.

"I don't know if we're dating," I replied. "But we're spending a lot of time together."

"You're dating. How many nights have you been apart since your first date?"

"Again, I don't know that it was a first date."

"Stop with the semantics, Anna. You know what I mean!"

"Okay! Jeez, relax."

"You even walk different now. Like celebrities walk, or someone who just won the lottery, and now they're billionaires, and they walk past you all like, 'I have something you don't have.'" She imitated a walk in an arrogant manner, with her nose in the air.

I laughed. "I do not! That's ridiculous." I rolled my eyes at her. "Maybe it's just happiness. That first-dating feeling. Sex is hot, can't wait to talk, every detail of each other seems ultra-important."

"So how many nights have you been apart since your first date?" She glared at me, obviously not wanting me to challenge her.

"Two," I said passively, looking straight ahead.

"Two nights?! You've been together every night, except for two? Why the two nights, for God's sake? Why not just move in together?" she shrieked.

I smiled and put my hand to my forehead like I had a fever. "You're making me blush."

She calmed down and laughed lightly. "You seem happy, so that's good. What do you think is going to happen here? Are you guys getting serious?"

"I don't know. We have an event this Saturday. It's a ball at the Bellevue?" I didn't know where the Bellevue was.

"The Bellevue is beautiful. Do you have a dress?"

"Not yet."

"You don't have a dress, Anna? It's Tuesday. You should already have it at the tailor!" She seemed very concerned.

"I've been busy!" I defended. It was true. I had finally presented to Benoit, and this time, also Bob and two other Procurement managers. The presentation was flawless, and the group was anxious over the potential money it could add back to its budget. Now, of course, the group expected results. Instant results meant I was working furiously to get people to do their jobs, a feat at Kahn & Hague. I also was losing much of my nighttime, time I used to do my best work, to dinners and tangled sheets with Benoit. I felt myself go warm thinking about him.

"We need to get you a dress. Let's leave at 4 o'clock today to go shopping. You'll have just enough time to get it altered before Saturday." Kelly exasperated.

I nodded.

"And you'll need to get your hair done, make up, too. I'll set you up with Sage. He's the best in Philly."

"Sage?"

"Yeah, so what? You got something against people who have names of herbs? He's amazing. He has this thick black hair that swoops like an ice cream cone." She twirled her finger above her head.

"Thanks, Kel." I wrapped one arm around her waist and squeezed. "You're a good friend."

"I know. I still can't believe you're dating him. What's he like in bed?"

The slow click of my heels descending the stairs stopped Kelly and Benoit's conversation.

Benoit stared as I walked toward him in my black off-the-shoulder dress; hair and makeup done masterfully.

"Wow," he said. "You are stunning."

I smiled coyly.

"I'm going to feed the dog and get out of here." Kelly had offered to take Polo for the night. "Have a wonderful time, you two!" she hollered as she led Polo toward the kitchen.

I stepped closer to Benoit. "Don't you look so…" I hesitated, searching for the perfect word…*handsome.* "You look so handsome." He did. He looked tall and fit in his impeccably cut tuxedo. His face was shaved close and his hair was combed neatly. He was, simply, a perfect gentleman.

He smiled and grabbed me by the waist and pulled me close, our faces inches apart, "You've taken my breath away again, Anna Reed. Should I get used to this?"

"Only if you want to." He kissed me with the lightness of a feather, so as not to smudge my lipstick.

"Shall we go?" He pulled back and offered his arm. I took it and he led me outside. A black luxury car was waiting for us.

The ride to the gala was quick. We sat with our fingertips interlaced as he told me about his dinner the night before, a resounding disappointment, as he put it, on every level: Food, company, business. He frowned and grazed my body as if to suggest that it was not worth missing time with me.

As we walked in, large signs that read, "Blue Hope Gala: Cure for Diabetes" flanked the reception table and blue circular decorations streamed throughout the lobby. I squeezed his hand as we headed toward the ballroom and found our table.

I recognized one of the men at the table as the brown-suited man leaving Benoit's office the day I went for our first meeting.

"Benny! Good to see you, buddy!" He thrust forward and gave Benoit a hearty man-hug.

"You remember Anna?" Benoit asked, introducing me.

"Yes, Anna, hi! We met briefly at the office. I'm Abe, and this is my wife, Madeline." He put one hand behind Madeline's back, and she reached her hand out to shake mine. "Your dress is beautiful," she said.

"Thank you," I reciprocated genuinely. "It's a pleasure to meet you, Madeline. And Abe, it's great to see you again." They seemed like a pleasant couple.

A waiter offered us a red or white glass of house wine, which Benoit politely declined.

"I'll be back, love. With champagne," he said with a smirk.

I winked at him with approval.

"So, Anna," Abe began after Benoit left, "Benoit has told us a lot about you. How are you enjoying Philadelphia?" I tried to seem unfazed by the fact that Benoit had 'told them a lot about me.'

"It's great. I'm looking forward to spring when I can get out and explore a little more. Are you both from the area?"

They looked at each other to see who would answer first. Madeline took the queue. "I'm from the area originally; Bryn Mawr. Abe is from upstate New York."

"That's how I know Benny," Abe said definitively. "His grandparents were the closest neighbor to us. We spent summers playing with sticks and dirt."

I smiled at the thought of Benoit as a little boy, Benny, his bright blue eyes shining through a face full of dirt. Did he have the imagination of Peter Pan? Or was he a more serious child who liked reading books in a hammock?

"Near Lake George?" I longed to know more about this little boy who grew to warm the bed beside me.

"Yes!" Abe beamed, delighted that I knew this piece of their past.

"Don't go fishing with them, Anna," Madeline chimed in. "They're intolerable with their fishing contests – who can catch the most, who can gut the fish the fastest, who caught the most the summer of '91. You get the idea. It's better to stay in the cabin and drink wine." She winked at Abe.

"Ah, we're not that bad," he contested.

"They're that bad, Anna," she said with smiling eyes.

I laughed. "I'll keep that in mind if a fishing invitation comes my way."

"Well, the way Benny talks about you, a lot of invitations will be coming your way," Abe said. "This is the first time he has brought someone to this ball. He always RSVPs for two, but comes alone."

"Abe!" Madeline chided. "Don't embarrass him!"

"It's true though, Madeline, and you know it!" Abe resisted. "He's had plenty of women—er, sorry." He looked at me apologetically, then back at Madeline. "But this is different. Where's the waiter?"

"It's different for me, too."

They looked at me with approval. "I'm glad. Benoit's a really great guy. He…," Abe paused. "He's just a really great guy, and it's good to see him look so happy."

I nodded my head. Benoit was lucky to have a friend in Abe. It was evident that he and Madeline were protective of him.

Benoit returned with two glasses of champagne. Salads were being served to each guest. Polite conversation amongst the table ensued, deciphering who knows who from where, and which acquaintances everyone had in common. The missing couple from our table showed up in the middle of the main course, drunk, and cursing that the filet at these things—gesturing disgustedly toward the ceiling—always was overcooked.

Benoit put out his hand. "Dance with me?"

I placed my hand in his and followed him to the dance floor. I silently prayed that he wasn't going to be a fancy dancer. I hadn't graduated much beyond the high school "sway" and an occasional dip. But we danced like we made love: Naturally, and in sync.

"You know you are the most beautiful woman here," Benoit tilted his head back to look at me while we danced. "I think you are the most beautiful woman I've ever met," he added seriously.

"Now you're just reaching," I teased. "Thank you."

"You are special, Anna." He had a nervous look on his face like he had more to say but couldn't find the words to say it.

I smiled and tipped my head. I soaked in the tenderness of his face as we swayed to the music, the soft light bouncing around us.

"I'm falling for you, Anna," he finally said. "No, I've fallen already. I love you. And you don't have to say anything back, but I've loved you for a while. Maybe even from the beginning."

I could feel his heart beating next to mine; both hearts pulsing loudly as if they were trying to escape our chests to run away together. I panted something between surprise and longing as I searched for the right words to respond. Though it had only been a few weeks, our connection was undeniable. It was beyond lust and newness. It was a connection that had honesty and intention.

"I love you, too," I replied. "From the beginning."

He relieved a sigh and pulled me close. We could feel each other's smiles as we danced cheek to cheek, our hearts soaring as the song lulled from middle to end.

"I don't usually stay the entire event," he broke the silence. "I think this is the first time I've made it to dessert."

"Perhaps we should not break tradition. Room service dessert?"

I could feel his smile widen on my cheek. "See? This is why I love you."

"And I thought maybe it was something else," I suggested.

He pulled back to look at my face. "It's that, too."

We kissed playfully as the song ended, then found Abe and Madeline to say goodbye. They watched us walk away with the look of parents watching their kids leave for the prom.

That night, we made love with more meaning, followed by chocolate cake and champagne in bed.

Chapter Nine

The second time I met Joel was in the summer.

Benoit and I had replaced snowy weekends by the fire with city strolls to the singing of cicadas and evening tapas on the patio. My life was unrecognizable from six months ago, and I had subconsciously separated it into two categories: Life before and after Philadelphia. My mother would call periodically, mostly to make sure I was still alive, and I would tell her that I was staying busy with work and enjoying the weather. She would ask if I had new friends or if I was seeing anyone, and I would reply with vague answers: "I've made a couple of nice friends, and I've been on a couple of nice dates." I felt a need to keep my new life, and Benoit in particular, all to myself; like a child hiding candy under her bed so that she didn't have to share with siblings.

Benoit and I were sitting by the patio doors at La Castagne that opened to Chestnut Street enjoying a glass of wine and watching the city operate. Polo lay lazily on the ground, head on my foot.

Joel rushed into the dining room from the curtain that led to the back. He looked agitated as he approached our table. He stuttered back when he saw Polo, who had lifted his head and groaned a yawn-like growl. I quickly grabbed Polo by the collar and shushed him. "It's okay, Polo. Relax." I was hoping to avoid another lunging incident. This time Joel didn't have a foot of snow to break his fall.

"Hello again, ma'am," he said with a quick nod; his eyes locked on Polo. He hesitantly turned his attention to Benoit. "Benoit, I need to speak with you."

Benoit didn't change his posture, though his demeanor had turned sober. He took a sip of his wine. "Can it wait, Joel? This is not a good time. Or *place*."

"Yeah, I know. I'm sorry. But I need to talk to you." He looked at me warily. "I wouldn't come here if it weren't important." He shifted his weight from one foot to the other and moved his hands in and out of his pockets as if he were looking for something. I wondered how anyone could wear a leather jacket in this heat.

Benoit set his glass down heavily. "I'll meet you in the back." He nodded toward the curtain indicating that Joel should leave.

"Thanks," Joel said apologetically. "Good to see you again, ma'am." He looked indirectly at me as he narrowed his eyes at Polo. Polo growled cautiously.

"Yeah, Joel, it's good to see you again, too. Maybe next time you can join us for a glass of wine," I said cheerily, trying to make up for my dog's poor manners.

Benoit and Joel exchanged a reserved look. Benoit sat up and put his napkin on the table. "This will only be a minute. I apologize, love."

"It's okay, no worries. Take your time. Just don't expect any of this wine to be left when you get back." I lifted my glass and winked at him.

He leaned over to kiss my forehead before chasing after Joel. I sipped my wine and stared out toward the bustling street. We had been to La Castagne at least a dozen times, but Benoit had never gone "behind the curtain," and it gave me an unsettled feeling. It was the same feeling I had the first time I met Joel and realized he was the man I saw the day of my interview: Apprehension. I had dismissed that he might have been talking to Benoit in that alley, but now I was less inclined to refute that notion.

Polo sat up and put his head on my lap, sensing my anxiety and offering comfort. I took another sip of wine and stroked Polo's bear-like head.

"What do you think, Polo?" I asked him, his eyes opening to my voice, then half-closing again. "They're probably back there cooking pasta and I'm acting as though they're hiding a body," I laughed at myself. "I should just relax, right?"

Polo tilted his head to the side the way he does when he hears a familiar word such as "treat." I patted him, grateful for his loyal companionship. I picked a piece of prosciutto from a platter Benoit and I were sharing and tossed it at him. He skillfully caught it mid-air.

"Good catch!" Benoit praised Polo, approaching the table hastily. He sat down with heightened energy and put his napkin back on his lap. "Sorry about that. Are we ready for another bottle of wine? Or did you save me a little?" He picked up the bottle and gauged that there was still enough to pour himself a generous glass.

"Everything alright? I mean, with Joel? Is he okay?" I asked curiously, just short of being nosy.

"Joel's okay. He just needed me to help him figure something out." Benoit was reaching for an olive.

"Oh good. He seemed a bit…distressed," I said, hoping he would sense that I was fishing for more information.

"Joel can get wound up easily. Sometimes he just needs someone to tell him what to do to get back on track."

"On track with what?" I asked lightly.

He smirked. "With life. With basically everything in life."

I nodded. I could tell Benoit was not interested in sharing details, but six months into our relationship, I felt like I should have a little more information about this mysterious man who showed up randomly with bottles of wine and emergencies that required private conversations.

I gently probed. "It seems Joel is lucky to have you. How long have you known him?"

He looked up while thinking, "A few years? I met him shortly after moving to Philly."

"I see. Well, Joel seems like a very nice guy," I lied.

He looked at me bemusedly, his brow slightly furled. "Joel? You're being serious? Joel's alright," he continued. "He doesn't intend to do harm to anyone, except himself maybe. He wants to be a good guy. He just sometimes can't get out of his own way."

"I've known people like that," I lied again.

"Sometimes people only know what they know. Joel's had a rough life. He's been around things that most people can't imagine; stuff you see in movies. But he wants a better life. He tries, at least."

"I guess that's half the battle," I offered.

I had met Benoit's desire to stop talking about Joel. Though I had many unanswered questions about him, I figured his story would unfold in due time. Besides, talking about Joel was stifling my afternoon wine buzz. "Want to take this picnic to the bench at the dog park? Let Polo run around a bit? Maybe later we can go see that new foreign film."

He clapped his hands together. "Yes! Great idea, you brilliant and beautiful woman!"

Chapter Ten

"Hey, Anna." Bob peeked his head through my office door.
"Hi, Bob." Bob had crept his way to the top of my favorite
sort-of-boss list. He asked only pertinent questions, involved himself
only when needed, and mostly left me to do my job at my discretion.
Until now.

"Karen Tietz reached out. You know that report you ran on the
payables for the Philadelphia and Norristown office last month? Fire
catches fast, and Karen is asking that you do the same analysis in
Illinois, the Almond Hills plant."

My eyebrows raised. "Okay. But I can do it from here. She just
needs to send me the data. I can reach out to her and walk her through
what I need."

"That's the thing. Karen is old-fashioned. She's also an institution
here, so she makes demands and usually gets what she wants. And she
wants you to go there to show her in person. Show her how to run the
reports in the system, all that. I told her you could talk her through
it over the phone, but she hollered, *'What's the good in having a fancy
consultant if they can't fancy consult in person?'*"

I sighed. "No problem. Where is Almond Hills?"

"Outside of Chicago. The site is somewhat remote. You'll need to rent a car."

"When would you like me to go?"

"As soon as possible. Karen is a squeaky wheel. She'll drive us crazy until you do."

"I'll go this week."

"Thanks, Anna," Bob said. "By the way, how's everything else going? You seem to have acclimated well. I'm glad that you and Kelly have become friends. I knew you'd hit it off," he said proudly.

"Everything's good, Bob. I have acclimated well," I replied, then added, "Moving here was everything I had hoped for." *And more.*

He was pleased.

Almond Hills, IL was nothing like I had pictured. With a name like Almond Hills, I imagined, well, rolling hills full of almond trees. Instead, Almond Hills was barren and expansive on both sides of a lonely highway. The occasional warehouse dotted the dry, endless landscape, like a sailboat dots the sea. I was glad the rental car had a full tank of gas. This was not somewhere I wanted to get stranded.

I signed in and waited as Karen Tietz was paged. I checked my phone for messages in case Doggie Day Camp had tried to get a hold of me. No reception in Almond Hills, it seemed.

Karen emerged from a secure door, her wrist jewelry jangling loudly. "Hi!"

I guessed that Karen was in her 50s. Her burnt auburn hair was cut short with bangs; and she wore a frumpy, but well-made, maroon suit with pantyhose and low pumps. She led me to a conference room where four other people were waiting.

We worked through lunch and finally I announced that I'd better get going; I had an hour's drive ahead of me to my hotel near the airport.

"Thank ya so much for coming," Karen said as I left. "You're really so good with numbers!"

I turned up the radio and sang to '90s Pop hits on my drive back, and as I neared Chicago, I heard my phone beep to life as reception became available. I glanced at it. No messages from Benoit. I frowned.

I checked into the hotel and collapsed on my bed, exhausted. I rechecked my phone. Still nothing. I sent Benoit a text:

Done with training.

I'm at the hotel and about to order room service.

Wish I was ordering chocolate cake and champagne with you.

I smiled, remembering the night Benoit first told me he loved me. We fed each other chocolate cake in bed and chased it down with expensive champagne, making love endlessly that night.

I didn't see the spinning wheel that he was replying, so I ordered room service and took a shower. Twenty-five minutes later, I was sitting in my pajamas and flipping through TV channels when my chicken salad, wine, and carrot cake arrived. I propped myself up in bed and landed on an episode of *Friends* while I ate.

Around 9 p.m., I still hadn't heard from Benoit. This was unusual. He and I kept a steady highway of communication even on the busiest of days. I grimaced as I typed another message to him:

Hey, love.

I'm sure you got caught up with something, but let me know you're alright?

I'd love to hear your voice before going to bed. xo

I hit send. My stomach was roiling with apprehension, but I shushed it away with a cold water from the minibar and pulled out my laptop. Work was always my best distraction. I was writing some post-meeting notes to send to the Almond Hills group when my phone dinged with a new message. I jumped to grab the phone, but grimaced when I saw Kelly's name:

Hey. How's the windy city?

I replied:

Good. Hey, have you seen Benoit today by chance?

I haven't heard from him, which is no big deal.

Just wondering.

I pictured Kelly laughing at me, the desperate, pitiful girlfriend, and waited for her snarky reply. She never disappointed:

You haven't heard from him for a whole day? I hope you packed some Xanax.

I heard yoga is good for withdrawals.

I laughed and shook my head. I loved Kelly and wondered if I had told her that lately:

Alright, alright. Thanks for the laugh.

Going to bed soon. Have a good night.

Spinning circle, then Kelly's reply:

Ha. You too, you psychopath.

I finished my notes from the day, looked again at my phone, and decided to go to sleep and let the ding of a late-night text wake me with something like: Love, I'm so sorry, I got caught up in a dinner meeting. The bed is cold without you.

Instead, I woke to the sound of someone filling a bucket from the hallway ice machine. I felt for my phone on the side of the bed and pressed the button to illuminate the screen. No messages. Time: 4:33 a.m. Why hadn't Benoit called or messaged? My concern was tinged with a small stain of anger.

I took a deep breath and contemplated sending him another text. No, it was too early. I'd send him something before boarding my flight. I anticipated our first argument when we finally spoke: Me trying to make a valid point of being concerned for his safety, him defending that we're adults and he doesn't need to account for his every step with me. That was true, but it was just a matter of respect, I reasoned. I wasn't looking to put a leash on him; I just want to know that the man I love was not floating in a river.

I was catching a 6 a.m. flight, so I got up, showered, and turned on *Marketwatch*. The market was anticipating an upswing in packaged foods.

Where was Benoit? I couldn't push the question back far enough in my head to forget it.

I landed in Philadelphia at 8:08 a.m. and waited anxiously for my phone to wake. No messages. The span of time in which Benoit would have woken up and realized he needed to call me had passed. Benoit never slept past 8:00 a.m. I called his phone while coasting on the tarmac, but the call went straight to voicemail. Anxiety replaced the anger from earlier this morning.

Something was wrong; I could feel it.

I texted Kelly:

Kel, please walk past Benoit's office this morning and see if he's there. I haven't heard from him still.

She immediately replied back:

Sure. Be at the office in 20 mins.

The lack of sarcasm in her response disturbed me. I tapped my finger nervously on the phone and realized just then how secluded our relationship was. I didn't have a phone number for anyone who knew him; not Alfonso, not Joel, not Abe, not his sister. My closest link was Kelly.

After disembarking the plane, I walked to the taxi line and hazily gave the driver my address. I stared at my phone. Fifteen minutes had passed since texting Kelly. She should be getting back to me soon. I scanned my brain for ways to get ahold of Benoit. I called the hotel and the front desk transferred me to his room. After three rings, voicemail. Short of calling the police, which I had no reason to do yet, I had exhausted my options.

I leaned my head against the back of the seat and closed my eyes. My phone buzzed. Kelly.

"Hello?" I answered the phone quickly.

"Hey. Benoit's not in his office," Kelly replied. "Are you okay, Anna? I mean, it's not unusual for people to not be in the office at 8:30 in the morning-"

I cut her off and redirected the driver. "Excuse me, Fourth & Chestnut please, and hurry!"

Chapter Eleven

I knew it before the cab rounded the corner and I saw the rotating red and blue lights whirring in front of the hotel, creating a sickening disco effect. Instantly, I felt as if I was looking up at an avalanche, and realized that even if I survived this, I'd walk away damaged.

When I reached the hotel, I rushed to the entrance where a police officer stopped me. "Are you a guest of the hotel, ma'am? Only hotel guests are allowed in at the moment."

I scanned behind him as I replied, "I'm not a guest. My-my-boyfriend lives here. He's a guest who lives here."

I saw Abe sitting on the arm of a lobby chair, talking to another officer; his slumped shoulders confirmed my worst fears.

"Abe! Abe!" I hollered desperately, my eyes filling with tears. "Abe, what happened?" I strained against the hold of the officer. "Let me in!" I shouted at him.

The officer speaking with Abe nodded to the officer holding me, who ushered me through with a benevolent nudge. Abe stood up and walked toward me, his eyes red and swollen. Not a shred of hope infused his face; it was the face of someone who had accepted defeat.

"No, Abe, no!" I shouted as I reached him, tears suspended, waiting for a definitive response. He grabbed both of my elbows and tried to pull me to him, but I resisted. "Where is he?" I asked frantically. "Is he hurt?"

Silence.

"Oh, God," I said disbelievingly. "No. Is he dead? Is he dead, Abe?" The words felt unnatural to say.

Abe sorrowfully nodded, "Yes, Anna. Benny's gone."

"No!" I panicked. "No! They're wrong. They have to be wrong. Where is he?"

Abe's tired eyes looked pitifully at me. "They're not wrong, Anna. I saw him." A quiet whimper escaped him. "I saw him just lying there. Just…just…lying there. I came to check on him when he didn't show up at work or answer my calls and..." His voice cracked into an alto pitch. "And there he was."

"Was he hurt?" I couldn't comprehend. "Did he fall? Did he look hurt?" I was desperate for answers as if knowing them would somehow make sense of this unfathomable occurrence.

"No, he looked fine," he sniffed. "He was wearing a bathrobe. He looked like he just got out of the shower, like any other morning."

My mind flicked memories of Benoit in his bathrobe on and off like an old movie projector. I recalled the mornings we would shower together and drink coffee by the fireplace still wrapped in our robes, sometimes glancing at the clock to see if we had enough time to make love before our morning meetings; sometimes not looking at the clock because we didn't care.

Rage crept into me like a snake slithers into a nest. "No, I don't believe it. You're wrong, Abe."

He shook his head.

"Someone missed something. Where is he?" I shouted and looked around frantically.

"He's gone, Anna." He cried and grabbed my elbows.

"Don't fucking say it again!" I yelled. "Don't say it!" I was screaming and shoving him between words. I genuinely wanted to hurt him and everyone else for telling me lies and keeping me from Benoit. Abe grabbed me tighter on the next push and pulled me in. The fight left as despair took over.

"No, no, no, no!" I sobbed violently, burying my face deep into Abe's chest. He was crying into my hair as a guttural moan wailed from my heavy body. My limbs were paralyzed, and if it weren't for Abe holding me up, I would have buckled to the floor. Bizarre thoughts whirled in my head: *It smells like ham in the lobby; Am I out of dog food?* I was in shock, Kelly would explain to me later.

The officer who was interviewing Abe interrupted. "Excuse me, I'm sorry, but I would like to finish your statement if possible," he said gingerly to Abe.

Abe nodded obediently at the officer, then whispered to me, "It's going to be okay, Anna. I'm just going to set you down right here on this chair. You're going to stay there while I get you some water." He spoke with the cautious cadence one might use to talk someone out of jumping off a building ledge.

I shook my head violently, refusing to let go for fear of facing this horrifying reality. A female officer pried me from Abe's arms. "I got her. Frank, go get some water please," she said to another officer standing by.

She led me to the chair. "I know, honey. It's okay, shhh." She held me to her cushiony bosom and rocked me. Her maternal comfort softened my cries, which had mellowed to an anguished lullaby.

"Can I see him?" I choked out and looked up at her hopefully.

"No, you can't see him," she said with sincerity. "He already has been put in the ambulance."

"I'll go to the ambulance. I can see him there?" I pleaded.

"I'm sorry, sweetheart." She nudged my head back down and rocked me again. "Shhh, shhh, there now," she repeated over and over, as my heart liquefied and poured out of me.

Chapter Twelve

I sat in the police station with Officers Long and Harley. My eyes were pink and swollen, and my cheeks were chafed from tears. Kelly had brought me a thick, oversized woolen cardigan that wrapped around me like a warm hug, although nothing could remove the chill from my body.

"I'm so sorry again for your loss," Officer Long said as she put a cup of coffee in front of me. "This won't take long. We just have a few routine questions. Mostly about the events leading up to Mr. Massenet's death."

I nodded. A swell gathered in my throat.

"We understand you spent a lot of time together before he passed away."

I nodded.

Officer Long continued, "Can you tell us where you were the morning of August 27th?"

"I was in Chicago, then Philadelphia. I was flying home from a business meeting."

"And you worked at Kahn & Hague with Mr. Massenet?"

"Yes. Well, kind of. I technically work for Manley-Collins bank, but I work at the Kahn and Hague building as a full-time consultant."

"And that's where you met Mr. Massenet?"

I wished they would just say Benoit. The way they pronounced Massenet was offensive. I nodded, "Yes."

"This might be personal, Anna, but I understand you had an intimate relationship with Mr. Massenet. Is that correct?"

I inhaled sharply and exhaled out my agitation. "That's correct."

Officer Harley sat quietly in a chair next to Officer Long. A look of discomfort settled on his face.

Officer Long acknowledged me. "Thank you for being open, Anna. I only ask because you might be able to fill in some details that we need for our investigation, considering your relationship with Mr. Massenet. Were you aware of any relationships that Mr. Massenet had that one might consider unhealthy?"

I shook my head slightly while thinking. "No. I mean, we were only dating for six months, so I only know of the relationships he had during that time. But no, I don't recall any unhealthy relationships."

"You weren't aware of any altercations or arguments he had with anybody?"

I recalled the last time Benoit and I were at La Castagne, when Joel came to have a word with Benoit. Benoit seemed agitated, but certainly not confrontational. Aside from that, I don't recall seeing Benoit so much as have a frown on his face.

"Uh, no. No, I don't recall any confrontations or altercations, or anything of the sort."

They nodded and took down some notes.

"Were you aware of any medical issues or ongoing needs that Mr. Massenet had?"

"He was diabetic. Type 1 since he was a boy. He took insulin to manage it and aside from that, he was healthier than most people I know."

Officer Long smiled briefly. "Okay. I'm going to switch gears. Do you know of any friends or contacts of Mr. Massenet's who would have been known simply as, 'B.P.'?"

I shook my head; not Abe, Madeline, Eloise, Alfonso, Joel, Kelly, me. I even thought about Kahn & Hague colleagues and the hotel staff. "No."

The officers sighed in unison.

"Why do you ask? Did you find something with those initials?"

The officers exchanged a look, then Officer Long apologized. "We can't disclose that to you, unfortunately, Anna. I know this tends to be a one-way stream of information, but that's just how investigations go."

I nodded in understanding.

"Is there anything at all that you can recall that you might think we'd have interest in? Anything or anyone that seemed a little 'off' during your relationship with Mr. Massenet? Maybe a circumstance or behavior that didn't add up? Or a friend that didn't make sense? Anything at all? No detail is too small to mention."

I thought about it and debated bringing up the only thing that never did add up to me: Joel.

"He had a friend, Joel," I said. "I only met him twice, and he seemed like a nice guy, if not a little unusual. He only came around once in a while, and whenever I'd ask about him, Benoit would just kind of laugh it off like their relationship was not worth talking about.

I don't know why I am even mentioning it. I mean, nothing weird ever actually happened. It just seemed like an unlikely friendship."

"Unlikely, how?" Officer Harley chimed in.

I looked over at him, regretting that I mentioned Joel. "I don't know. It's just that Joel didn't work with Benoit. He didn't go to dinner or have drinks with Benoit. He mostly just helped Benoit with errands and stuff."

The officers shifted in their chairs. "Helped with errands? Do you know what kind of errands? Did Mr. Massenet ever describe his relationship with Joel?"

The conversation was starting to make me nervous and I reached for the glass of water sitting beside my coffee. I took a cold gulp. "Benoit called Joel his helper. He said he did things for him. Kind of like an assistant."

"What kinds of things did he do for Mr. Massenet?" Officer Long asked.

I shook my head. "I don't know exactly. As far as I knew, it was things like bringing an overnight bag when he needed one and fetching wine. I honestly don't know beyond that."

They both inhaled and wrote something down.

"And do you know anything else about Joel? A last name? Where he lived? His background?"

My stomach ached with anxiety. "No. I don't know anything about him other than what he looked like."

"Can you give us a description of Joel?"

"Short, maybe five feet, maybe shorter. Very small. Shaved head, blue eyes. He had scars all over his head. He sounds scary-looking, but he was actually not that scary. He was almost, I don't know, sweet-looking. Like a boy who never grew up, but was rough around the edges."

They wrote down what I assumed was my description of Joel.

"And you don't know his last name or where he lived?"

"No."

"Okay. Well, you've been very helpful, Anna. We appreciate you coming in and taking the time to meet with us, especially at such a difficult time," Officer Long said gently.

"So, what's next? Do you know how Benoit died?"

They shook their heads. "No. He will have an autopsy performed because of the unusual circumstance surrounding his death, and pending that our investigation finds no foul play involved in his death, the results of the autopsy will be released to his family."

"Eloise," I said softly.

"I'm sorry?" Officer Long asked.

"Oh, nothing. Eloise is his sister."

"I have one more question for you before you go," prompted Officer Long.

I nodded.

She reached into a bag beside her and pulled out a plastic bag with an object inside. She lifted it up for me to get a closer look. "Do you recognize this button?"

I squinted to see it better. It was silver with an emblem or engraving on it; I tried to make it out. Officer Long pulled the plastic taut against the button's face, and the embossing of a panther head became clear.

I furrowed my brow. "I've never seen that button before."

Officer Long held the button. "Are you sure? You've never seen Mr. Massenet wear it? On a coat, or a blazer, or a bag?"

"No. That is not something he would wear."

They exchanged another look.

"Okay," Officer Long said as she put it back in the bag beside her. "Anna, thank you again for coming down. We will contact you if we have any further questions, but you've been very helpful. Officer Julep will take you home."

I nodded and stood up slowly.

At home, I collapsed on my bed with a heavy, overtired plop. I didn't move for the next 10 hours.

Chapter Thirteen

"I'll get you another cup of tea," Kelly said as she pulled herself up from her position beside me on the couch. "Can I get you anything else?"

I shook my head as she took the tea cup from my loose grip.

"Maybe you should try to sleep. It's been a long day." She looked at me pitifully. She was wearing her fuzzy pink slippers with the button-up black dress she wore to today's funeral services; a string from the hem of the skirt was dangling behind her knee. I hated myself for noticing these things. It seemed wrong to notice pink slippers and loose strings when my heart felt like it was barely beating blood through my body.

"You can sleep in the office. There's a sofa that pulls out," Kelly said.

I shook my head again and stared blankly at the string.

"Okay. Just relax then. I'll be back."

Polo lay at my feet, occasionally lifting his head and resting it on my lap to check on my state of being. Once satisfied, he'd go back to sleep.

The past week had been a dizzying series of events.

The coroner ruled out suicide. After a brief and fruitless investigation, the police ruled out foul play. The toxicology screening came back clean. The official cause of death: Sudden cardiac death.

I couldn't make sense of it, and it did little to give me closure. The broad cause of death only filled me with more questions and doubt about what might have happened, and I pleaded with myself to just accept it so that I wouldn't stir at night searching for answers.

Benoit's sister, Eloise, flew to Philadelphia on the earliest available flight. Benoit's father didn't come with her. According to Eloise, he proclaimed with an intoxicated slur, "*The next funeral I'll attend will be my own.*" Then with a drunk laugh, he had added, "*I'll probably be the only one there.*" Eloise pleaded for him to come with her; she needed him. She'd help him stay comfortable, she told him, which meant she'd keep him drunk. But he refused. As she walked out of the bar that nursed the remaining black part of her father's soul, she took one look back and through her glassy gaze of tears, saw her father bang his head on the bar, shoulders shaking with heavy sobs. It would be the last time Eloise would see her father alive.

I was nervous to meet Eloise. I was nervous about the entire funeral, candidly. There was a fine line to walk between being involved enough, but not too much. Over the past six months, Benoit and I had been inseparable, but our world together was a sliver of the lives we had lived before, and nothing shows rank of relationship better than a funeral. Aside from Abe and Madeline, I only knew the people of Benoit's past in stories, and I didn't know if they knew anything about me. The awareness made me feel insignificant, which was a stark contrast to how I felt while Benoit was alive.

This particularly mattered with Eloise. I knew how much she

meant to Benoit, and I was anxious to find out if he had ever mentioned our relationship to her. If I stripped it down, I could admit that the importance of my role in Benoit's life was somehow tied to Eloise's validity of me. So, when she entered Abe's and Madeline's house, 24 hours after Abe found Benoit in the hotel room, I cried tears of relief along with those of grief when she walked straight to me and burrowed her face into my shoulder and sobbed. "He's gone. How is he gone? Why was he taken from us?"

I held her head in my hands and whispered hoarsely, "I don't know. I'm so sorry, Eloise."

Her body was limp in my arms and the validation I was seeking was encompassed in this act of surrender: Eloise sought *me* for comfort, perhaps the way she would have sought comfort from Benoit if he were here. I felt protective of her and a trace of strength returned in my resolve to ensure Eloise would be okay.

Benoit hadn't left much by way of funeral wishes: How many 34-year-olds would have? But Eloise knew he would want to be buried next to his mother and grandparents in upstate New York. Abe put Eloise in contact with Benoit's attorney, who confirmed, much to Eloise's surprise, the will's designation of her as the executor and trustee of Benoit's assets. Eloise was overwhelmed with the responsibility, and Abe stepped in to help her sort it out.

Madeline took the lead in coordinating the funeral arrangements. I stayed busy helping Eloise with non-estate related matters. She needed a dress for the funeral, and she needed help packing Benoit's belongings from the hotel room. I didn't feel ready to walk into that hotel room again, but I knew I was the most qualified to sort through Benoit's personal life.

The plastic key card beeped, and a flash of green unlocked the hotel door. I pushed the door open and peered into the room. The bed was made, the tables were cleared and dusted, and the curtains were open, letting the bright Philadelphia daylight in. The room looked as though Benoit could return from work any moment; clean, but lived in. I swallowed hard as I stared at the bed. Tears welled in my eyes as I remembered the passionate nights and intimate mornings knotted in those sheets with Benoit's warm body next to me.

"This must be hard for you," Eloise said with a cracked voice. She was standing behind me, careful not to push me in; she probably knew I'd fall and not get back up.

I whimpered, "I miss him so much." I held onto the door to keep from collapsing. I looked up at the ceiling, closed my eyes, and wept. "I don't know if I can go in. He's in there. He's everywhere in there and I don't know if I can be so close to him and not be able to hold him, touch him."

Eloise wrapped her arms around me and cried, our shoulders heaved in unison.

"I need a drink." Eloise motioned back toward the elevator.

I nodded and wiped my nose and eyes. "I'll have what you're having."

She left, the door clicking with a heavy shut behind her. I walked slowly toward the bed. I ran my finger along the pillow cases, then walked to the closet and fingered through the suits and shirts hanging neatly. I found the shirt Benoit wore on our first date and pulled it off the hanger. I brought it to my nose and breathed in. It still smelled like Benoit, and I convulsed with grief.

"Come back," I pleaded, and though I was alone, I knew he was there. "Please come back. I wasn't done. We weren't done." I could feel his presence wrapping around me like the morning sun warms the dew from frosted blades of grass. I sobbed quietly into his shirt. "We weren't done yet."

After what felt like an eternity, I finally kissed the chest of his shirt and whispered, "You always took my breath away, Benoit; and now you've taken my heart with it."

I folded the shirt and put it in my bag. Eloise would be back soon, and I needed to be strong for her.

Eloise returned with a bottle of vodka and two glasses.

"The bartender asked me what I felt like, and when I told him I felt like standing in the street and letting a bus hit me, he handed me the bottle and a glass," she laughed. "Then I told him I had a friend who wanted to join me, and he handed me another glass."

"Remind me to give him a nice tip on the way out."

She poured us two generous shots and lifted her glass. "To Benoit, who would've wanted us to have a laugh between the tears."

"To laughing through the tears."

We clinked and threw the vodka back quickly, both of us coughing out the fumes with laughter.

"Another!" We threw back another shot.

We laughed hysterically as we sat on the floor enjoying our vodka picnic.

"When our mother died, Benoit took care of everything. He sheltered me from the pain of losing her by constantly doing things that she would've done. He tried to make me laugh through the pain, the same way my mother made us laugh when we scraped our knees. He practiced for weeks making crepes the way she would make them. He finished my schooling in the same manner she would have. He never complained, but I always felt bad that he had to grow up so quickly, and that he prolonged going to school himself. I felt like I was keeping him prisoner." She looked serious and her eyes filled with tears.

"He was proud of you, I know that. He talked about you all the time. He described your patisserie and he complained every time we ordered a croissant, saying it wasn't as good as Eloise's."

She sniffed.

"I also know that he wouldn't have wanted you to feel an ounce of guilt." I wished I could offer her more.

"I know that he was going to ask you to marry him," Eloise confided.

My eyes widened and my lip quivered. "What?"

"He called to ask if I could help him plan a proposal in Paris. He wanted to take you there this fall when the city is quiet and the air is crisp with love." She grinned and poured us another drink.

Tears streaked my face, this time with joy. "I had no idea."

"I can see why he liked you. You remind me of my mother. You're beautiful, smart, and easy to be with. You two made a good match, I can tell."

I looked at Eloise lovingly. "I would've said yes. And I would've been proud to call you my sister. I always wanted a sister."

She lifted her glass: "To almost sisters."

I mirrored: "To almost sisters."

The alcohol was setting in sharply now. She went to pour another glass and I giggled. "Last one. We should probably focus on packing this room."

"I'm procrastinating," she said. "I know that once his stuff is packed in a box, I have to accept that he's gone, and I don't want him to be gone, too, Anna. Everyone is gone. He was all the family I had left. I have no one now. No one." She cried heavily, her glass slipping from her hand.

I set the glass and bottle on the table and pulled her to me. "You have me, if you'll have me, Eloise. I'll be your family."

"It's not the same," she sobbed.

"I know it's not," I said, and I meant it.

Neither of us could substitute the loss of Benoit.

The funeral was perfectly orchestrated, thanks to Madeline.

Services were held in a small Presbyterian church near Lake George; the same pastor read the same passages in the same church that held the services of Benoit's mother and grandparents before him.

I was surprised by how many people attended. Many people were from the town where Benoit spent summers: Friends of his grandparents and mother, Abe's parents, and a couple of boys—men now—with whom Abe and Benoit used to run around. Several people from Kahn & Hague drove up for the funeral, Bob and his wife among them. Kelly and her fiancé, Tom, made the trek, mostly to support me and bring me home. Alfonso and his wife, along with their two children, came. The most surprising guest was the former dean of Oxford, who heard of Benoit's death through some of his Oxford friends, most of whom flew in for the services. The church was full, and I felt content to see the reach Benoit's friendship and love had in this world.

After church services, we followed the casket to the cemetery and watched as it was lowered next to his mother, a spot for Eloise on the other side of her. No plot for their father, I noticed.

As the line of people walked past and threw flowers on the casket, I looked up and noticed a figure standing back from the crowd, near the tree line. A short man with a small build, dressed in black slacks and a black leather jacket, hands in his pockets. I squinted and made out Joel, standing back with his head down, shuffling his feet.

"Anna, you ready to get up?" Eloise's nudge broke my stare, and I nodded. We got up and trailed the procession of people.

I glanced back at the trees, but Joel was gone.

Chapter Fourteen

I felt nauseous as I swirled my chai latte around in my mug. Kelly and I were on a coffee break for the first time since I returned to work. I had taken two weeks off, the most I'd taken in my career. My Salt Lake City boss was unaware of the circumstances surrounding my requested time off. I told him I was sick, and he didn't ask questions. Bob, who had learned at the funeral that Benoit and I had a relationship, encouraged me to take the time I needed.

For the first time, I found myself unmotivated by work. I hoped my apathy was just a product of circumstance, but the possibility that I might never feel excited about my job again gnawed at me like a rat gnawing through a wire: Either the rat would give up, or the wire would break.

"How are you holding up?" Kelly asked.

I looked up from my mug. "Okay, I guess. Sorry I'm so blah. I'm not known to wallow in misery for long; I'll get better."

"Anna, it's only been a couple of weeks. Everyone grieves differently. This isn't something you can run a formula on. Be patient with yourself."

"I know. Walks help. It's nice that the weather has been pleasant; Polo and I have been walking all around the city. I think he's losing weight." I chuckled dismally.

Kelly guffawed. "He fucking needs to. Tom fed him bacon every day he was with us. I told him to stop, but he'd say, 'aw, he likes it!' Can you imagine what he'll be like with our kids?"

I was surprised to hear Kelly mention kids. She always referred to kids as, "those things." She'd say, "Let's choose a table away from *those things*," or, "She used to be cool before she started having *those things*."

"Kids, Kel? I'm proud of you, all grown up."

She rolled her eyes. "Whatever. It's what humans are supposed to do, right?"

I smirked. "I think we've evolved past needing to reproduce for survival. I think we just do that for fun now."

"Well, Tom wants to start now, like, now as in today. I told him I don't want to be a pregnant bride."

"I don't blame you. Tell Tom to keep his biological clock ticking slowly, just until January," I said. "You can have a honeymoon baby."

She banged her hand lightly on the counter, "I know! And I just bought a smoking hot bikini for our honeymoon. How would I wear that with a belly? He's so weird sometimes. Let's have a baby, Jesus; like it's just that easy to stop the Pill and get pregnant."

I chortled, then my face turned pale with panic. The Pill. I hadn't taken it since Benoit's death, and I hadn't gotten my period. I was due. I was past due.

"Oh my God." I clutched my purse and searched for my phone.

Kelly looked at me nervously. "What? What's wrong? You okay? You need something in there?"

"I need my phone. What's the date?"

"Uh, the 12th, I think?

"Shit." I found my phone and pulled up my calendar. "Shit, shit, shit, shit, shit."

"Shit, what? Are you late for a meeting?"

I found the date entry for when I should have started my period. My stomach dropped.

"No, I'm not late for a meeting, Kel. I'm late for the month."

Kelly's eyes widened and her mouth dropped open. "Oh shit, Anna. Late, as in your period is late?"

My eyes started to water; I nodded yes.

"I'm never late, Kelly."

Eight pregnancy tests later, one of each brand available at the pharmacy, left me with a pile of plastic applicators showing two lines, plus marks, and the word "pregnant"—all confirming that I was, indeed, with child. Still, I remained unconvinced.

"There are no false positives with these tests," Kelly said. "False negatives, yes. But not false positives. You're pregnant, my friend."

I sat on the edge of the bathtub and cried.

Kelly sat next to me and put a hand on my shoulder. "I know this could not be worse timing, Anna, and I know this is just fucking mean of the universe to do to you right now...But this could be okay." She said it almost as a question.

I sat there staring at the bathroom floor tiles. I was trying to figure out when and how I got pregnant. Was it when I missed two days of the Pill, so I doubled up when I remembered? Was it just a bad pack of birth control pills? It had to have been the missed pills, but how? I'd had friends who intentionally went off the Pill and couldn't get pregnant. What are the odds that I'd get pregnant from a couple of missed pills? Slim, I guessed, but possible.

"Do you think I hurt the baby?" I asked apprehensively. "I was still taking the Pill and I drank, not a lot, but I drank wine…and vodka shots."

"No," Kelly snickered. "Please. I've seen women do far worse than that. The baby will be fine."

"I should probably call the doctor in the morning," I said.

"You should probably call your mom first," she retorted.

My mom. How was I going to tell my mom that I was pregnant; and oh, the father passed away a couple weeks ago? I had kept her and my dad in the dark about Benoit. They knew I had been dating, that I had been spending time with someone I worked with; but they didn't know who or how serious our relationship had been.

"I'm not going to tell anyone until I'm sure."

"Anna, you're pregnant. You should consider at least calling your mom."

"She doesn't even know I was in a relationship, Kelly. We don't have that kind of thing where I'd gush about who I was dating or how I was feeling."

"Is she going to freak out?"

"My mom has never freaked out over anything. She will probably say, 'That's so great, honey, congratulations!' Then she'll start telling me about how Grandma needs a new hip and Aunt Mary is running a triathlon…."

Kelly looked confused. "Really? My mom would freak out."

"My mom is oblivious to things like this. It will just bounce off her bubble."

"Her bubble?"

"Never mind. It just means that she will choose to see the positive in this; she'll dismiss any unpleasant details."

"She sounds wonderful," Kelly said, still confused. "Will she come to help you?"

"You know she can't. She has to take care of my dad."

Kelly nodded.

"It's okay. I can do this," I said.

Kelly clicked her tongue in agitation. "I feel like I'm reminding you a lot of this little fact, but you're fucking pregnant, Anna! You're not having a small procedure done, then you're back at work. You're going to have a live little thing to feed and change and shit. Not to mention the pregnancy. I really don't know how I am sounding like the only responsible one here!"

I groaned. "I know, I'm sorry! I'm not trying to sound insensible. I'm just used to doing things on my own. I will figure this out like I figure everything else out. I'll be fine."

"I'm sorry, I'm not trying to stress you out, but I'm stressing here! It's just so much to process. You just lost your boyfriend, and now you're having his baby? It's a lot."

We both stared at the bathroom tiles.

"I'll call the doctor in the morning. Once I know for sure, and how far along I am and all that, I will call my mom. I promise. Then I'll make a plan. Until then, there's nothing else I can do."

She nodded her head in acceptance.

"You're going to have a baby." A slow grin spread on her face. "You're going to have a cute, genius, supermodel baby."

I looked down at my stomach. I was going to have a baby, Benoit's baby. The realization was sinking in. I would get to raise our child; a child that represents everything good and pure about love.

I smiled. We were not done after all.

Chapter Fifteen

T he hardest part about grieving is the cloud of guilt that looms in the aftermath.

Guilt for all the would haves, should haves, could haves. Conversations that play over in your head, all ending with the same sickening conclusion that it doesn't matter: There's no chance for do-overs.

If that's not bad enough, everything you do is scrutinized. You're acting too angry, too depressed, too quiet, too emotional. Later, as you begin to heal, the guilt of healing kicks in. Smiling and laughing seem offensively inappropriate. Moving on too quickly feels wrong, yet taking too long to move on feels worse. The guilt cycle spins until you don't know how to feel, except that you're supposed to feel something other than how you actually feel.

After learning I was pregnant, I was overwrought with conflicting emotions. I didn't want grief to affect my pregnancy, but I couldn't find a way to process the pain of losing Benoit with the fear and joy. of being pregnant. I hadn't yet told my family, and I couldn't burden

Kelly as she prepared for her wedding. So, I looked up a psychologist: Jack Horn, Grief Counselor. That'll do, I thought.

My first experience with Jack caught me off guard. I pulled up to an old house that had been converted into offices in a little suburb outside of Philadelphia. Jack's name was not on the sign outside, but a law firm, accounting firm, and wedding planner touted signage. I checked the address again and determined that this was the correct address. I walked into a small reception area with eight empty chairs and looked for a sign or a plaque that would offer a way to Jack's office, but I couldn't find one.

This is bullshit, I thought. Jack is probably a serial killer who lures women into this house. There's likely a basement full of momentos he has collected from all the stupid women who actually came to see Jack the psychologist and ended up down in a well, "putting the fucking lotion in the basket."

I turned around to leave just as a door opened. Out walked a tall, broad, linebacker-looking man, sniffling with red eyes and a handful of tissues. "Thanks, Jack," he said hoarsely.

"I'll see you next week," Jack said impassively as he followed the man out.

The man nodded toward me as he walked out the door.

Jack stopped in front of me, "Anna?" he asked warmly. Jack might have been able to throw me down the stairs and into a well about 60 years earlier, but not today. Jack was old, with thinned white hair and a sea of deep lines in his face. He looked as frail as a dried flower; if you touched him, he might crumble. He walked with a limp and wore reading glasses on a cord that hung around his neck and rested on his sweater.

I nodded.

"Right this way," he said, and turned to lead me into a room.

The room was the size of a large bathroom. A small loveseat sat at one end of the rectangular room; each arm touching opposite sides of the wall. Jack's large office chair sat across from the loveseat; a round coffee table with a box of tissue in between. Two diplomas from Temple University hung on the wall and crammed in the corner was a filing cabinet topped with a fake plant and a wooden plaque that read: John A. Horn, PhD, PsyD. Jack for short.

Jack motioned for me to sit on the loveseat. He sat in his chair, grabbed a clipboard, and licked his finger to turn his notebook to a fresh piece of paper.

"So, what brings you here today, Anna?" The way he spoke invited a calm wave to sweep over my body, like warm honey on a sore throat. For no reason I could make clear, I started crying.

"Well, in a nutshell, I am pregnant," I sniffled. Jack offered a subtle congratulatory smile and reached over to hand me a tissue. He sat back and stared at me attentively.

"I'm 12 weeks along and, well, that would be exciting news, under normal circumstances. But mine are not normal circumstances. Mine are not normal at all."

I waited for Jack to ask me what made my circumstances abnormal, but he just stared at me with his grandfatherly eyes and waited for me to continue. Nevertheless, I felt compelled to keep the one-way dialogue going.

"They're not normal because my boyfriend, the father of my baby, died four weeks ago. He had a sudden cardiac death, or some bullshit like that."

I held the tissue under my eye and realized it was no use; tears were coming faster than I could catch them. Jack stayed disconcertedly quiet.

Finally: "What do you mean by *bullshit*?"

I stared at him incredulously. *Really, Jack? That's what you're interested in? Why I used profanity?* Jesus, this was a waste of time. Except that I was crying, and this crying felt good. This crying felt cathartic; it wasn't laced with the guilt of burdening someone else, or the emptiness of crying alone. This crying was pure.

"It's bullshit because it doesn't fucking make sense," I whined angrily. "He was only 34, and he had a heart attack in the middle of the morning that killed him. No warning? No prior heart condition?" I said as if someone owed me an answer.

Jack stared at me.

"And it's bullshit because we were in love, newly in love, and it was the kind of love that would have lasted; I know it. We were starting something unique; our own little love story that belonged to us and no one else. And then he was just gone. Just one day, gone. Before we even got to the good stuff. Before we got to meet each other's families and get married and have babies and bicker over bills. Before any of that." I choked on tears. "Before we were done."

I sobbed uncontrollably. A quiet wail of frustration seeped out. "*We weren't done.* That's all that keeps going through my head, and it feels so goddamn unfair." I put my head on my knees, my arms over my head, and wept as my body shook out feelings of anger and frustration, despair and fear, sadness and unjustness.

I sat up and wiped my eyes. I was drained.

"And it's bullshit because I had to go on that stupid business trip that was a waste of time and if I hadn't gone, I would've been there to call 9-1-1 and he might still be alive. Instead, he died on the floor of a hotel room with no one to help him. No one should die like that, alone and helpless."

Admitting the guilt made me shift with discomfort.

"And now I'm pregnant and I didn't get to see the look on his face when I told him. He would've been so happy," I cried softly. "And it's bullshit because this baby will never know his father, and I'll only have a snippet of information to offer about him. And it's bullshit that when I can't feel any more lonely, any more empty, I'm going to be raising a child on my own, and that's scary, and sad, and pretty fucking terrifying."

Jack stared empathetically. My body felt tired; I wanted to lay down and sleep, actually sleep, for the first time in four weeks.

"I think the most bullshit part right now is that I want to be happy about this pregnancy and just stop crying so much. When will the crying stop, Jack?" I pleaded. "When do I stop crying all the fucking time?" I grabbed a fresh tissue, discarding my last tissue onto a mountain of used ones.

Jack waited a moment to answer, then said pragmatically, "You'll stop crying when you're ready to stop crying. It will be gradual, and you might not notice it. But one day, you'll cry a little less than the day before. Then one week, you'll cry a little less than the week before. Until one day, you'll realize you can't remember the last time you cried."

I looked at him with renewed hope.

"But you'll never stop crying because those tears of anguish will turn into tears of happiness as the memories turn from sharp to sweet. You might find yourself yearning for and welcoming crying as a sign of remembrance and love. So, the answer is: Never. You'll never stop crying; the crying will just serve a different purpose."

I smiled weakly and nodded my head as his words took root.

"I'm looking forward to that," I said. "I'm really looking forward to that."

Later that day, I called Eloise. We spoke regularly after the funeral, but had fallen short of conversation lately.

"Allo?" She answered.

"Eloise, hi, it's Anna!" I said warmly.

"Anna! Hi, how are you?" she asked, switching to English.

"I'm great, how have you been?"

"Oh, same as usual. Very busy, which is good. It keeps my mind occupied."

"That's good. Well, I do want to catch up on everything, but I actually called to tell you some exciting news."

"Oh?'

"Yes." I paused. *Why was this so hard to spit out?* "I am calling because I wanted to tell you that I'm pregnant."

Silence.

"I'm 12 weeks along."

Silence.

Then I realized she hadn't connected that the baby was Benoit's.

"It's Benoit's baby. I'm pregnant with your niece or nephew." I hoped this would evoke reaction.

"Oh my God!" she screeched. Her voice cracked into an elated cry, "I'm going to be an aunt?!"

"Yes! You're going to be an aunt!" I laughed. Eloise's joy gave me renewed energy, like a boxer getting motivation from the crowd in the 10th round.

"Anna, when are you due to have the baby?"

"June. June 5th," I said.

"I will be there, if that's okay?"

"Of course! I would be so grateful to have you here!"

"Anna, you have made me smile for the first time in a long time."

My eyes watered. "I'm so glad, Eloise."

"I'm going to be an aunt!" she squealed.

I giggled.

"Anna, do you know what this means?"

"What?"

She got serious. "It means that Benoit lives. Benoit lives in that baby. I'm not alone. I have family."

I held back tears. "Yes, you do. You have family in us, Eloise."

Chapter Sixteen

"**I**s that seat taken?" An attractive man was pointing to the seat next to me on the train.

I glanced at the unoccupied seats around us as people shuffled past in the aisle. Boarding Track Five at Philadelphia's 30th Street Station resembled opening the doors to a major retailer on Black Friday.

"Uh, no," I tried to mask my confusion. It was impractical to think that I would have gotten away with keeping the window seat occupied with only my briefcase on a 7 a.m. ride to D.C., but as of now, there were plenty of other seats available. I grabbed my briefcase and placed it under the seat in front of me, then stood up to let him through.

"Thanks," he said as he shimmied in. Normally, I would have gone back to minding my business, but there was something entertaining about the way he fidgeted and talked to himself while pulling out his laptop that kept my interested eye on him.

"I was at a concert late last night," he looked at me and smiled. His smile was alarmingly beguiling, and I hoped the awe in my face wasn't obvious.

"I was entertaining clients and stayed out way too late," he continued. "I didn't think I was going to catch this train! I literally woke up, took a shower, grabbed my stuff, and ran to the train station. I don't even know if I have socks on. Do I have socks on?" he asked, as if we were old friends.

We both looked down at his feet. "You are wearing socks," I smiled amusedly.

"I'm not gonna lie, I'm shocked."

I chuckled curiously. How was I charmed by a stranger asking me about his socks? Ignoring further thought about it, I turned to fish out my phone. I should check on Eloise and Nathan. I left the house this morning before either of them were awake.

I dialed Eloise.

"Allo?" She always answered in French.

"Good morning, Eloise."

"Bonjour! How is your morning?" she replied cheerfully.

"Good. I'm on the train now, but I wanted to check in. Reception can get spotty once we're moving. How's Nathan?"

Nathan Benoit Reed was born on a sunny May day, 10 days before his due date. My one-year contract at Kahn & Hague had expired, and I had declined their renewal offer. Walking to the building each day, entering only from Market Street to avoid Chestnut Street, where Benoit and I had shared now painfully sweet memories, was something I was happy to leave behind. Instead, my Utah-based employer offered me a full-time position managing a portfolio of large-market clients in the eastern region. I accepted gratefully, which allowed me to work from home, supplemented with travel from New York to the Carolinas. All day-trips, no overnights, which was manageable with a baby.

"Nathan is wonderful," Eloise chimed. "He's eating and making a mess right now. We have big plans to go to the park today and later we are going to make some carrot and pear popsicles, aren't we, Nathan?" she said to me, but more so to Nathan.

"That sounds lovely. Call if you need me, but I may not be available if I'm in a meeting. I'll let you know when I catch the train home."

"Of course! Don't worry about a thing. We've got it all under control!"

"Thanks Eloise, give a kiss to Nathan for me. Goodbye."

I hung up and sighed thankfully for Eloise, who had moved to Philadelphia to help me with Nathan. She stayed for four weeks after he was born, and by the end of her stay, I begged her to be my nanny. I didn't have much to offer by way of compensation, but I promised that I'd always provide a roof over her head and food to eat; and most importantly, a family. She went back to Paris, sold her part of the patisserie to her business partner, and moved to Philadelphia with two suitcases and an old French mixer.

The train was now moving. Time of arrival to Washington D.C.: 8:47 a.m.

"You have children?" I realized, embarrassed, that the guy next to me had listened to my conversation, although how can you not when you're sitting shoulder-to-shoulder with someone?

"Yes, a son. He's eight months old," I answered proudly.

He slackened sincerely. "That's amazing. Congratulations."

"Thank you. Do you have kids?" I asked politely.

"No, I wish. I was married. She left me with a lot of bills, but no kids," he laughed.

I liked his candor.

"I'm Anna, by the way." I held out my hand as introduction.

"I'm Marco." He shook my hand.

He was a good-looking man. Just short of 6 feet tall, I estimated, with olive skin, as if he just returned from sailing on the Mediterranean. He had dark hair, green eyes, and the most contagious smile I had ever seen.

I looked away, annoyed that I didn't want to. Since Benoit's death over the past year and a half, I had been grossly involved in pregnancy, work, baby, and now, work again. I hadn't had the faintest interest in men or where one might fall in my future. I was content with just being a mom. But Marco had gotten my attention.

"You live in the city?" he interrupted my thoughts.

"I used to, but I live in Manayunk now."

"Oh, I like Manayunk. Great town. What made you leave the city?"

"Well, mostly Nathan. I needed more room after the baby. It's less expensive and easier to find bigger places with better parking in Manayunk."

"Oh, you're divorced too?" he asked eagerly.

"No, not divorced."

"Baby daddy?" he asked, nonoffensively.

"Not exactly. My son's father passed away while I was pregnant. Actually, before I even knew I was pregnant."

"I'm so sorry."

"No, it's okay. Obviously, it was rough at first, but we're good now. Thank you, though."

"Do you have a picture of him? Nathan, I meant?"

I reached for a picture I carried in my briefcase.

"He's beautiful," he said as he stared at the picture. "You're very lucky."

I am very lucky, I thought, and I appreciated that he saw it that way, too.

Just then, another train passed closely from the opposite direction, creating a thunderous noise and causing the entire car to shake. I impulsively grabbed the arm rest with my left hand and my knee with my right, and Marco did the same, but with opposite hands.

"Jesus! That scares me every time!" I laughed as the train finished passing and the sound went back to normal.

We looked down and realized our hands were practically bracing each other's. He grabbed my hand and lifted it up. "I thought Nathan's picture and this hand were going to be the last things I saw and felt before dying!" he laughed, easing the awkwardness.

"Me, too!" We laughed from our bellies as the fright of it resolved.

We talked a little bit about business; he was in IT and going to his headquarters for a meeting. He hated his industry, just too much bureaucracy and politics in the corporate world. He was good at it, but he wanted a simpler life; something more fulfilling.

"Like what?" I asked, intrigued.

"I don't know. I've always wanted to open a biscotti shop. My mother makes the best biscotti—an old family recipe—and I always dreamed of having an Italian-style coffee shop where you walk in and choose a flavor of biscotti to have with your coffee."

That sounded nice, I thought. I could relate to wanting a simpler life. Since having Nathan, I found my job, and the entire corporate world, less enchanting. The drive I once had to impress those at the top had waned as I compared being Nathan's everything to being a replaceable object paid to make the bank money, a lot of it. This morning, before leaving, I lingered over Nathan's crib watching him sleep; his chubby cheeks puckering his softly opened mouth. I wanted to stay home just a little bit longer and be the one to take him to the park and make carrot and pear popsicles with him.

"You don't like coffee, do you?" he asked. "Or you're one of those 'Ameri-cahns' who drink year-old coffee from pods?" He said "Ameri-cahns" with an accent, rolling the 'r.'

I laughed. "No, I despise the pods. I'm quite the coffee snob, if you want to know the truth. I only drink coffee from an old French press. Otherwise, I stick with tea. It's hard to mess up tea; it's unassuming and simple."

He smiled.

"It sounds nice though, your biscotti shop. I think you should do it," I said confidently.

"Really? Just like that?"

"Why not? Life is too short not to do it. You never know if you'll have the opportunity to do it later. If it's what you really want, then go for it."

With his charming smile, he enticed, "On that note, let me take you to dinner."

"I really set you up for that, didn't I?" I flustered.

"Just dinner. Tonight, when we get back to Philadelphia."

"It's not that easy for me. I have a baby. I have to get home."

"Okay, another night then."

I contemplated his offer. "How about this? If you and I end up on the same train back to Philly, I'll let you take me to dinner."

"I don't know if I can take that risk. I mean, I made a pact with myself many years ago that if I ever found a woman who could make me want to drink tea, I was going to have to marry her. Now I have to gamble on whether or not I'll see you again?"

I laughed. "Oh my God! Stop!"

"You think I'm joking? I am dead serious!" he said playfully.

I shook my head. "I guess you're going to have to hope you make it back to the train station before I do."

"Oh, I'll be there. Just a second while I cancel all of my meetings." He pretended to cancel his meetings on his laptop. He stopped after a second and stared at me. "Okay, Anna, I accept your challenge. But if I don't see you this afternoon, it might mean eternal disappointment for me."

I shrugged, "What's the Italian saying: *Que Sera Sera?*"

His face lit up. "Yes. What will be, will be."

My meetings ran longer than I anticipated after my client insisted that we break for lunch. I was intent to finish the few last items on the agenda and have a late lunch on my way back to the train station, but they had other plans.

"There's a new sushi place across the street. We've all been dying to try it." It was typical for clients to wait for the bankers to show up and pay for a meal on which they'd otherwise not splurge.

I checked my watch. "A quick bite, but I have to catch a 3 p.m. train, so we'll have to work through some of these items while we eat."

They may as well have high-fived each other, they seemed so pleased.

We worked through sushi, which was, admittedly, amazing. Then, I packed my briefcase and waited for a cab to Union Station. I tried to convince myself that I was just anxious to get home to see Nathan, but I finally owned up to the fact that I was curious, excited even, to see if Marco would be there.

I arrived at 2:34 p.m. with plenty of time to catch the 3 o'clock. I went to the bathroom to freshen up my hair and apply new lip gloss. As women bustled past, I stared in the mirror, realizing that preening was something I didn't expect to do for a long time. But dammit, it felt good to be noticed again, and to notice someone else.

I walked toward the terminal to where the train would depart to Philadelphia. Union Station was overwhelmingly crowded. Nearly every seat was occupied, and people were standing idly waiting for the train to arrive. I walked casually, trying not to look like I was eagerly searching for Marco, when I heard, "Anna! Anna!"

I turned my head in the direction of my name and sitting on a chair was Marco, waving his arms and beckoning with that huge, contagious smile. I laughed. He did it; he earned his dinner date with me.

I waved modestly and he motioned for me to come toward him. When I reached him, he held up a cup. "I got you a coffee, I mean, a tea," he said.

I took the tea in both hands. "What kind of tea?" I asked playfully.

"Uh, green tea."

I took a sip. "It's good."

"But it's not your fave. Shit, you're an Earl Grey girl, aren't you?"

I shook my head.

"Straight black tea?"

I shook my head.

"How many other kinds of tea are there?"

"Chai. I'm a chai gal, a soy chai latte gal."

"Not gonna lie, never would've guessed that. Like ever. I don't think I even know what a soy chai latte is."

I laughed. "But green tea is my second favorite."

He smiled proudly.

"It's still hot," I said quizzically.

"I've been sitting here all day, getting a fresh tea every half hour," he said with a serious face.

My eyes widened. "You have?"

"No. I did go to my meetings. But I rushed through lunch to make it here by 2 p.m. I think I left lunch before paying. It's okay, Gary owed me."

"So, I guess this means we get to have dinner?" I asked as if it were a suggestion more than a question.

He confirmed with a flashy nod.

Marco was first-generation Italian, I learned on our ride back. He was the first in his family, as far back as "the books" went, to be divorced; his wife ran off with her high-school boyfriend.

"It broke my mother's heart," he said. "I mean, it broke my heart too. I never saw myself being divorced."

"That must have been hard," I empathized.

He winked at me. "It's all good. Things happen for a reason, right?"

I nodded. It was hard to imagine anyone cheating on Marco. Aside from being charming and good-looking, he also was playful and sincere. He had the sort of whimsical bravado that was confident, but not offensive; like he could tell you that you stink, but you'd laugh instead of feel hurt. His demeanor was just so carefree and animated, which naturally made him intriguing and entertaining.

Our conversation on the ride back was lively and dynamic. There was a different level of energy that surrounded Marco. My stomach muscles ached from laughing as we approached Philadelphia; I was surprised to feel a speck of apprehension about the train ride being over so quickly.

"So, Anna, are you going to give me your number, or are you going to challenge me to guess a date, time, and place for our third date?"

I resigned, "I'll give you my number this time, but don't get all cocky about it."

"I'm already cocky about the fact that you went on two dates with me."

I chuckled and took his phone to enter my number.

He walked me to the entrance of the corridor where I would continue walking to the parking garage. He would veer off in the opposite direction to walk home to Center City. We stopped and stared at each other awkwardly.

"I'm glad to have met you, Anna."

"I'm glad, too. "

He kissed me on the cheek and flashed his irresistible smile again. My stomach lurched with butterflies.

"Until next time, then." And he turned to go. I almost expected to see him jump and clap his feet together as he walked off, a la Dick van Dyk as the chimney sweep in *Mary Poppins*.

I grinned from ear to ear as I walked toward my car, and put a hand to my cheek to lock in the lingering warmth of his kiss.

"Hey," Kelly answered the phone quickly.

"Hey."

"Hey," she said more inquisitively.

"I met someone. A guy. On the train."

Short silence, then, "Mmm-hmm?"

"His name is Marco."

"Geez, you sure know how to pick men with unconventional names. Italian?"

"Obviously."

"Italians make great husbands. They're loyal, and like kids, and usually cook."

"So much for stereotyping," I teased.

"Well, it's true," she said.

"Anyway, he asked me to dinner."

"So, go," she said encouragingly.

"I don't know if I'm ready to be dating again."

"I don't think there's a rule about this kind of thing, Anna. It's just dinner. If nothing else, it's good practice to get back out there."

"You're right. Okay," I said.

"Did you meet on the way there, or on the way back? Don't know why I'm asking, just curious."

"Both."

"Both?"

"Yeah, it's a long story, but we sat next to each other on the way there, then ended up on the same train back."

"Cute."

"It is pretty cute." I couldn't help the smile from spreading across my face.

"Is he good-looking?"

"Very. And funny. He made me laugh. He's very energetic."

"That's good. This will be good for you."

"Thanks. I'll let you go. I'm sure you're busy unpacking."

"Yeah, I finally picked up all our shit from storage that we got for the wedding, now that I have the room to unpack it." Kelly and Tom had, as predicted, recently bought a house in Cherry Hill, New Jersey.

"Yikes, good luck," I said.

"Yeah, don't feel obligated to come help me. It's not like I've ever been there for you or anything," she said sarcastically.

"I'll bring Nathan this weekend and help," I laughed.

She giggled. "Okay. Are you going to bring Polo and Marco, too? Oh my God! You'll be dating a Marco and have dog named Polo! That's funny! I mean, if you call Marco's name, does Polo perk up and bark, "Polo?"

"You're nuts, Kel," I laughed. "Gotta go."

Chapter Seventeen

"Have I told you today how much I love you?" Marco asked me as we loosened oysters with a little fork and shot them down with vinegar and Tabasco sauce. It was date night and Eloise was watching the kids.

"Hmmm, not today," I frowned teasingly.

"Shame on me! I love you, and you look beautiful tonight." He leaned over to kiss my cheek.

As certain as the sun rises and sets, Marco adored me. Even after five years and three kids, Marco made me feel like the most important and beautiful thing in his life. From the outside looking in, one might think Marco doted on me more than I doted on him. But our relationship was anything but one-sided. I adored Marco to the point of nausea; I was just a little less vocal or openly demonstrative about it.

"Did I tell you what Lucas told me the other day when he came home from school?" I asked.

"Oh no, what?" Lucas was the jokester of our family.

"I was making the kids a snack after school, and I asked how their day was, if anything new happened, all that." I implied. "Without missing a beat, Lucas looked up and said, 'Well, I met God today.'"

Marco's eyebrows rose and he chuckled. "He did *what*?"

"That was my reaction!" I laughed. "I kept a cool face, but said, 'That's pretty amazing, bud. Where did you meet…God?' And Lucas replied casually that he saw God at school during snack."

Marco giggled with anticipation.

I continued. "They sing a little prayer over their snack to the tune of Superman, 'Thank you God for giving us food,'" I demonstrated. "And after the song, Lucas said that God walked in and gave them all Goldfish crackers and cheese sticks!"

Marco looked at me, amusedly confused.

"Apparently, the janitor, Mr. Wolfe, was filling in for Mrs. Brillo, who usually brings the snacks into the classroom. So when Mr. Wolfe walked in with food, Lucas figured he was God because they had just thanked God for giving them food in their prayer!"

Marco guffawed and almost started choking. "That is hysterical! Oh man, what are we going to do with that kid?"

"Well, at the very least, it might be time to talk to our kids about God," I laughed.

"You're much better qualified for the job," he said. "I got kicked out of CCD. Whenever my name showed up as the altar boy, the priest did the sign of the cross."

"I'm not sure what I can offer, either. I was hoping that putting them into a Methodist preschool would kind of help us out in that regard, but clearly they're messing it up as badly as we would."

"I say we just let him go on thinking Mr. Wolfe is God. I mean, he seems like a nice enough guy."

I chortled and shook my head. "It's funny, but it's also kind of not funny. I mean, our child thinks the janitor is God. Can you imagine what the teachers must have said to each other? They're probably still praying for the real God to forgive our poor parenting and not send us straight to Hell."

He rolled his eyes. "I'll call my mom. She'll take them to church with her. They'll be fixed in a few weeks."

"Oh geez, your mother's dream," I laughed exasperatingly.

The bartender, who after many years of serving us, had anticipated our order and set down our bronzino and salad, then topped off our glasses of wine.

"Changing the subject, how are things at the shop?" I asked casually.

After a whirlwind courtship of only six months, Marco and I had married and moved to Doylestown, a suburb 35 miles north of Philadelphia. With my commission bonus and the sale proceeds of Marco's Center City apartment, we bought a modest four-bedroom home in a crowded neighborhood that was "good for trick-or-treating," Marco observed when we first pulled up to it with the realtor.

We also used some of the money to open a biscotti shop in downtown Doylestown, which was a quaint and bustling series of streets with restaurants and shops. The plan was for Marco to run the shop while I continued to work for the bank. But plans changed when I found out I was pregnant with Lucas, then later, Lily. I stayed with the bank until Lucas' birth, after which point, I resigned. Taking a break from a career I worked so hard for was admittedly tough to do, but as it turned out, I was surprisingly good at domesticity and found a calm sense of order in managing our lives at home. And at least owning the coffee shop, I had equity in something. The shop wouldn't afford any more studded Valentino shoes, but we were rich with love, and that felt much better.

Marco took a sip of wine. "Things at the shop are good, same as usual."

I could sense avoidance in his answer. He never looked me in the eyes and his voice took on more of an alto pitch when he was hiding something.

"Is that new coffee shop down the street taking any business from us? Or not really?" I probed.

He looked preoccupied while chewing. "A little, maybe. Nothing to worry about though."

His distracted demeanor told me things were worse than he was saying.

"You sure, honey?"

He kept chewing and nodded.

"Marco, you can tell me if things are not great. I can handle it, you know. I'm a pretty tough woman," I winked.

He looked up with a weary smile. "I know you're tough, but I don't want to worry you. Let me worry. That's what I'm built for."

I tipped my head to one side. "How bad is it?"

He was scraping the fish bones with his fork for the remaining pieces of meat.

"How bad is it, babe?" I repeated a little more seriously.

"I'm behind on a couple of flour invoices." He sighed, then shifted uncomfortably, grabbing his glass of water.

"That's not too bad," I inhaled. "Busy season is here. We should catch up pretty quickly, I would think?"

He grimaced.

"Babe, what is it?" I asked softly. Marco rarely showed distress. He was the fixer, the hustler, the no-loss-only-opportunity guy, which was why we were such a good team. And it also was why I hadn't worried much about the shop, until now.

"Nothing. I'll figure it out, I promise," he said.

"Marco, tell me. Is it worse than that?" I asked.

He let out a sharp exhale. "I had to dip into our line of credit at the bank to pay a couple of bills."

I nodded composedly. "Well, that's what it's there for; to float us during a bad month."

He shifted.

"Oh God, how many months, honey?" I asked.

"Six."

I gasped. That line of credit was backed by a personal guarantee, and if we got behind and became delinquent, it would impact our personal credit. I panicked, thinking of my 730 credit score taking a dive. But it was more than that: The bank could come after our house, our everything.

"Maybe seven," he resigned. "I don't know. When I catch up on one bill, I get behind on another, and the shop just isn't pulling in the revenue that it used to."

I swallowed hard and tried not to overreact. If we were seven months behind on bills, and hitting our line of credit to keep afloat, that meant we were essentially seven months in debt while interest continued to build. It had been some time since I managed the books at the shop, but some quick head math calculated that at best, we were $30,000 behind.

"What does our revenue look like right now? And what's our biggest expense?" I asked calmly.

"Well, aside from flour, it's my and Eloise's paychecks."

I got a pit in my stomach.

Marco and Eloise had worked together since Biscotti opened its doors. Eloise spent countless hours with Marco's mother, Rosetta, perfecting her biscotti recipe. The French baker had quickly become a biscotti master, infusing a dash of French flair to the Italian cookie. The result was a biscotti in all of its crunchy, twice-baked glory, with a hint of softness from a little extra French butter. Marco and Eloise's partnership came as naturally as their friendship did; and with her baking expertise, Eloise became head baker, while Marco managed the business side of the shop.

"Eloise would understand if we had to let her go," I said, not meaning it.

He looked up at me sharply. "I can't let Eloise go. You know I can't. We can't. No way." Marco had become more protective of Eloise than perhaps I was. He sighed, "I called Gary to see if I could maybe get back into IT Sales for a bit."

I gasped. "You called Gary? You hated that job. Are you even still up-to-speed on their products, or services, or whatever?"

He looked slightly offended. "I'm not some dumb coffee shop baker, Anna. I'll be fine getting back into IT."

"And I'm not some dumb stay-at-home-Mom, either, Marco," I retorted with more defensiveness than I liked. I toned it down. "I'm sorry. It's just that you could have talked to me earlier about this. You might recall that I have a pretty good brain up here," I tapped my head with a muted smile. "One that's good with business and numbers. I could've helped sooner."

We both took a sip of wine to formulate our next words.

Marco grabbed my knee. "I'm sorry. You're right. I didn't keep it from you because I thought you were incapable of helping. Hell, you can do pretty much everything, and usually better than anyone else. I just didn't want to worry you; you're so busy at home with the kids and everything else. Besides, I made this mess. I should be the one cleaning it."

"That's not exactly how it works, honey. You know that. We are the best team I've ever known. I'd bet on us every day of the week. If you had let me in, we could have figured this out together."

He looked at me apologetically.

"Hey look, it doesn't matter what has happened. You and I can fix this," I reassured him. "If you're certain you want to go back to work with Gary, I'll run the shop. Lily is almost potty- trained, which means she can start preschool soon. This will give me something to do. I'm going to be bored without the kids," I lied. I secretly had been counting down the days to when I'd have freedom to read a book again and enjoy an entire cup of coffee before it went cold.

"Are you sure? I know you were looking forward to getting some time back to yourself. Were you still thinking about going back to banking?"

"Ah, no. We both know that it's not realistic for me to go back to banking full-time. I'll never be able to be the mom I want to be. This will be a good in-between for me. Biscotti will keep me busy and it's flexible enough that I can still make it to school bake sales and field trips. I really never pictured myself saying that when I was in my 20s," I laughed.

Marco smiled, then turned sober. "I'm so sorry, babe."

I knew that Marco kept the problems at Biscotti from me to protect me, and likely because at first it was one bad month that he thought he could catch up on, but then it led to two bad months, which led to seven. Regardless, I felt a tinge of resentment that he didn't trust that I could help. I knew it wasn't conscious on his part, but somewhere in the midst of changing diapers and baking zucchini muffins with flax seeds and whole wheat flour, I had become someone who couldn't handle the operational details of a business—at least in Marco's eyes. And that fact bothered me more than any other.

The even more unsatisfying facet was that it was no use trying to figure out how we got here, or what we should have done differently. There always was only one answer for Marco and me: Us. And choosing Us meant that we just had to move forward together on a solution.

"It's okay. I mean, I wish you would've told me about this earlier, but it makes no difference now. We're going to fix this. You focus on getting back into the swing of things with Gary, and I'll focus on Biscotti. I can do this, trust me."

"I really don't deserve you, you know?" Marco said.

"Stop it," I grinned. "Honestly, I'm looking forward to getting involved in the shop and using that part of my brain again. This will be good for me."

"Yeah, I'm a little excited to get back into IT. It's funny how things change. Five years ago, I couldn't wait to have a slower paced life. But now, I kind of miss the cut-throat hustle and bustle."

"Change is good, as long as we're changing together. Us First, right?" I winked at him.

"Always. Us First." He raised his glass.

Chapter Eighteen

The first thing I did when I took over Biscotti management was change Jared's role. Jared was a 26-year-old, good-looking, works-to-feed-his-soul kind of guy who was a baker at Biscotti in the mornings and a mixology student in the afternoons. When I learned Jared was about to graduate, I asked if he would consider becoming our coffee mixologist. "Sure, could be cool."

"How are you with people?"

"You mean, do I like them? Of course. You have to be a people person to be a good bartender."

"What if we made a challenge for you that would be fun for our customers? When they come in, you guess the perfect coffee for them; and if it's not the best fit, the coffee is free?"

He smiled reservedly. "I don't know. What if I end up giving a lot of coffee away?"

"Don't worry about that. Coffee margins are huge. The idea is to get customers through the door. Even if we have to remake the coffee, they're likely to buy something else with higher margins while they're in here."

He nodded, understanding the concept.

"It doesn't hurt that you look like Jared Leto either," I added, "with a beard. Circa *My So Called Life*."

Jared looked at me quizzically.

"Never mind. The point is that all the high school girls will come in and spend their parent's money to have Jared guess their coffee." I said *Jared* with the tone of a struck love girl.

He laughed modestly. "I don't know, but okay. I'm down with it. Let's give it a try."

The next day, Jared came in with three questions he would ask each customer, which would lead him to guess her favorite coffee:

1) *Do you prefer red or white wine?* This question was meant to test acidity preference.

2) *Milkshake or water ice?* This question was meant to test milk preference.

3) *Plain cupcake or cupcake with frosting, sprinkles, and cherry on top?* This question was meant to test appetite for embellishments in the coffee.

Jared tested his theory on the staff and nailed an 80 percent accuracy rate. I posted an oversized trifold sign on the sidewalk outside the shop, challenging the walking traffic to "Beat the Barista, or Get a Free Coffee!"

Word spread fast, and walk-in traffic more than doubled, with customers loitering to watch other customers take the challenge. I would soon need to hire another Jared as a backup if the original Jared quit, I thought to myself; and added that task to my list.

Eloise wouldn't admit it, but I could tell she was a little resentful of the attention Jared was getting. Her biscotti creations had been the center of our shop (hence, the name); but now, people were showing up just as much for the coffee experience. I encouraged her to work with Jared in creating a "perfect pairing" challenge, like a sommelier would pair a wine with a certain dish. She smiled, but I knew getting to that point would take some work.

Meanwhile, it had taken me about two weeks to balance the books, or rather, determine how out of balance they really were. I reached out to vendors, and in some cases switched vendors, to negotiate lower costs on products. I let the early afternoon staff go; surely I could manage serving biscotti and making lattes for those four slow hours. I even found a way to transfer some of the debt we had accumulated to interest-free loans, with the catch that they be paid off in six months.

Despite all these efforts, I couldn't see a way to catch up in six months. The line of credit debt was worse than I thought: It had reached more than $35,000. It would take us at least one year, if we were lucky, to break even again. And if I didn't pay that loan off in six months, the compounding interest, waiting like a lit firecracker, would skyrocket to an amount that would be nearly impossible to rectify.

As I sat in the back office, which I had modestly redecorated with items from our basement, I contemplated the future of Biscotti. It pained me to think about closing its doors; it had become more than what we "did;" it was part of who we were, as so often happens with having a small business. And my stomach churned at the thought of letting Eloise go. I was determined to find a way to dig us out of this hole, and as thoughts of catering or birthday parties swirled in my head, I heard Eloise cursing loudly in French. I walked out to find her tinkering with the mixer.

"The goddamn pin fell out again," she said as I approached. "It took six weeks for it to ship from Korea, or wherever, last time." She kicked the base of the mixer.

"That's the only place to get this 'pin?' From Korea? There has to be somewhere closer," I said skeptically.

"I don't know where else to go. I called the restaurant stores in Chalfont and Plymouth Meeting. They both said the same thing: They could order it, but it would take six weeks."

That seemed ridiculous. There were hundreds of bakeries and pizza shops using the same industrial-sized mixers in the Greater Philadelphia area. Surely, they all couldn't halt business for six weeks if the pin broke.

"I'll find the pin. In the meantime, do you have a way to manage until I can track one down?"

She looked at me doubtfully. "I can make small batches in the countertop mixers. It takes double the time, but I can manage for now. Last time, I had to use Sweet Thing's mixers to make all my dough at midnight before they came in for the day, then transport it here. It was miserable."

"Do the best you can with the small mixers, and I'll find the pin. Write down exactly what it is for me, please?"

She put her hands out as if to say she gave up, but she nodded compliantly. She walked slowly over to a sticky pad and wrote down the part number.

"Thanks. Just give me an hour."

"If you track that pin down in an hour, your next date night is on me!" she said provokingly.

"It is anyway," I scoffed. "But I accept the challenge. Have I ever lost a bet?"

She knew the answer: No.

Chapter Nineteen

I pulled off the Callowhill exit and continued down Second Street toward the restaurant equipment store in Philadelphia. Driving into the city, seeing the skyline and bridges, still made me tingle.

It had taken some convincing for the restaurant store manager to sell me the pin, though he alluded to having access to one. He clearly had his favorite customers and didn't welcome special requests from outsiders, but he finally relented after I told him I'd come down and wait in person while he tried to track it down. I had nothing to do today, I told him, and I'd be happy to wait with him. He put me on hold and somehow found the pin.

"Can I help you?" An unkempt, overweight man sat on a stool behind the counter as I walked in, the door chiming. I recognized his voice; he must be the manager.

"Frank?"

"Yeh."

"I'm Anna. I called you about the mixer pin?"

He stared at me, then heavily dismounted the stool without saying a word. I watched him curiously as he waddled past me and toward the back of the store. I was unsure if I was meant to follow him, but I did, anyway. He grabbed a plastic bag from off the shelf.

"This what you lookin' for?" He handed me the bag.

I opened the bag and pulled out the pin.

"I guess so. It looks like the same part. This is part number 30-2-80-8?"

He grunted, which I took as a yes ma'am, though God-forbid he exerted energy to say that. I despised laziness.

"That's great, thank you, Frank. This is really helpful. Do I pay you up at the counter?"

Another grunt.

"I'll follow you, then."

He took a minute to rev up the energy to waddle back to the counter.

"Cash or credit?" he asked as he walked.

"I can do either. Which do you prefer?"

"Cash," he answered in a gruff voice. He reached the register and plopped back down onto the stool with a clumsy groan.

"Okay, how much?" I asked.

"Seventy-five."

"You told me $65 on the phone."

We stared at each other, waiting for the other to draw first.

"It's $75."

I glared at him and thought about taking the pin and running. I mean, what could he really do? He couldn't catch me if I was blind and running with both legs tied together, through molasses. I wished I had the guts to do it.

I intuitively glanced toward the door as the thought ran through my mind and the shape of a man outside the large storefront window caught my eye. It was an undeniable shape, like that of a horse jockey; small and spindly, but it was his mannerisms that drew my attention. He wore a leather jacket as he lit his cigarette, shuffled his feet.

"Just a minute," I said to Frank without breaking my gaze, and I walked toward the door.

"Okay, $65!" I heard Frank holler crabbily after me.

I heedlessly opened the front door. "Joel?" I called.

The man turned around and there stood Joel, all 110 pounds of him, his bright blue eyes darted at me, then stuck in recognition.

"Uh, Anna, oh shit, wow, uh," he stuttered as he contemplated the best way to put out his cigarette.

"Joel, I thought that was you!" I beamed, walking toward him. "How have you been?"

He shuffled nervously and looked toward my waist, which was practically at his eye level. "Uh, good, good. I've been alright. Ya know, just same as usual," he ran a hand over his shaved head. "Shit. How have you been?"

"Good, I've been good," I said. "You're still in Philly, I see."

"Yeh, I mean, where the fuck else would I go?" he snorted. "I don't think I'm the Florida type."

I smiled. "Philly suits you."

I wanted to end the conversation there with a conclusive pleasantry, but something was nagging at me: The image of Joel at Benoit's funeral, his tiny body lingering in the trees. Why hadn't he come closer? Why hadn't he reached out to anyone since Benoit's death? More intriguingly, but pointless now anyway, what was his relationship with Benoit?

"I saw you at Benoit's funeral. You were standing by the trees." I waited for his reaction.

A flash of panic ran across his face, then he ran his hand over his head again and scratched behind his neck. "Uh, yeah, well, I didn't want to intrude, but…" he paused, "I wanted to be there, too, ya know."

"Why would you feel like you'd be intruding? You and Benoit were very close. You worked together for years, right?"

He paused before answering. "Right," he cleared his throat. "Right. We knew each other a long time."

"Then, why would you have been intruding?"

"I don't know," he sighed. "It's just like, we knew each other a long time, but I don't know, shit like that makes me uncomfortable."

There was more to learn, but I chose not to press it.

"I understand. Everyone deals with death differently."

He nodded and shuffled his feet.

"Hey! You probably wouldn't have known this, but did you know that Benoit has a son?" I asked.

"Really?" he asked, confused. I couldn't figure out how he kept his teeth so white with all the smoking and God-knows-what-else he did. Joel was blessed with good teeth genes.

"Yeah, turns out I was pregnant when Benoit passed away. His name is Nathan. Nathan Benoit. He's six now. He has Benoit's eyes. And hair."

"Wow, that's crazy. I mean, congratulations."

"Yep. He's amazing. The world has a funny way of working, I guess."

"Yeah, I guess so. So, do you guys live in Philly, still?"

"No, we're in Doylestown. I got married. I have two other kids, another boy and a little girl."

"Doylestown, huh?" He said *huh* in a contemplative way.

"Yeah. The 'burbs. You remember Eloise? Benoit's sister? I don't know if you two ever met, but she lives near us. She used to live with us, but now she lives nearby and works with my husband."

"Oh?"

"Actually, she did work with my husband. Now she works with me. It's a long story, but the short of it is that we run a coffee shop in Doylestown."

"A coffee shop?"

"Yeah. Eloise bakes the biscotti. She's a baker, you might remember?" He looked blankly at me. It seemed he didn't know much about Eloise. "Anyway, we run the shop now. That's why I'm here. The pin on our mixer broke, so I tracked one down to this store."

He nodded in understanding, but didn't respond.

"Anyway, I better get back in there," I gestured toward the store. "The manager's a real asshole, but I have to get this pin or Eloise is going to have a goddamn breakdown."

"Frank?" he asked.

"Hmmm?"

"Is Frank the asshole you're talking about?"

"Oh, yeah. He was trying to give me a different price than he quoted me on the phone, but I think I was winning the battle when I came outside. He'll get to my price. I'm not worried about it," I said confidently.

Joel opened the store door and proffered me to walk through. I hesitated, but went in. He walked in front of me with a quick gait, went behind the counter to where Frank was rooted, whispered something briefly in his ear, then walked back to me.

"I gotta go, Anna. It was real nice seeing you. I'm glad to hear Benoit has a baby, well, a boy now, I guess. But that's good stuff. Real good."

I was a little taken back, but I nodded. "It was good to see you again too, Joel. Take care."

He smiled awkwardly, then walked off in a distracted manner.

I sighed and looked back at Frank to settle up.

"It's on the house," Frank said gruffly, then shoved the bag with the pin over the counter to me.

Chapter Twenty

Though time had melted most of my city memories into a warm place, seeing Joel again stirred some of the colder ones to the surface. Over the next few days, whenever there was a lull in the shop, or as I lay in bed at night, memories related to Joel would reel in my head.

I remembered the first time I saw Joel, standing in that alley, then again outside my gate in that Philadelphia snow storm. I pictured Joel's small frame in the dense tree line at Benoit's funeral, and a flutter of discomfort gnawed at my stomach as it brought back all the questions I had about their relationship. Questions I thought I had made peace with were back like a nagging fly.

I didn't tell Marco that I had run into Joel for two reasons. I would be surprised if he remembered who Joel was; and I didn't want him to think that it stewed feelings about Benoit. Marco was far from jealous when it came to Benoit; we made it a point to speak freely about him with Eloise and of course, Nathan. But it's one thing to speak fondly of someone you loved; it's another to dwell in things that have no real relevance to the present.

The only person who wouldn't judge the fact that seeing Joel impelled thoughts about Benoit was Kelly, but she hadn't been available for that type of conversation lately. I spoke with her briefly while she was going through the car wash, then again when I was with Marco and the kids, then I missed her call another time.

So, I just pushed the interaction to the back of my mind and filed it under a "who cares" folder.

It was a rainy afternoon in Doylestown as I cleaned the espresso machine, so business was naturally slow. Eloise had finished her morning baking and had left to run some errands before coming back to prep dough for the next day. Jared was scheduled to come in shortly before I would need to pick up Lily from preschool.

The front door chimed, and I was startled to see Joel walking in briskly. My insides rolled a little.

"Joel! I didn't expect to see you here!" I said bewildered.

Joel looked around the shop. "Yeh, I was in the area, so I thought I'd stop by."

That was a lie. No one was ever just in the Doylestown area. Doylestown is tucked out of the way, heavy traffic in, heavy traffic out. Plus, Joel was a city rat: They didn't leave unless they had to.

"Just in the area, huh?" I asked warily.

He nodded. "Yeh."

"In that case, can I get you some coffee?"

"Uh, sure. Just regular coffee. Black."

I turned around to grind some coffee. "How'd you find me here?" I asked over my shoulder.

"Not a lot of coffee shops that bake biscotti in Doylestown. The name kinda helped, too."

He was right, there were a lot of coffee shops. But they only sold the prepackaged, brand-name biscotti; not freshly baked.

"Guess that's true," I said. "It's a shame you won't meet Eloise. She won't be back until later. I'm sure she'd love to meet one of Benoit's old friends."

He shifted uncomfortably. "Yeah, maybe next time."

Next time? Why was Joel really here? Joel caught me on a day that I wasn't in the mood for fluffy conversation or for vague answers that didn't add up. I poured his coffee and stared at him, deciding how to probe.

"You in Doylestown often?" I asked.

He was looking around the shop. "Nah. I had an aunt who lived here when I was little. She died, but I remember coming up and playing on her swing set. She'd take us to movies at the County."

"Not sure if you saw it, but the County's still here," I said, tipping my head east toward the County Theater.

"Yeah, I saw it. Just right down the street. They're still playing old movies," he smiled nostalgically.

I smiled back, but enough with the bullshit.

"Why are you here, Joel? I mean, don't get me wrong, it's great to see you again, but you and I weren't on a 'stop by, old friend' basis. I'm just surprised to see you all the way up here."

He stared at his coffee for a minute. "I have a favor to ask you."

"Favor? What kind of favor?"

"Well," he scratched behind his neck. "I was wondering if you could hold a bag for me, maybe behind the counter or something, until a friend of mine comes to pick it up."

"You need me to hold a bag?" I asked incredulously. "Like a gym bag? A suitcase? What for, anyway?"

"It's just a bag. Not that big. I just need you to keep it safe until my friend picks it up. If you can do that, I can offer you a little bit of money, you know, for your troubles."

I laughed as if I were waiting for the punchline. "Joel, are you being serious? I honestly can't tell if you're messing with me. You want to pay me to hold a bag? Until your friend picks it up? Why would you pay me money for something like that?"

"Look, the less you know, the better. It's just a bag. Keep it safe until my friend comes and I'll give you $500 for it."

"Five hundred dollars? To hold a bag?" I asked with a slight shriek in my voice. I laughed mockingly. "No, I don't think so, Joel." I stared at him while he held his mug in both hands, gazing at his coffee. "I think maybe you should leave."

He shifted and drank the last gulp before setting down the mug noisily on the counter.

"Okay, yeh, no problem. Sorry. Sorry to have bothered you." He got up and put on his jacket. "Good to see you, Anna. Sorry."

I resented that my piqued curiosity left me feeling unsatisfied that he was about to leave so easily; like telling your boyfriend to *just get the hell out!*—but not meaning it. He wanted me to hold a bag for $500? I contemplated his offer and pictured a bag sitting mundanely behind the counter. I mean, $500 could do a lot for us right now. I had reduced our take-home pay to catch up on some bills, and Marco was making little, very little, at his new job because it was mostly commission-based and it would take time to build back his pipeline, likely months. After reconciling our budget and accounting for obligatory bills such as mortgage and cars, I had separated the scant leftover money into buckets of "other expenses," and grimaced. I didn't know how I was going to pay for the boys' football uniforms, never mind the weight of the shop's debt that now haunted my dreams.

"Wait, Joel."

He turned around.

"You've got to tell me what's in the bag."

He put both hands into his leather jacket pockets. "I can't. It's just a bag. That's all you have to know."

Shit, that means that whatever is in there is probably illegal. Or maybe not, I wanted to tell myself. Maybe it's something embarrassing that he just doesn't want me to see, like a bag full of dildos. Then, who am I to judge? If my friend walked in and asked me to hold her purse until her husband came to get it, I would; and I wouldn't third-degree her on what was in her purse. It wasn't the same thing, maybe; but I was just holding a bag, nothing else. For $500. If there was anything illegal in it, I'd never know. Truth is, I didn't want to know. I needed that $500.

"When will it be picked up?" I asked.

"Tomorrow morning," he said.

That would work, I thought. I always came in early to prep the store before opening; then I went home, packed lunches, and saw the kids off to school before coming back again for the afternoon shift.

"Okay," I said thoughtfully. "And who will be coming?"

"A guy named Panda. He'll pick it up and bring you a bag to return to me."

"You said I'd only be holding one bag," I retorted.

"Well, only one bag for Panda to pick up. But I guess technically, you'll be returning one back to me, so two," he said apologetically.

"And how will I get paid?"

"I'll come tomorrow afternoon, same time at 2 p.m. to get the bag that Panda left and to give you your money."

How easy it seemed. And though my gut was telling me it wasn't a good idea, my brain was overriding my gut.

"Okay, I'll do it," I said reluctantly.

Joel stood still. "Yeh, ok. Then just hold this behind the counter, I guess, and I'll tell Panda to come meet you." He picked up the duffel bag and slung it toward me. I took it with apprehensive hands.

"I'll have to hold the bag in the back," I said. "But I'll bring it up when he arrives. Tell Panda to stand at the end of the counter by the register, and to set his bag close to the cabinet." I pointed at exactly where. "When I bring my bag up, I'll set it next to his, which he'll take when he leaves."

"Yeh, that'll work," he said. I almost could detect a satisfactory smile, which I resented.

"Six a.m., no later. And you can't tell Panda my name, or that I run the shop. Just tell him that I work here and that I'll be wearing a red scarf. He can ask for a black coffee and a cinnamon biscotti. Tell him that I'll go in the back to get the biscotti, which of course won't be true—I'll be retrieving the bag instead."

Joel nodded. "Yeh, okay. See you tomorrow, then."

I nodded in return, and watched Joel walk out the door, taking the air out of the room with him.

I stared at the bag as I sat at my desk sipping coffee.

It looked symmetrically packed, but there were no sharp corners showing through the duffel bag. Maybe it was padded with those air packets. It felt evenly heavy when I moved it from behind the counter to the small office in the back. Maybe it was bottles of booze. No, I'd hear it sloshing, right? Stacks of cash? Don't be ridiculous.

"Excuse me, Anna?" Jared knocked softly on the side of the door. I jumped imperceptibly.

"Hi, Jared."

"Kelly's here to see you." Shit, today was Wednesday. I forgot Kelly said she was bringing the girls up today.

"Oh, thanks! Send them back!" The girls liked helping Eloise make the dough, but I quickly remembered the bag. Kelly would have a million questions about a black utility-looking duffel bag. "Never mind, Jared. I'll come up."

I passed Eloise on my way up. "Kelly and the girls are up front. Come say hi."

"They're not going to help with the dough?" she asked.

"I'll see, but probably not today."

"Okay, I'll be up in a few."

Kelly was sitting at a table with her four-year-old twin girls, Cam and Micaela.

"Hey Kel!" I heartily hugged my best friend. "And you brought princesses to the shop?!" I squatted and pulled both of the girls in for a hug and kiss on the side of the head. They were dressed as Disney's Aurora and Belle, crowns and all.

"I don't even bother making them take it off," Kelly said, pointing at their elaborate princess costumes, which were tattered and stained black on the hem from dragging along sidewalks and across streets. "Not worth it. If they feel comfortable going out like that, why shouldn't I? Can I get a coffee? And a vanilla orange biscotti. Two of them. Or three."

I looked over at Jared, who nodded in acknowledgement. He already was making the girls hot cocoa.

"What's new? You look good," I said.

Kelly had a rough several years. After she and Tom moved to Cherry Hill, they ran into fertility problems. It took two years for them to get pregnant, but they finally had Cam and Micaela, and all seemed well. Except that shortly after the girls were born, Kelly's mother was diagnosed with Stage Four breast cancer and died six slow, painful months later. Then, Tom got laid off from his job, which put a financial stress on them for almost a year until he found another position. Things finally seemed in the clear when Kelly learned she'd contracted Lyme's Disease from a tick bite. She had battled severe lethargy and inflammation for the past year, but she was finally starting to feel better; hence, the one-hour field trip to Doylestown.

"I feel good. I've been having a few good days here and there. I can see the light!" She raised her hands in a hallelujah gesture. "How long has it been since I've been up here?"

"You and Tom came for Marco's birthday, so I guess six months or so?" Since it was more than an hour's drive from Cherry Hill, even in good health, visits were only occasional.

"Yeah, feels like it has been forever," she said.

I nodded and looked out the window.

"You okay? You seem distracted," Kelly asked.

"Just tired," I lied. Kelly's spidey-senses were always spot-on.

"Oh right, waking up early now that you're running the shop?"

I nodded. "Even earlier than before. I come in around 5:30 a.m., stay for two hours to prep for the day, then go home so Marco can get to work. I come back after I take the kids to school."

She raised her eyebrows and cocked her head sideways. "Phew, I'm exhausted hearing about it. I'm glad Marco's enjoying being back in the corporate world. It's better suited for his energy. He was probably going crazy during the lulls here."

I never thought of that possibility, but Kelly was right. Marco was a high-energy, ambitious person. As alluring as a simple life seemed at one point, running Biscotti had weighed him down, like strapping a backpack full of bricks on a jogger. He wanted to run into the fire or war zone; I wanted to organize and command it from a post.

"He's doing well. It's a slow start for sure, really slow. Between you and me, too slow. But Sales is one of those jobs that just takes some time, I guess. He'll get there soon, *hopefully*," I emphasized, as I drew my lower jaw back in a desperate manner.

"I hear ya," she sympathized. "But be patient. He'll do great once he gets going." She dunked her second biscotti into her vanilla-almond latte with a dash of cinnamon and coriander, her favorite, thanks to Jared.

The girls were taking turns playing a game on a learning app on their electronic tablet. Tablets, another great babysitter, I thought, especially in restaurants. And I didn't care how much the older generation scoffed at it. They gave their kids crayons and paper to keep them occupied: What was the difference? Both required motor skills and imagination. I would argue some tablet games also required a fair amount of problem-solving skills. Take that, crayons! Although I did love crayons, and I was not above staying up past bedtime finishing an elaborate coloring page with one of my kids.

"Oh my God, I haven't talked to you much this past week, but you won't believe who I ran into down in Philadelphia," I exclaimed, as if I just remembered.

"Who?"

"Do you remember that guy, Joel? I don't know if you ever met him, but he was Benoit's 'assistant' or whatever?"

"I think so. The guy who brought you wine during the snow storm?"

"Exactly. Him. I ran into him. At the restaurant equipment store on Second Street. Small world, huh?"

"Yeah, it's weird that you even recognized him after all these years."

"Well, he's very easy to recognize. He has a distinctive look."

"How so?"

"For starters, he's short and small, like really, really short and small. And he has a buzzed head covered in scars. And he's really jittery. He shuffles his feet all the time. I don't know. I recognized him."

Kelly nodded, waiting for me to tell her why it was important I was mentioning this. I couldn't will myself to tell her that he also stopped by, and oh, he asked me to hold a bag full of I'm-not-sure-what. Embarrassment flushed over me at the thought of explaining the scenario to Kelly. She would tell me I was crazy, then run back to look into the bag.

"Anyway, I just thought it was weird to run into him. I don't often run into people from that time in my life."

"Um, you practically live with Benoit's sister," she said jestingly.

"Well, aside from her. She's more ours now than she ever was Benoit's." Eloise often joked that she had become Italian; trading in her croissant for a biscotti.

"So, what's this guy, Joel, up to? Is he still an assistant, or whatever?" Kelly asked.

"To be honest, I'm not sure he really was Benoit's 'assistant.' I don't know what he was. I only saw him once in a while, usually for a minute, and whenever I asked Benoit about him, he would just say, 'Joel does things for me. He doesn't mind. He owes me.' Stuff like that.'"

Kelly looked confused, but uninterested. "Hmmm. Well, it's neither here nor there now, right?"

"Right." I wished I had the courage to tell Kelly my recent interactions with Joel. It wouldn't matter anyway; I was only holding a bag for one night; I'd likely never see Joel again.

"Should we take the girls to the park?" Kelly asked.

"Sure, let me just tell Eloise that we're going. She'll want to give you all a hug first."

I walked back and told Eloise we were leaving. She took off her apron. "I was almost done. I was going to come out and have a cup of coffee with Kelly. Sorry. Just ran longer than I thought. Watch this dough while I go kiss the girls?"

I nodded and she proceeded toward the front.

I went to my office, saw the bag tucked safely under my desk, and locked the door. I didn't always lock it, but today I would. Hopefully, no one would notice.

Chapter Twenty-One

P anda arrived at the shop at exactly 6 a.m.

I assumed Panda was not his real name, but quickly understood how he earned the nickname: His eyes had unnaturally dark rings around them (probably hereditary), but ominous, nonetheless.

He walked in briskly, carrying a black duffel bag identical to the one I had in the office and wearing a scally cap and a zipped-up gray jacket. Aside from the dark-rimmed eyes, he was handsome and nicely dressed. I was relieved that Panda wouldn't stand out from typical Doylestown men, whose lives ran the same cycle of playing high school football, going to college, then ending up back in their hometown as real estate agents, wealth managers, and attorneys—none of which they would have accomplished without old money and connections.

Panda came directly to the end of the counter, set down the bag next to the cabinet, and asked for a black coffee and a cinnamon biscotti, just as instructed.

"Sure, the baker hasn't brought them up yet," I said with a slight quiver in my voice. "But let me check in the back to see if they're ready. I'll only be a minute."

He nodded and leaned on the counter and took a cautious glance around the shop. It was quiet this early in the morning; only the hum of refrigerators, muted music, and twirling crank of the mixer coming from the back made for sound. I quickly went to the office and grabbed the bag, each step feeling heavier than the last. *Calm down*, I willed myself. *You're just giving someone a bag, for God's sake.*

I came back to the front, set my bag down next to his, and steadied my shaky hand as I brought it up to the register and said politely, "Sorry, but the baker doesn't have the cinnamon biscotti ready yet. Would you like another kind of biscotti or just the coffee today?"

"Just the coffee," he said.

I poured him a cup of coffee to go. "My treat," I said seriously.

He grabbed the bag Joel gave me and left.

I stood still, staring at the fiery trail Panda left behind as he walked out, like a fairy's dust fanning behind her as she flies. My pulse was racing, and I braced the counter while processing how to look casual as I grabbed the bag he left and headed toward the back.

"Ma'am? Are you open yet?" A customer had come in as Panda was leaving, but I hadn't heard him approach.

"Oh, I'm sorry." I turned around and set the bag next to my feet at the register. "What can I get for you?" Although we opened at 6 a.m., we usually didn't see traffic until closer to 7 a.m., which was when the barista started the shift. I could manage making basic coffees until then, but nothing fancy. Of course, today *would* be the day heavy traffic flowed in earlier than usual.

"I'll have a latte with whole milk," a half-bald man in a blowzy blue suit said as he thumbed through dollar bills in his money clip.

"My pleasure," I smiled.

I turned to the espresso machine, removed the portafilter (which I was happy to see was properly cleaned by the closing crew), and gave the machine a quick purge. My hands felt like jelly as I filled the portafilter with 14 grams of espresso, tapped it evenly, and twisted the handle back onto the machine. In seconds, two thick, dark strands of liquid streamed out like chocolate fondue.

I glanced at the bag sitting on the floor, as if it was a naughty kid sitting in time out, as I poured the milk into the carafe. Steaming the milk was easy now that I was used to it, but it took a while to learn how to get the correct temperature and consistency. Fortunately, this latte was to-go; it saved me from performing my amateur latte art, which was limited to only a heart at this point. Jared was trying to teach me a fern leaf; it was coming along.

"Will that be all, sir?" I asked politely.

"Actually, no," he said, scanning the glass jars of biscotti behind me. His delay in leaving felt monumentally long as I glanced at the idle bag. "I'll take an almond biscotti, as well, please."

I handed him the almond biscotti in a paper bag. He paid and left, the door chiming behind him. I glanced around for any other customers I may not have noticed. None to serve, so I picked up the bag and headed swiftly toward the back. This bag felt significantly lighter; possibly empty.

Eloise and her baking assistant, Maribel, were completing the morning baking as I passed them. I was grateful for their loud conversation and the radio blasting Andre Bocelli (Eloise's preference, not Maribel's). They didn't even glance at me as I walked into the office and set the lighter bag under the desk.

I sat for a moment to catch my breath. *What now?* Joel would be coming into the shop that afternoon to retrieve the bag Panda left behind, and to pay me my $500, but was that all I had to do? Nothing else? It seemed too simple. Yet my sweaty palms and racing pulse screamed that it was anything other than simple.

I stared at the bag and nudged it with my foot. It felt more hollow than the last bag. I hated admitting to myself that the mystery of the bag's contents stroked my curiosity strings like Carlos Santana playing, "Maria Maria." When was the last time I felt a rush like this? I couldn't remember. But I realized that the slight smile on my face might be more than just nerves; it might be excitement.

Joel walked in, head stooped and hands in his pockets. "Hey." He took a seat at the counter. It was exactly 2 p.m., right on schedule.

"Hey," I replied. "Coffee?"

He nodded, then as an afterthought, "Please. Thank you."

I made his regular coffee, black. I wasn't sure how to lead into the imminent conversation about the bag, and more importantly, my money.

"How was traffic?" I asked.

"Not bad."

"Traffic is usually pretty mild this time of day," I commented casually.

"Yeh."

Silence while I finished his coffee and poured it into his cup. He sipped it. "Mmm. That's real good coffee. What kind of coffee you use?"

I shrugged. "Just a local brand."

"Guess you need a fancy machine to make it taste good, huh?" He laughed a little nervously.

"Not really." He hadn't watched me use my tried-and-true method: A $40 French press.

"So, Joel?" I leaned both elbows on the counter and stared at him with a close-mouthed smile. I enjoyed making Joel shift uncomfortably. "The bag was picked up safely, just like you asked. So, now what?"

"Uh," he cleared his throat. "So, I guess I owe you this." He reached into his jacket and pulled out an envelope. He laid it on the counter. I picked it up and thought about opening and counting it, like payoffs work in the movies, but I hadn't earned that kind of swagger. Yet.

"You have the bag Panda gave you?" he asked.

"Yes. I'll go get it." I walked to the back office, grabbed the bag and put the envelope of cash under my computer keyboard, but not without a quick peek. Five Benjamins were filed neatly inside. I paused for a moment, smiling at my loot; but suddenly, the door chimed. I jumped a little, contemplated whether to leave the bag in the office or take it to Joel, and decided to keep with the plan.

I walked up to the front and casually set the bag down at the end of the counter. "Hi, can I help you?" I asked a pair of women with matching ponytails and expensive workout clothes that they certainly didn't work out in.

"Oh, yes! We've never been in here before. Are you the owner? Look how cute the jars are, Meg," the brown ponytailed woman said in a slightly southern accent to the blonde ponytailed woman, as she pointed to the rows of jars with different flavored biscotti.

"They're very cute," Blonde ponytail said.

"She just moved to Doylestown," Brown ponytail pointed to Blonde ponytail. "From North Carolina. And I came to see where she moved to," Brown ponytail rambled. "The shops, the restaurants…I think I may just wanna move here, too!" Her energy was a bit much for me, but I found her entertaining.

"Doylestown is charming," I agreed, glancing nervously at Joel at the other end of the counter. "What can I get you ladies to drink?"

Blonde ponytail was staring blankly around the shop, following our conversation with a distracted nod here and there. She brought her gaze back to me. "Just a skinny vanilla latte for me, please."

"I'll do the same," Brown ponytail chimed in cheerily.

"For here or to go?" I asked, hoping they would be leaving.

They looked at each other. "Let's sit a while?" Blonde ponytail answered as a question.

A wave of nerves pressed over me. I needed the shop to be empty to finish talking with Joel. I cleared my throat. "Have you guys walked down Ashland Street? There are some amazing houses to see, and the Mercer Museum is neat to wander into." I tried to subtly convince them to go.

"Oh, shoot," said Brown ponytail. "Maybe we should go check out more of Doylestown. What do you think?"

Blonde ponytail smiled her affirmation.

I winked at them. "Two skinny vanilla lattes to go, then."

As I made their lattes, I glanced at Joel again. He was staring at his coffee, hunched over the counter. He had experience appearing ordinary enough not to be noticed, I observed.

The Ponytails chattered about the cobblestone alleys and the old brick buildings in Doylestown, which filled me with a residential pride.

Even after five years, I felt nostalgic and comforted by the quaint and charming feel of Doylestown. The people were polite, but not phony. There was a general sense of happiness here, maybe from the wealth, and kids were able to grow up with a degree of innocence lost in some other Philadelphia suburbs.

"Here you are. Can I offer you biscotti, as well?" I asked as I set down their lattes.

"I shouldn't. I ate all those carbs last night, Meg," laughed Brown ponytail.

"But doesn't a cherry-almond biscotti sound good?" said Blonde ponytail.

"What is an-ees?" asked Brown ponytail, pointing to a jar with anise biscotti.

"Anise. It's a popular Italian flavor. Sort of black licorice-like, but subtle. How about this? I'll do one anise and one cherry-almond biscotti, my treat, as a welcome to Doylestown." I put the biscotti in the brown paper bags with tongs.

"Y'all are so nice!" said Brown ponytail. I assumed I was *y'all*? I liked Brown ponytail and wished I had more time to chit-chat with her.

"Thank you," said Blonde ponytail as I handed her the bag. There was something less enthusiastic about her, something almost defeated. For a different reason, I wished I had more time to spend with her, too.

The Ponytails jauntily left the shop and I turned to Joel. He stood; cup long empty. "I gotta run. Can I have the bag?" He gestured impatiently toward the bag lying on the ground behind the counter.

"Uh, yeah, here," I reached down to retrieve the bag, agitated that I wouldn't get to play out the conversation I had prepared for Joel. And before I could process the ramifications of what I was about to say, I handed him the bag and asked, "Do you have another bag for me?"

Joel looked at me, surprised, but answered simply, "I can bring one tomorrow. Two p.m.?"

I nodded, pulse pounding in my ears.

"See you tomorrow." He swung the duffel bag over his shoulder and left.

And just like that, I dove over the moral line without knowing what awaited to break my fall, if anything at all.

I licked my thumb and counted the five $100 bills on my desk, crisp and new-smelling.

I hadn't anticipated asking Joel for more bags, but I couldn't ignore the fact that in one day, I had made more money than Biscotti would allow for us to take home in almost a week. This $500 meant I could buy the boys' football uniforms and pay half of Lily's preschool tuition without dipping further into our savings.

I bit my lip deep in thought, then turned to my computer and shook my mouse to wake it. I opened our accounting books. I clicked through until I found the sheet I was looking for, full of red figures in parentheses, the debt sheet. I sighed. I hated looking at this sheet. Its numbers seemed to taunt, "Nah-nah-nah-nah-nah." I almost could hear the ticking noise of a clock nearing the stroke of our midnight, when the interest on the six-month personal line of credit would come due.

What I hated even more about looking at this sheet was the small pinch of resentment that sprinkled over me; resentment that Marco had gotten this deep into debt. It had become more evident to me, after realizing the state of the books, that Marco didn't know how bad it was. Though he was a smart man, not everyone had a knack for accounting, and many smart people have fallen prey to the delicate handling of cash flow. This was especially true for small business owners who managed their own books, only hiring an accountant to do their taxes once a year. I couldn't be mad at Marco for his lack of accounting skills, but I couldn't help hold a small grudge that he hadn't asked me for help sooner. In fact, I wasn't convinced he ever planned to ask me for help, and I wondered at what point I would have found out we had lost everything.

A memory of my mother sitting at the table late at night, with scattered bills and a cup of coffee, flashed in my head. It was right after my dad's accident; he lay in a coma in the hospital. My mother didn't hear me creep downstairs to get my history book from my book bag, but I stopped abruptly on the bottom step, watching her cry softly into her hands, her shoulders shaking lightly. I wanted to hug my mom, even though we didn't hug much, and tell her not to worry. But I knew she had a lot to worry about. And I was frustrated that this bright, charismatic woman had never gone to college nor otherwise pursued a career outside our home, leaving her to rely entirely on my father's income to carry our family—as her mother had, and her mother's mother. And now, she sat crying at the table, helpless and hopeless, piles of bills underneath her shaking elbows.

I never did hug my mom nor reassured her, something I regretted. Instead, I used that image to fuel me into a resolve to never end up in that situation. I wanted to be my own rock, create my own destiny.

But like many women, and surely like my mother had, and my mother's mother, I had underestimated how much motherhood would change me. My ideology of being a career mom, kissing my kids good-bye while passing them to their nanny, talking quickly into a cell phone on my way to the office, was alluring at one point. In reality, it was soul-crushing. I couldn't think of another person raising my children. I wanted to be the one who packed their lunches, showed up at their school for read-alongs, and tucked them in at night with a silly chant and tickle.

As I stared at the red debt on my computer screen, then glanced at the five, crisp, hundred-dollar bills, I knew what I had to do. I had to hold enough bags to climb us out of this hole so that my kids wouldn't watch me cry at a kitchen table or work three jobs, too tired to read them a book at night.

It wouldn't take me long, I gauged with renewed purpose. I built a spreadsheet that would account for holding two bags a week, or $1,000. Good, but not enough, I determined. Four bags a week? Better. Even better was five bags a week. If I could do five bags a week, that would bring in roughly $2,500 a week. At that rate, I could pay off the business loan in just over three months. Of course, I needed a little bit more than that for the other expenses, so four months, max.

I nodded my head as I deliberated the numbers. It would work; I knew it would. I just had to treat this like any other job, I told myself casually. But of course, the pressing matter of what was in the bags weighed on my conscience. Could I do a job without knowing what was in the bags? I supposed it was not that different than a delivery person's job, transporting boxes full of who-knew-what. I knew, deep down, it wasn't the same thing, but I couldn't think too much about this. I would talk to Joel about holding more bags tomorrow.

Now, I had to get ready to go. Tonight was date night.

Chapter Twenty-Two

"How's the shop?" Marco asked me. "I feel like I haven't been there in so long."

Marco and I sat at the counter of a BYOB Mexican restaurant, sharing Coronas and a heaping bowl of chips and guacamole. Oysters and wine were not part of the new budget.

I tipped my head back and forth. "It's okay. The hype of the Beat the Barista challenge is wearing off, so it's a waiting game at this point. We just have to catch up on some of the bills and hope that business sustains." My stomach lurched at the thought of telling Marco what I had done, holding a bag of unknown contents. But I also couldn't help but think that if he truly knew how bleak things were at the shop, he might have understood.

Marco nodded guiltily. "I hear you."

These days, I didn't like talking about the shop with Marco; it made him feel as if he failed us. And despite myself, talking about it provoked an itch of irritation, and I had to hold my tongue to avoid hurting his feelings.

"I have to tell you, I think you're better at running the shop than I was," he said.

"Oh, come on, that's not true," I sneered. "I think it's just more my pace." But I knew he was right.

He kissed my hand. "Are you at least happy working outside of the home again? I mean, I know it's still hard work at the shop, but is it nice to have a little bit of freedom from the kids?"

"It's different work, and yes, I'm happy to be using the part of my brain that calculates numbers and strategizes beyond how much toilet paper to stock up on again," I laughed jokingly. "Although, I still have to do that on top of this job, so there's that."

"I can help," Marco said. "We're a team. Give me more house responsibilities; you shouldn't be left feeling like you have two jobs."

"I think that's just a working mother's curse, honey."

"I know. Women are so much tougher than men," he said seriously. "I would crumble if I tried to do all that you do. You're amazing, you know that? And I appreciate you."

I smiled at Marco. I knew he meant it, even if it didn't make my jobs, or the weight on my shoulders, any lighter.

"I'm good, honey," I said reassuringly. "I love being busy. You know me."

"I know, but just let me know if it gets to be too much. We'll figure something else out," he said as he crunched a hard tortilla chip.

I couldn't help but resent his effortless comment, as if figuring out "something else" was so easy to do. If it were as simple as clapping your hands, and a new job with higher salary appeared to pay your bills, surely we wouldn't be in this financial mess. *Stop it*, I told myself.

Dwelling on this is not going to get us anywhere; I had to push my irritation aside.

"Enough about me. Anything new at your job?" I asked eagerly.

"No, nothing really new," Marco said. "I have to build my client relationships back up again, which is harder than I thought it would be," he shrugged. "But I'm getting there. Just wish it were quicker."

Me too, I thought. *Stop it. Stop dwelling.*

"Well, as long as you're happy, I'm sure the rest will fall into place soon enough," I said.

"I am happy," he said proudly. "I'm feeling good, to be honest. Even though it's hard, I like working with Gary again. He took me to the best steakhouse in D.C. the other night. Oh my God, the steak was a bone-in filet; it had a bone handle that was this long," he demonstrated a distance of about 10 inches. "And it just melted in my mouth. Babe, it was so good."

That must be nice; to feel good and to enjoy bone-in filets while I ate the leftover mac and cheese from the kid's plates at night, and picked up the broken pieces of the glass he shattered. *Stop.* I could feel the lava creeping up the inside of the volcano. *Please don't erupt,* I pleaded with myself.

I nodded duplicitously.

"And then Gary ordered this dessert that came out on this rolling tray thing, and the server lit it up, and it went, Boom!" he gestured an explosion with his hands. "And this lotus flower or something opened to reveal this chocolate swan thing. It was crazy," Marco said, right before crunching down on another tortilla chip.

I held back the lava. "That sounds amazing."

"Hey, you okay?" he asked casually.

"Mmm-hmm," I smiled.

"Uh-oh, what'd I do?" Marco became suddenly aware of my body language, like a scientist seeing a spike in waves on a seismograph.

"Nothing," I said curtly.

"Oh no, that's the worse answer. I know it's something. Come on, give it to me."

I shrugged my shoulders, maintaining my pithy smile.

He put his beer down and braced himself. "Anna, tell me. What'd I do?"

The volcano erupted.

"I just don't want to hear about your two-pound steak or lotus flower desserts when this is the fanciest meal I've had in four weeks!" I exploded, a glob of guacamole plopping off my chip. I dropped the chip on my plate and shook my head. I hated losing my temper, and I hated fighting with Marco. We weren't a couple that fought often. We were usually so in sync with each other that there was rarely cause for argument.

And maybe that's what bothered me more. Marco was busy working and traveling to D.C. several times a week. I was pre-occupied with the shop and the new routine with the kids. Our weekends were brief and filled with kids' activities and leftover work. Even date nights had become a hasty to-do, instead of a night I counted down.

"I'm sorry," Marco said sincerely, but with a hint of defensiveness. "I won't talk about my business dinners anymore."

I sighed. It wasn't about his dinner, and he knew that.

"It's just, I'm just, a little overwhelmed, and I'm probably just taking it out on you," I said resignedly, though that wasn't entirely true. Part of my explosion was stoked by the resentment that I had let build, and I was tired of resenting Marco. I knew our problems weren't entirely his fault, and I knew that if the tables had been turned, he would've jumped in to solve the problem like I had. And he wouldn't resent me for it.

"I'm sorry you're so overwhelmed, babe," he said with a gentle rub of my arm. "Like I said earlier, let me help more. What do you need me to do?"

"I guess maybe you could help with the kids' lunches in the morning?"

"Easy! Done! What else?" he smiled. I couldn't help but giggle lightly, thinking of how many times that smile had coaxed me into forgiveness; it still made my heart flutter.

"And I know dinners and travel are all part of the new job. But maybe just say 'no' to the ones that aren't critical," I said.

"Well, I'll try, but I can't say no to all of them."

"I know, but Gary doesn't have a family. I know it's easy for him to invite you out for dinner or a drink after work, but I really need you here. Just be choosy is all I'm saying." It was hard for me to ask for help, especially after so many years of handling everything when it came to the house and the kids.

"Got it. Done," he said. "What else?"

I looked at my almost-gone Corona. "And grab me another beer because I don't plan on going home sober tonight."

He laughed. "That makes two of us! We'll walk home!"

"Let's not go home until the kids are certain to be asleep," I suggested.

"Oh, we'll wait until way past bedtime! And do not sit and chit chat with Eloise when we get home!" he threatened jestingly.

"I won't," I winked.

Despite the rough patch, our taco and beer night would prove to be just what we needed to smooth out our troubles. For tonight, at least.

The next day, Joel trotted into the shop at exactly 2 p.m. carrying a new duffel bag identical to the first one.

I was hoping to have a conversation with him about how many bags I could hold a week, or if I could hold more than one at a time. But he stayed only long enough for me to make him a coffee, then left with urgency. The conversation would have to wait for tomorrow when I would see Joel again, I frowned.

The bag sat on the floor in the corner of my office while I went about my afternoon taking inventory, reconciling accounting books, and placing orders. The occasional customer came in for her afternoon jolt of coffee, but it was otherwise a typically quiet afternoon. I was finishing payroll in my office, standing by the printer as it spat out paychecks, when I glanced over at the bag sitting idly in the corner. It looked back at me with a daring glare.

I picked up the bag, the sound of the printing checks repetitively grinding in the background, and I placed it on my desk. This bag felt the same weight as the last bag, roughly 10 pounds. I squeezed it like someone squeezes a yoga ball, with little give. There was something hard in the center of a layer of padding. I shook the bag. Nothing rattled or sloshed. I wished I could make out the shape of what was in the middle, but the padding was in the way.

"It's just a bag." I could hear Joel's rough voice echoing in my ear as I thought about unzipping the bag just an inch to see what color the padding was. If it was a cotton material, I could conclude that maybe it was clothes. But why would I be holding a bag of clothes for $500? Maybe it was full of Gucci scarves and Louis Vuitton shoes. That would make it an expensive bag to hold. If I just unzipped it a little….I thought with burning curiosity.

"Hey!" Eloise startled me as she stuck her head casually in the office doorway. "You going away?" She nodded toward the bag.

"Oh," I gulped. "No, I just…shit, you scared me," I laughed. "I had a bunch of football equipment and stuff to take to the boys' game and I couldn't find their football bag. So, I used this old thing," I tried to look natural putting the bag back on the ground. "What's up? You're back early?"

"Not really. It's almost 4 p.m."

I glanced at the clock. Shit, it was almost 4 p.m. I had lost track of time. "Guess it is. I have to go get Lily soon. Is Jared here yet?"

Breathe slowly. Look natural, I willed myself.

"Dunno. I just came in through the side door. You okay? You seem distracted."

"Yeah, yes. I'm fine. I was doing month-end stuff, which always fries my brain a little bit." I gathered all the paychecks from the printer and formed them into a neat pile. Just then, Jared walked through the side door.

"Hey, ladies!" he said, as he walked past us and toward the front of the store.

"Hey, Jared," we said in unison.

"I've been giving some thought to your suggestion about pairing a biscotti with a coffee," Eloise said. "To get more people coming into the shop. I thought I could work with Jared to figure out which combo works best and we can write suggestions on the board. It's not a Beat the Barista challenge, but it's something new."

I could tell she was trying to make peace with her biscotti's current role at the shop, which had, despite its namesake, taken second place to the coffee. But maybe Eloise also felt a sense of responsibility to help with getting the shop back on its feet. Though we didn't talk about it with her in detail, she certainly knew that financially, we weren't where we used to be.

"That's a great idea. The biscotti have always been the star of this shop. Let's highlight them again; make them *irree-zees-ta-ble.*" She smiled as I said *irresistible* in a French accent.

"Yes ma'am," she nodded.

I rolled my eyes. "Stop it. You know I hate when you call me that. By the way, Marco has to go out of town next Friday night. Want to come over and watch movies in bed with me like old times? There's a new foreign film that just came out on rental?" I tried to lure her in playfully. Eloise loved foreign films as much as I did.

"It's a date," she said delightedly. I hadn't seen the old Eloise in a while. The Eloise who uprooted her life in Paris to help me raise Nathan in a tiny apartment in Manayunk. The Eloise who understood the pain of losing Benoit and stood by my side as I said "I do" to Marco. The Eloise who followed us to Doylestown, helped us open a business, breathed with me during each of my children's labor, and helped raise each of them as her own. Though Eloise and I didn't become sisters through marriage, we had become sisters by choice, and we would always have that.

"Be careful how you present that to Jen," I teased. "I don't think she'd appreciate you saying that you're going to be lying in bed with another woman on Friday night."

"Hmph," she bellowed. "She'll probably be excited to have a night alone with her reality shows!"

"I'll pick up the champagne."

"And I'll bring the chocolate cake," she winked.

I waited until I heard the side door close behind her, then I picked up the bag and plopped it back on my desk with a dull thud. I weighed the consequences of opening it. If I was going to continue holding bags, shouldn't I know their contents? The analytical part of my brain told me that I must solve the equation to find the answer; and to solve the equation, I had to know what x was. Or did I? Maybe I could just let the equation sit with an idle x as long as I got paid.

Maybe I could, but I doubted it.

Chapter Twenty-Three

When I was a little girl, I used to sneak out of my room in the middle of the night to the Christmas tree. I'd tip-toe softly down the hallway to avoid the patches where the wood creaked until I finally made it to the tree, where I quietly dropped to my hands and knees. I'd fish out one of my presents, inch-by-inch like a Jenga piece, so as not to disrupt the packages around it; and when it was finally free, I'd start the next process: Gift surgery. I would carefully peel away the scotch tape, slowly enough that the paper wouldn't pull away with the sticky side of the tape, until both ends gaped open. I found that it was best to do this ritual nightly because once the tape cured for a few days, it was hard to peel it off cleanly. Then, I'd carefully slide the gift out of whichever end seemed easier and marvel at the contents. After careful examination of the item, checking that it was the correct name brand or the right color, I'd slip it back in and fold both sides with the same creases as before. The tape might have lost a little bit of stickiness, but if I carefully set it back with the seams facing other gifts, no one noticed.

Nine out of ten times, I'd be elated at what I found inside the package. I'd creep back into bed with a smile on my face, dreaming of what I'd do with my new item once Christmas came. But once in a while, I'd gently tug at something from one of those ends with great anticipation, only to be gravely disappointed. I'd go back to my bedroom with a sense of helplessness because I couldn't tell my mom that I said the *purple* one, not the *pink* one! I knew I'd have to wake up Christmas morning and pretend that I didn't know a pink stereo was waiting for me, then try hide the preemptive expression of disappointment on my face.

But never did I open a package and jump back in terror.

"Good morning, babe," I kissed Marco on the forehead and set a cup of coffee on the nightstand next to the bed. "I'm going into the shop a little early. We have a big order I need to help with."

"What time is it?" he asked without opening his eyes.

"It's almost 5 a.m."

"It's so early."

"I know. I'll be back at 7:30 a.m. to get the kids ready for school. The monitor's on for Lily. She should be fine, but just listen for her. Oh, and no TV for the boys until they've done their jobs. They always try to sneak around that rule when I'm gone."

He reached blindly for my hand and squeezed it. "Love you."

"Love you, too."

Polo slowly followed me to the mudroom. He still made it a point to see me out every time I left the house. I bent down, gave him a vigorous rub on the sides of his big head, then pulled out a bag of his favorite treats. "Don't tell anyone I gave you dessert before break-fast." He stared at me with the treat hanging out of his mouth, his tail wagging, until I walked out the door.

I drove the two miles into town and parked in the rear of the building. The lights of the shop shone cheerily through the darkness of the morning, and I could see Eloise's and Maribel's silhouettes inside baking. I walked in the side door and nodded to them. Eloise said something to me, but I couldn't hear her over the mixer and the radio, so I mouthed, "I can't hear you." She waved me off, and we smiled and continued with our respective work.

I went into the office and hesitated as I closed the door, but I knew Eloise was too busy to notice, and I only needed a minute alone.

I hung my coat and put my purse down, then turned on my computer. As it woke up, I grabbed the bag from under the desk and rested it in front of me. I drew one short breath, then unzipped the bag slowly. A yellow packing material resembling insulation in an attic became visible as I drew open the zipper fully. There didn't appear to be an opening at the top of the padding, so I stuck my hand carefully inside, wedging it between the yellow material and the wall of the bag, my fingers searching for an opening along the side. My hand reached the bottom of the bag and I withdrew it slowly. I went back in on the other side, and before I was halfway down, I felt a slit in the padding. I tucked my hand into the slit and felt for the center. My fingers touched something. It felt like hard plastic wrap. I withdrew my hand quickly and panted.

I shook my fingers out and contemplated on whether to try again. I had come this far. I had to know what was inside.

I reached back into the bag and opened it a little wider, careful not to disrupt the padding, but enough to see the opening. It was still too dark to see what was past the slit, so I pulled the side of the bag down and let the yellow padding fray open. There was something wrapped in tape just beyond the opening. I reached my hand in and took hold of the side of the hard object and wiggled it free. The moment the light fully revealed the package, I knew what it was, and I gasped in alarm. My heart pulsed in my ears and I stuck the package back in as quickly as I took it out.

I frantically stuffed the yellow padding back into place, zipped up the bag, and threw it back under my desk. I felt my eyes well with tears and a sour taste filled the back of my throat. *What the fuck have I gotten into?*

It would be the first and last time I ever touched cocaine.

I sat at my desk for 30 minutes, dry heaving only once, while I castigated myself for opening the bag. Panda was coming for the pickup in 20 minutes and I needed to get myself together before then. First, I needed to make some decisions on how to move forward now that I knew the bags held a brick of cocaine. I laughed at myself pathetically: I didn't even know how much a brick of cocaine contained. A kilo? I guessed from seeing enough movies, but beyond that, I knew nothing about drugs. Of any kind.

I shuddered. I could feel my plan of paying off our debt falling apart. There was no way I could go on holding bags, now that I knew there were drugs in them. I had suspected something illegal could have been in the bags, but I didn't want to believe that it was drugs. I felt foolish to have convinced myself otherwise.

But now that I knew it was drugs, I would have to tell Joel that I couldn't hold any more bags, even though he was bringing another one today. He wouldn't be happy that I was backing out of the arrangement; his eyes had lit up when I asked if he was bringing another bag. Surely, he had started calculating the potential of our new arrangement the same way I had, and I was afraid he would not go away easily.

I could call the police. I sloshed the thought around in my head. I'd explain that I thought I was just helping a friend out by holding his luggage, but that at some point, I didn't feel right about not knowing the contents, so I looked, then called authorities the minute I suspected it was drugs. That would be the most responsible thing to do. Surely, after vetting me out, they would realize that it was an innocent, however stupid, judge of circumstance on my part, and I'd get a slap on the wrist. I would likely need a lawyer, though, and I couldn't afford one right now. And what if they didn't see it as innocent? And why would I hold a friend's luggage twice? For someone else to pick up? I couldn't risk it. Calling the police didn't seem like the right answer.

Then there was the reason I held a bag in the first place: The money.

Of course, there were other ways to make money without holding bags of cocaine. I could go back to banking now that all the kids were in school, but the thought of going back to that once-loved world haunted me. Besides, it would take years to build my portfolio, and we didn't have the luxury of time. On top of that, I'd have to commute to Philadelphia or New York, and the hours would mean I'd barely get to see my family. No, not banking. Maybe a retail job such as clothing, or hey, even retail branch banking? Nah, retail was never my thing; even running Biscotti bored me to tears some days. Besides, I would never make enough in retail to pay off the loan in six months. And someone shoot me down dead if I become a pyramid-type consultant selling cosmetics or handbags to other women.

As I negotiated my thoughts, one kept making its way back to the forefront, despite my effort to shoo it away. What would happen if I just kept on holding bags? Of course, drugs were bad, but I'm not making them or dealing them. I was just a middle man, or woman. I was just holding a bag, much like a pharmacy holds drugs; what happened to it after it left my possession was none of my business. And it was the option that made the most money in the shortest amount of time, while allowing me to still take care of the kids and my family's needs.

My next move became clear: I needed to run the numbers. Numbers never lied to me.

Chapter Twenty-Four

M oving one bag a day, Monday through Friday, could bring in
$2,500 a week. But I had calculated that before I knew how
valuable the cargo was. Now, I was certain I could negotiate more
money, maybe double.

After I dropped the kids off at school the next morning, I drove
over to the local library. I wasn't foolish enough to use the Internet
for my research, or to check out books in my name. I'd be able to
find enough resources to read at the library that would give me the
information I needed.

I started with—who else? —Pablo Escobar. This would prove a
fruitful beginning. There were dozens of books about his rise as the
Columbian drug lord who, at one time, supplied more than 80 percent
of America's cocaine. I stood in the aisle, pulling out one book at a
time, and found myself grossly immersed in the sophistication of his
operation. At the height of Pablo's operation, he was making $420
million a week and had a reported net worth of $25 billion. That's
billion, with a *b*, I scoffed impressively.

While I recognized Pablo was a scumbag criminal—thievery

and murder commonly listed on his resume—I couldn't help but be impressed by the sheer magnitude of his cradle-to-grave business. He sourced and processed raw materials; manufactured and produced a high-quality product; put that product into circulation; transported and distributed it; and kept his product competitive and available. This from a man who didn't go to Wharton Business School to learn how to run a business and make money off of money. In fact, Pablo didn't even go to college. And Pablo didn't have lobbyists in Washington, D.C. fighting to protect the interests of his business: Instead, he had all of Washington, Columbia, and God-knows-where-else trying to shut him down.

I stopped on a quote from Pablo and read it aloud: The business is "...Simple: you bribe someone here, you bribe someone there, and you pay a friendly banker to help you bring the money back." I remembered a time when I was in banking and a colleague in our investment group mentioned that he was taking our client to Monte Carlo, on a private jet, to stay on a yacht. Rumor had it that same client also received an Aston Martin Superlegerra right before allocating the rest of his fortune to our bank and running for office. I shook my head. Pablo Escobar might have been a scumbag, breaking the law to rise to the top, but at least he owned it. The criminals in government and big corporations hid behind Armani suits and bent the laws so far that when they snapped, they'd just make a new one to tape it back together.

I moved on from Pablo and after an hour of sitting in the aisles with books spread on my lap, I finally found what I was looking for: Current street value of a kilo of cocaine. Turns out that the little brick in the center of those duffel bags could fetch anywhere from $20,000 to $38,000, depending on where it was going. Typically, rural areas fetched more street value than urban areas; it was simply savings in logistics. I guessed that Doylestown, being a rich suburb, fetched a good amount of money. That's probably why Joel sought me out after seeing me in Philadelphia. Perhaps he had been looking for a way to infiltrate these suburbs for a while. If that was the case, surely, he was happy about his newfound relationship and would hate to have it interrupted so quickly.

The bile that occupied my throat this morning had been swallowed down, replaced with a flutter of prospect in my chest: I could easily get double.

A nervous anticipation sat on my shoulders as I prepared for Joel to come in that afternoon.

I had to address two things before continuing with any kind of business arrangement. The first was a guarantee that no one, beside Joel and Panda, knew about me; not my name, not my business, not even my gender. The first was important because I only planned to do this for a few months, four max. When I exited, I wanted to do that cleanly, ensure I couldn't be traced back to anyone else. I could handle Joel, I figured, and Panda didn't even know my name. For all he knew, I was just a woman who worked at a coffee shop. I'd deny anything other than serving him coffee if he ever claimed to know me otherwise.

The second item I needed to address was the duffel bag. The duffel bag, in all its stereotypical glory, would eventually raise questions. I needed the bag to be something more practical for everyday use, something a little more inconspicuous. Something like, I looked around my office and landed on my diaper bag: Bingo. I needed something like a diaper bag. Though Lily was out of diapers, for the most part, I still carried a diaper bag. Most moms do long after they're not carrying diapers, because the diaper bag basically becomes a bag full of Mother's essentials, which she pulls out like a magician pulling items out of a hat. It holds an endless amount of random supplies such as wipes for dirty hands, Band-Aids, snacks, water bottles, electronics, extra clothing, bug spray, sunblock...the list goes on.

I had an extra identical diaper bag, thanks to a duplicate baby registration error, that I would pick up before Joel came in. Why would Joel care which bag carried his cargo?

He said it himself: It's just a bag.

"Coffee, Joel?" I asked as he took a seat at the bar that afternoon.

"Yeh, thanks. Do those almond biscotti have peanuts?" he asked.

"I don't think so," I said, looking behind me at the jar. "I should probably know that, right? Are you allergic to peanuts?"

"Yeh."

"I'll ask Eloise when she comes in, but I don't think so. We don't have peanut butter back there. Are you allergic only if you eat it, or like, can't-touch-things-processed-on-facilities-with-peanuts allergic?"

"The super allergic one."

"Ah, well, better stick with coffee, then, until I can verify the biscotti are safe to eat."

He nodded.

I filled the press with coffee grinds. As it steeped with boiling water, I leaned forward on the counter to meet Joel's eye level. "Joel, we need to talk."

He stiffened slightly. I still made him nervous, which I appreciated because what I was about to say would catch him off guard.

"Joel, what the hell were you thinking giving me a bag full of cocaine?"

He looked at me wide-eyed, then slackened a bit and sighed. "You looked."

I stared at him without answering.

"Fuck," he ran a hand over his head. "I told you not to look. I didn't want to get you in trouble if anything happened. If you didn't know what was in there, then, you know, you wouldn't get in as much trouble and shit."

"Plausible denial? That's how you were protecting me, Joel? How about not giving me a bag of illegal drugs to begin with?"

He sighed. "We've been trying to get into this area for a while. So when I ran into you and you said you had a shop up this way, I don't know; it just seemed like the perfect setup."

"What do you mean when you say you've been trying to get into this area for a while?"

"You know, 'cause Doylestown is full of rich people. Rich people do a lot of coke, and they pay a lot of money for it."

"Doylestown? Has a lot of coke-heads? No way." I pushed back off the counter and grabbed the French press to pour his coffee.

"Yeh, full of 'em. Mostly executives. They all live here because of the pharmas up in Jersey and the big companies in New York."

He was right. Every other husband in Doylestown seemed to be a pharmaceutical or New York City executive. Living in Doylestown was less expensive than living in Northern New Jersey or New York City, and the commute by train was easy.

"Huh," I said quizzically. "I never would have thought. I guess I wouldn't know how to notice that kind of thing."

We sat there in silence for a moment. Finally Joel said, "I'm real sorry, Anna. I wasn't trying to get you in trouble. I was mostly just trying to, you know, make a mutually beneficial thing happen here." He said "mutually beneficial" in the same unintelligent, yet endearing, way Rocky Balboa would have said it.

He timidly sipped his coffee.

"Where do the bags go from here?" The business aspect intrigued me.

"Uh, mostly they stay local. If we can get more bags moving, we can expand into different suburbs and areas. That's kinda how it works."

That's how it works. He said it as casually as someone might mention rain rolling in, and I wondered at what point does one become that desensitized about trafficking drugs. I had already replaced some of my repulsion with excitement, but I was doing it to save my family's future. Joel was doing it for what? Because it's what he knew? Because he was trying to save something, too? I guessed it didn't really matter.

The door chimed and a man in a suit walked in.

"Can I help you, sir?" I asked pleasantly.

"Hold on one sec," he said loudly to someone on his Bluetooth ear device, then to me. "Just a coffee and chocolate chip biscotti to go please." I nodded politely and he resumed his noisy conversation. As I prepared his order, I stole glances at him, wondering if he was one of the coke-head executives Joel claimed infested this area. He talked loudly into the air while waiting for his coffee, cursing at the person on the other end of his phone call, barely looking up as he handed me his credit card. He grabbed his coffee and biscotti with one hand, and left.

As soon as the door chimed shut, Joel looked at me. "So, I guess you're out then?"

I assumed he was asking if I was done moving bags.

I inhaled deeply. "I'm not out. But the price to hold the bags went up to $1,000 per bag."

"No fucking way! I already gave you a good price at $500."

"And you move a kilo of coke for what, $30,000? Maybe more in this area? My price is fair," I said.

"I thought you didn't know much about this profession?" he asked, irritated.

"I do now. I'm a quick learner."

"I can't give you $1,000 for one bag. That's insane," he said.

"Price just went up to $1,200," I said easily.

Joel exhaled loudly. "You're out of your fucking mind! $1,200, no way!" he laughed smugly.

"Price just went up to-"

"Okay! $1,000 per bag," he stopped me in a panic.

"But the price had already reached $1,200," I reminded him.

"One thousand, Anna. Really, that's the best I can do," he said, running his hands over his buzzed head. I could see a glaze of perspiration shining off his forehead.

"Okay, $1,000 per bag. And what if I held two bags?" I asked. If I was only going to be doing this for a short while, why not double what I had just doubled?

He looked up sharply. "You can't hold more than one bag. It gets too suspicious. One bag per person."

"Okay, what if I had more than one person?" I had no intentions of involving anyone else, but I was curious.

"Do you?" he asked with a raised eyebrow.

"I'm just asking," I shrugged indifferently.

"Well, a couple more people in Doylestown would be good, but not too many. You need people to branch out, you know? Get into some of the other places that make a lot of money."

"Like where?"

"I don't know, like anywhere. I mean, the cities are pretty much full, there's a lot of competition. But the suburbs are harder to get into."

I nodded. "Another thing: Who's Panda and what does he know about me?"

He clicked his tongue. "Panda? Panda's nobody. He goes from place to place. I don't even know him much, really. He's getting transferred soon."

"Does he know my name?"

"No. You told me not to tell him. He just knows you as my contact."

"Well, I don't want Panda to know my name or anything else about me, other than I work at a coffee shop and have a bag for him to pick up."

He nodded nonchalantly.

"In fact," I continued, "I don't see a reason that any of your contacts should know anything about me. Period. I need your guarantee, Joel, that I remain anonymous." It dawned on me that Joel didn't even know my last name. Not my married one, at least, and I would be surprised if he ever would have learned my last name when I knew him from before. Joel's not someone who would ask that sort of thing, nor would he have had a reason to. I didn't know Joel's last name when the cops questioned me after Benoit's death. Come to think of it, I didn't know it now.

Joel looked defensively amused. "Okay, I got it. No one will know anything about you. No one has to, really. They don't care what I do with my-" he looked around the shop, then said quieter, "-product. As long as it gets where it needs to go."

I nodded apprehensively. "I'm serious about that, Joel. I only plan to do this for a few months, and I need to trust that you can protect me."

He looked at me curiously. "A few months? A minute ago, you were asking to take two bags at a time and said you had someone else to help."

"No, I didn't say I had someone else to help. I just asked what would happen if I did, and for the record, I don't. But if I'm only doing this for a while, just to make some extra money, I might as well maximize on it. But it seems that is not an option, so we'll stick with our plan. One bag a day for $1,200."

"One thousand," he said quickly with a worried look on his face.

I laughed. "Just keeping you on your toes, Joel. One thousand it is. Paid daily, and if you get behind paying, the bag sits undelivered."

The door chimed and a woman in all black wearing a hairdresser's apron walked in. I looked at Joel quickly for confirmation. He nodded and I tapped the bar with a casual wink, then walked over to the register.

"Hi Lindsay!" I said cheerfully. "Same as usual?"

"Yes, thanks Anna. I'm going to sit here while I wait. My back just can't handle standing all day long anymore." She rubbed her lower back and twirled her neck around.

"I hear you. I look forward to doing paperwork in the office after a few hours of standing at the counter."

She smiled and looked over at Joel. Joel sat crouched over his cup of coffee, tapping his foot up and down on the barstool ledge. Joel didn't exactly fit into the Doylestown scene, with his beat-up head and zero-eye-contact rule of socialization. Lindsay stared at him curiously, and I wondered what questions were circulating in her mind. Hairdressers were more astute than FBI agents, and they loved talking about anything they saw, heard, or thought they saw or heard.

"I need to get into the salon soon." I attempted to distract Lindsay. "My roots are grown out." I pointed to my hair.

"You always look gorgeous, Anna. You're one of those people who never age," she said, breaking her gaze from Joel.

"I don't know about that, but thank you."

"Really though, I don't know how you look that good after three kids. How do you keep the weight off?"

I grinned blandly. "Lots of coffee and biscotti?"

"My ass would be the size of Texas if I did that," she sighed with a passive laugh.

I rang her up and she left, but not without a long look from Joel's head to his feet. I could already hear her asking, "*Who was that guy?*" the next time I went to the salon.

"You know, you might consider dressing a little differently when you come here," I said to Joel as I walked back over and leaned on the counter across from him again. "Or at least smile or act like a pleasant townie."

He looked down at his clothing. "What's wrong with what I have on?"

I tipped my head to the side. "Everything's wrong about it in Doylestown. Leather jacket and jeans? You look like you just walked off of a movie set. *Bronx Tale*," I clarified. "Not *Dead Poet's Society.*"

"I like my clothes," he said defensively.

"They're great clothes, Joel. But if the objective is to stay off the radar, then you might want to buy a sweater vest or something," I snickered softly. The image of Joel in a sweater vest was humorous.

"A fucking sweater vest?" he asked. Then a little louder, "A sweater vest, Anna? No fucking way." He shook his head.

"Alright, just a suggestion. But speaking of fitting in...I need to change the bag up a bit. I can't be holding duffel bags around here. Eloise already asked questions about it and if my husband comes in, he'll know it's not my bag."

"What do you have in mind?"

I reached under the counter. "This." I dropped the diaper bag in front of him.

He stared at the diaper bag, gray with white paisleys. "Uh-uh. I don't think so."

"Uh-huh. I *do* think so."

He stared at it thoughtfully.

"And I was thinking you could pad it with diapers," I added.

"Diapers?" He looked at me disgustedly. "I'm going to look ridiculous carrying that. Didn't you just tell me I needed to fit in?"

"Maybe you should find a baby to bring with you." I held back a laugh. "Dads carry diaper bags all the time."

"This isn't funny. I don't think I can use that," he stared at the diaper bag as if it were diseased.

"You can, and I have two of them. One for drop off, one for pick up. And I just ordered another one for my everyday use. I'll never be in possession of more than two bags at a time, which is what I've always had, so my family will never ask questions."

He resignedly took the bag and sighed. "Okay. I'll pack tomorrow's product-"

"You mean formula?" I interrupted him insinuatingly. "This bag will hold tomorrow's baby formula?"

"What exactly is baby formula, anyway?" he asked impatiently.

"Baby formula, Joel, is a white powdery substance that you mix with water to feed to babies. In a bottle. It's a milk formula."

He picked up on my metaphor. "Right, the *baby formula* will be packed in this bag, this diaper bag, for tomorrow's drop-"

"You mean playdate." Then I added. "That's like a kid's hang-out session."

"For tomorrow's *playdate*," he repeated slowly.

"Excellent! Playdate at 2 p.m. See you then!"

Chapter Twenty-Five

I never understood which side attracted which in the law of attraction. Was it that the person attracted the "like" thing? Or was it that the "like" thing attracted the person?

Two weeks after Joel and I started moving bags regularly, I recruited my first "employee," someone whom I had sat next to every week for two months in Toddler Yoga. Yet until today, I didn't know anything about her except her first name. It didn't happen intentionally, but something drew me to her, or her to me....

Toddler Yoga was every Tuesday at 10 a.m. I slipped away from the shop for an hour to do yoga with Lily, which was meant to encourage the children's sense of balance and well-being in today's busy world. I found it mostly just showed whose kids were going to be the boss when they grew up, and whose kids were going to work for them.

Tara sat next to me on her purple yoga mat while her two-year-old son, Jeffrey, did somersaults, one after another. She leaned back with one hand on the floor behind her, the other hand rocking a car seat with a sleeping baby in it.

"I'm so goddamned tired. Is it Namaste or whatever time yet?

The part where we lie down and close our eyes?" Tara asked with a sleepy banter.

"Shavasana?"

"Yeah, whatever," she chaffed. "You have three kids, right? How do you do it?"

"Well, Lily is my youngest, so we're past all the sleepless nights. It's amazing how human you become when you start getting sleep again."

"Does your husband get nicer, too?" she asked.

"Well, it's easier to reconnect, if that's what you mean?"

"No, I mean, does your husband stop being an asshole?" she asked with an undertone of anger.

"I think if your husband's an asshole, he's just an asshole no matter what," I winked in jest.

"Good to know. I guess I'll have to keep going to therapy, then," she laughed sadly. "Retail therapy, that is."

"Well, at least he lets you do that."

"Oh, he doesn't let me. He doesn't even know," she laughed. She had a drunk sort of laughter, although she didn't appear intoxicated. Maybe she was just in newborn delirium—sleep- and nutrient-deprived. Maybe she was a pill-popper. Who knew?

"He doesn't know that you shop? Is it like you spend more at Target than you should've, but you tell him it was for extra paper towels and diapers type of shopping?" I asked.

She guffawed. "Oh, everybody does that. No, mine is more like shoes and coats that I tell him are from Target, but they're really from Bergdorf, Neiman, Bloomies…." The time in my life where I visited those stores seemed an eternity ago.

"He wouldn't notice what I'm wearing, honestly, unless I'm wearing nothing," she continued. "Then he cares, but only long enough to satisfy himself. Never me. You know how it is."

I definitely did not know how that was. Marco was a generous lover, but this conversation was about her, not me, and I was intrigued by her drops of autobiographical information.

"Do you have a lot of these shoes and coats that he thinks are from Target?" I asked.

She looked at me with a glean of pride in her eyes, like she was getting excited bragging about her dirty little secret. "Tons of them."

"What's a ton? Like 20 pair of shoes? Thirty? Forty?"

She looked down at her baby, smiling. "Like, hundreds."

"Hundreds of designer shoes?" I asked, wide-eyed. "Where do you keep them? Your husband doesn't ask where all your-," I gestured toward her feet, "shoes come from? Doesn't he see them piling in your closet?"

"I hide them in the attic. No one goes up there. I bought a couple of those portable closet things, the kind with snap-together frames and a zip-up cover. I hide all my clothes and shoes up there and bring down only a few at a time after he goes to work."

"And he just pays the bills, no questions asked? At least you have that, right?"

"Hell, no. That's one thing he would notice: Money. He doesn't even know about the bills. I hide those, too."

I lifted my eyebrows. This woman became more interesting by the moment.

"How do you manage to hide that from him?"

"Honestly, it's getting tricky. I opened as many credit cards as I could, and I just pay the minimum balance. I used to be able to take a little bit of cash out here, hide a little there, to keep the cards going, but the minimums are getting higher, and it's getting harder to keep it up." Tara's demeanor turned somber.

"I'm sorry, that must be hard for you."

"Which part?" she laughed. "That my husband doesn't give a shit about me? Or that I cover it up with a compulsive shopping disorder?"

I stayed quiet and smiled.

She continued. "Or that I'm about to get caught, which will make my husband flip out, and probably leave me with two kids and a mountain of credit card debt? He'll take me to the cleaners too, hiring the best lawyers. I could get a lawyer who would make him pay alimony and child support and all that, but I couldn't afford a good one. I'd have to find one of those shitty lawyers who will take a percentage of the settlement." Her eyes filled with tears. "I'm afraid he'd try to take the kids from me. He'd say I'm an unfit mother, and I'm not. I am a great mother." She looked at her baby, sleeping quietly in his carrier.

"Maybe you should just come clean. He might understand more than you think he would."

She looked at me as if I'd suggested she touch a snake. "Uh-uh, no way. He wouldn't understand. It would just give him a reason to leave me. I have to pay off the cards before he finds out."

"Do you have a plan?"

"Not yet. But I'm sure something will come up. I'm going to look into a job during the day while he's working. Maybe somewhere I can take the kids. Like a daycare or something."

"You'll never be able to pay off all that debt working at a daycare. Maybe you should look into something else. You could consign your clothes."

"It still wouldn't be enough. I've already started doing that. I only get about 20 percent of the clothes' and shoes' value, which barely covers the interest of the credit cards."

I nodded thoughtfully. "I'm sure there's something out there."

"Like what? What is out there that I can do during the day, with two kids, that my husband won't find out about, that will make enough money to pay off my credit card bills?"

My stomach churned with a solution too egregious to mention.

"Okay! Everyone back to their mats," instructed the yoga teacher. "We're going to learn the elephant pose! Who can show me how an elephant walks?" Free time was over, and the kids were returning to do poses with Mom.

"Is there an elephant pose in yoga?" I asked Tara in an effort to lighten the mood. "I'm no yogi, but I've done yoga enough that I think I would've run into this pose before today."

She laughed morosely. "I think Miss Ruth makes most of this shit up. I don't care though, gives me an hour where I don't have to entertain my kid."

We went through the motions of learning the elephant pose. I genuinely enjoyed watching Lily's pudgy toddler body bend and roll into silly positions, and hearing her sweet giggles when she accomplished a pose.

"Do you know how a mama elephant protects her baby elephant?" I whispered to Lily as we crouched side-by-side with both hands and knees on the ground.

She looked up with her big green eyes. "How, Mama?"

"Like this." I put my arm out imitating an elephant's trunk and swept her under my belly, making a barely audible elephant's trumpet sound while tickling her ribs. She squealed louder than I anticipated, and I stopped and playfully put my finger to my mouth, gesturing her to be quiet as we stifled our laughs.

"Good, so we'll *quietly* move on to a happy elephant pose," Miss Ruth said loudly, clearly sending the message that our out-of-turn playing was distracting.

"Back to your place now," I whispered to Lily. She giggled back into place beside me.

We finished our poses and ended with a short shavasana. I lay with my eyes open thinking about how Tara must wish she could melt into the floor with all of her problems. Selfishly, I felt grateful not to feel as miserable as she did. I had my own set of problems, but Tara just seemed so hopeless. And hopeless was a sad place to be.

As we were packing up to leave, I looked over at Tara's diaper bag. It was a black Yves Saint Laurent bag, which I never noticed before. I thought about how easy it was to assume someone's status based on her possessions. An hour ago, I might have assumed that Tara had oodles of money and an adoring husband who spoiled her with diamonds and designer bags. Meanwhile, Tara was desperately unloved by her husband and drowning her neglected heart with material items that fed her soul only temporarily, leaving more than just credit card debt. It left her entire being in debt.

Tara slung the nearly $3,000 bag over her shoulder, picked up the carrier with the still sleeping baby in the other hand, and walked over to me. "Hey, sorry I dumped all that shit on you."

"Oh, no, please. I'm glad you did. It's good to talk about things. I hope things get better for you. I mean it."

She laughed. "Well, unless you know how to grow a money tree...."

But hey, it was good to talk to someone about it. I feel like I live on an island sometimes. I'm from Allentown, but my mom and dad are too sick to travel, and Rick is from New York, so I'm basically alone. A lot."

Allentown? *Further reach*, I heard Joel's voice in my head.

"How often do you go to Allentown?"

"I don't know. I guess two to three times a week, depending on what's going on with them."

I blinked my eyes heavily with regret before inviting, "Tara, listen, I do know of a way you could make a little extra money, if you're interested."

"Oh, thanks, but is it one of those selling makeup or face product gigs? I've looked into that. No amount of face creams could pay my credit card bills," she laughed desperately.

"It's bigger money than that. It's a little unorthodox, but it might help you get out of your rut."

"I'm interested. What is it?"

"Come by my shop later. Around 3 p.m.? You know where the biscotti shop is in town?"

"Yeah, Biscotti? I love that place. I didn't know it was yours!"

"I've only been there full time for a couple of months. My husband ran it before."

"Great, I'll see you at 3 p.m., then," she said.

I nodded apprehensively.

Chapter Twenty-Six

The next morning, Lynn walked in with the appearance of a deflated balloon.

Lynn came in every Monday and Wednesday morning, but never the other days of the week, which I found interesting. Her normally neat hair was pulled back in a messy bun; she wore a skirt and a wrinkled button-up blouse that she tried to cover up with a cardigan. Her face was gaunt, and it looked like she hadn't slept well in a quite a while.

"Good morning, Lynn," I said sincerely. "Usual?"

She nodded as she sat down at the counter. She pulled out her makeup case and checked her face and hair in the mirror, wiping the smeared mascara from underneath her eyes.

"That kind of morning?" I asked as I prepared her usual Americano, four shots of espresso, and a lemon biscotti.

"That kind of life," she said resignedly. "These day trips to Newark are getting old." Lynn sighed as she fished out her phone.

"Do you commute for work?"

"Mmm-hmm." She looked down, scrolled through her emails.

"Remind me what you do?"

"I'm in Sales. Insurance. I sell policies. Actually, I don't sell policies anymore, my team does. My corporate offices are in Newark and I oversee the Northeast regional sales team. It's a shit job, but someone's gotta pay the bills."

I nodded in acknowledgement as I poured the hot water over her four espresso shots.

"You have kids, right? I've seen you around town on the weekends with them. Son and daughter?" I asked.

"Yes, Layla and Kyle," she smiled pitifully. "Kyle, for obvious reasons, is why I keep this job. It has good benefits." Kyle was in a wheelchair and had severe disabilities; to what extent, I did not know.

I kept quiet as I reached for her lemon biscotti. I found the best way to make people talk is by *not* talking, a page from Jack-the-dinosaur-therapist's book.

"I just don't know how long I can do this," she continued, shaking her head. "It doesn't matter. How are you, Anna?"

I ignored her attempt to deflect. "The commute killing you?" I asked.

"No, my fucking husband is killing me," she said seriously.

I grimaced with sympathy.

"No, really, he's killing me. Slowly, too. I actually would appreciate if he ran me over with a truck instead of dragging me through his bullshit over and over again."

I let out a quiet, empathetic sigh. Lynn had a very direct way about her that I enjoyed. She liked to say outrageous things for shock value, mostly to amuse herself, but also to gauge which type of people could keep up with her crude wit.

"Remember how I told you that Brent got a new job?" she continued. "You might not remember, but anyway, he already fucked it up. Got fired in the first week. It was his fifth job this year. I'm going to lose it, Anna. I really am. I might run *myself* over with a truck." She laughed pathetically as she took a swig of her Americano.

"I'm sorry to hear that. I know you were hoping that would work out," I said.

"Yeah, well, I should have known. I mean, he hasn't been able to hold down a job since coming back from Afghanistan. PTSD is no joke."

"I know it's serious. Does he get help for it?"

"Therapists, meds, more meds. Yeah, he's done it all. He's usually okay until he has to go back to work. Work stress is a major trigger, but I need him to work, you know? I can't carry our family by myself while he's home bird-watching or whatever the hell he does. Probably watches porn all day."

"Probably not, Lynn, Jesus," I snorted with laughter. "Brent's a good guy with a difficult disorder. It's nobody's fault," I said sympathetically. "But everyone's burden."

She looked at me solemnly and took a deep breath, "Yeah, Anna. Yeah, it is."

I put my hand over hers, gave it a little squeeze before turning to clean out the portafilter.

"I know it's not Brent's fault. I just have no one else to blame," she said with a sigh. "Tell the truth, I wish we could afford for Brent to stay home and manage things there. He actually likes being a Desperate Housewife," she smiled. "But we need his income. Even with insurance, I can't keep up with his and Kyle's medical bills. We've mortgaged our house twice and my mother's house once. It's just a fucking crime how hard it is to take care of a disabled child. Do you know that Kyle hasn't been upstairs in our house for almost a year because he got too big for me to carry, and Brent hurt his back in Afghanistan? We don't have a bedroom downstairs; he sleeps in the dining room. There's not a full bathroom downstairs so I have to bathe him with a sponge in the mud room. Once a week, I take him to the YMCA for a shower."

She threw her hands up and shook her head, demoralized.

I pursed my lips together. Hearing about Lynn's circumstance made me itch with repudiation; like reading an article on child abuse and quickly putting down the paper to shelter yourself from the horror of it. Lynn woke up every morning and faced challenges most of us couldn't comprehend, but all of us feared. She had more than a disabled child; she had a mentally disabled husband—to no fault of his own— and, if I had to guess, a significantly neglected daughter.

"I just don't see anything changing," she said in a cracking voice. "This is it for me. This is my life." She held a tissue with one finger at the corner of her eye, soaking up a heavy tear before it fell.

I stared helplessly at Lynn as she alternated her tissue from one eye to the other.

"Lynn, I'm sure you've explored every avenue, but there's not some government or non-profit organization that can help? Surely, Brent has veteran programs available?"

She scoffed. "You're fucking kidding, Anna? You've obviously never been to the VA. I've maxed out everything insurance can offer. It's harder than you'd think to take advantage of some of the disability programs out there. You practically need a PhD to apply for some of them, and don't even get me started about how much time it takes:

It's another full-time job. Listen, I'm sorry. I shouldn't be pouring this out on you like this. You caught me on a bad morning."

"No, please. I'm glad to listen, if nothing else."

"I'll be fine. I'll figure it out, like always," she said stoically as she stood up and grabbed for her purse.

"Today's coffee is on me," I said.

"Oh, come on. I don't need all of your pity, just some of it," she said.

"No, I wish I could do more. People like you deserve more in this life. You shouldn't have to bear so much burden."

"It's all good, Anna. Like I said, I'll figure it out, even if I have to hook on the side," she laughed. "I'm kidding. Kind of. I mean, it worked out for Julia Roberts in *Pretty Woman*."

I didn't think I could bring myself to broach the prospect of Lynn holding bags, even though I knew the extra cash would dramatically change her circumstance. But no one else was helping Lynn, goddammit. Why shouldn't I?

"Lynn, how much would a stair lift cost? For Kyle?" I asked.

"Oh, no, Anna, I'm not falling into that trap. I will not let you offer to pay for it."

"No, I couldn't even if I wanted to, unfortunately. But I'm curious. How much do they cost?"

"Well, lucky for me, we have an old curvy staircase, so around $5,000, I've been told."

"What if I could help you earn that money pretty quickly?" I asked, each word coming out like slow, sticky syrup.

"I can't quit my job. Is it something I can do after work or on the weekend?"

"Yes. And it won't take much time at all. You could probably afford a stair lift in a matter of weeks."

"Keep talking," she said, as she sat back down and leaned forward.

Chapter Twenty-Seven

B efore I could feel confident about bringing Tara and Lynn into the operation safely, I needed to iron out some details with Joel. There were the logistical aspects of bringing in more people, which meant a change in the way we moved the bags, but there also was the matter of protecting Tara and Lynn.

Joel came in at his usual time, 2 p.m., and sat at the counter.

"New shirt?" I smiled.

He looked down. "Yeh, well."

Joel was wearing a blue button-up shirt (unbuttoned to an inappropriate level), tucked into his jeans with a black belt. It wasn't a sweater vest, but he made an effort into stepping toward Doylestown attire, even if the effect meant he stood out more than before. Two tattoos peeked out of his shirt on either side of his chest, a series of scratch marks like those of a large cat and part of a face of an animal. I could only make out the eye and some whiskers. Joel's shirt hung loosely on his body, like a child wrapped in a rain poncho, and I wondered if Joel struggled shopping as he teetered between the Boy's and Men's sections of the store for best fit.

I passed his coffee and an almond biscotti across the counter to him. "They're peanut-free. I checked."

He nodded briefly, dipped his biscotti in his coffee, and took a bite. His shoulders slackened. "These are good. Real good." His shiny white teeth peeked through the biscotti.

"Listen, we have to talk," I said.

"I can't give you any more money for those bags," he said defensively.

"No, I know that. I have something to put past you; and I think you'll like it."

"Okay?" He asked through a second bite of his biscotti.

"What if I had a few more people to move bags? You said before that you would be interested if there was further reach. Any value to Newark or Allentown?"

He raised his eyebrows and licked the last of the biscotti off his fingers. "Possibly. Why?"

"Because I have two, let's call them *friends*, who go to those places regularly, at least twice a week, and could use some extra cash."

"Are they reliable?"

"Very," I replied confidently.

"And they're willing to," he hesitated, "enter this line of business?"

"Well, yes and no. That's another thing I wanted to talk to you about. I didn't exactly tell them what was in the bags, and I don't think I have to. Hear me out," I said.

He stared at me suspiciously, hunched over the counter, both hands on his coffee mug as though someone might steal it.

I reached beneath the counter and pulled out a 36 oz. can of baby

MICHELLE LEE

formula, setting it firmly in front of Joel. "You're going to put the product, the 'baby formula,' inside this. Naturally."

He stared at the can, then looked at me. "Right. You're crazy, Anna, you know that? I went along with the diaper bag and wearing nicer clothes, but this is crazy. No."

"Why not? It's the perfect size and it will look natural inside a diaper bag."

"Yeah, but that's a lot of extra work, and for what?"

"So that if my friends get curious enough to look inside the bag like I did, they'll only find this in there. That whole 'plausible denial' thing that you tried to protect me with? It's probably bullshit. But even so, I'm going to do that. Only I'm going to succeed at it."

"But they can just open the cans and see what's in there," he countered, confused.

"Or can they?" I pulled out a two-inch thick restaurant equipment catalog. I opened it to a page marked by a folded corner and pointed. "This machine seals cans."

He looked closer. "Yeh, so?"

"So, if you seal the cans before putting them into the bags, then it won't matter if they open the bags. They will only find sealed cans of baby formula."

"What if they got a can opener and opened the cans?"

"I highly doubt they'd go that far. Do you know how long it took me just to unzip the bag you gave me? I wouldn't have dared to tamper with the product. And I'm ballsier than most."

"You're definitely ballsy," he agreed.

"Besides, I'll make sure they don't mess with the cans. If they're tampered with, they won't get paid."

"You really think that will work?"

"Yes. People believe what they want to believe. Look, they're not dumb. They're going to suspect that there may be something dangerous or illegal in the bags, and they might try to look. But they won't find more than diapers and a can of baby formula. If they ask me questions about it, I'll tell them the same thing you told me: It's better not to ask; it's baby formula. They'll only have two choices at that point: To accept that and go about their business; or to quit. But it's hard to walk away from easy money." Trust me, *I know.*

"And if they do open the cans? What will we do, then?" he asked.

What will *we* do? This was the other matter I needed to settle: Ensuring complete anonymity of my network. I had a reasonable sense of assurance that Joel's "people" wouldn't know about me. But I had to ensure that Joel wouldn't know about anyone in my network, either. This meant that Joel could only deal with me, and I could only deal with my contacts, my mothers. It was a risky, single point of failure. But it was a critical protection plan.

"*We* don't do anything. *I* will deal with anyone who gets out of line," I said.

He scrunched his face up skeptically. "What do you mean, you'll deal with it? I'll have to help if I'm running these friends of yours."

"You won't be running them. Only I will."

"But I have to give them the bags," he said.

"You'll bring the bags here in the morning. I'll distribute them appropriately. They'll deliver them to your contacts in the locations we agree upon. Any problems on the other end of it, you let me know, and I'll deal with it. I'll take the heat."

"You must really trust them to deliver, then," he sneered.

"I do. The same way you trust me."

He tapped his foot thoughtfully. "Your contacts will deliver the bags to Newark and Allentown?"

"Yes, Allentown on Tuesdays and Fridays. Newark on Mondays and Wednesdays. So you'll have to arrange for contacts on the other end to pick up the bags."

"Starting when?"

"Starting whenever we have these little details worked out. I'll buy extra diaper bags, you call your buddy Frank at the restaurant store and inquire about the can sealing machine. I'm sure he owes you a favor. It shouldn't take us longer than a week to sort it all out."

He grinned widely and pushed up off the stool. "You're pretty fucking good at this, Anna. Even better than He was."

My face dropped. "What'd you just say? Better than who was?"

Joel looked up with a panicked face. "Oh, nothing. Never mind. I just meant I didn't expect you to be this good at, you know, this type of thing."

"No, I think you meant more than that. You said *better than he was*. What did you mean by that? Who's 'He?'"

Joel ran his hands over his head and cranked his neck sideways as though he had a kink in it.

"Joel?" I pressed. "Who's 'He?' What the hell did you mean when you said that?" I asked with mounting irritation.

He shifted uncomfortably. "You know who *he* is," he said as he stared at the floor.

My heart sunk. "Benoit?"

Joel stood silent.

"I'm better than Benoit was?" I asked. The room suddenly seemed smaller as it closed in on the questions racing through my mind. "Was he involved in this, Joel?"

"I just meant-" Joel started, but he was interrupted by the door chime and a giggly group of teenagers entering the shop.

I inhaled sharply and stared at Joel.

He nervously stepped aside for the teens to swarm the counter.

"Gotta go." Joel walked out the front door, the bell chiming behind him.

Chapter Twenty-Eight

J oel kept his distance for the next week as we sorted out operational details, partly because there was no real need to make plans in person; but also partly because he was avoiding my imminent questions about Benoit, which I could only ask him in person. Questions about a dead ex's involvement in cocaine dealings wasn't really text-worthy, which was why I was looking forward to seeing Joel again to continue the conversation where it left off. First though, we had to tie up some loose ends.

Joel verified that the can-sealing machine had been purchased, but not without trying to make me pay for it. I quickly dismissed him by reminding Joel that without me, he didn't have an operation; and I knew his buddy, Frank, had set him up with a nice discount. He relented easily.

I remembered a time not that long ago when Joel called me "ma'am" and shoveled my patio. Time and surely, experience climbing the cocaine ladder, had given Joel a more brazen edge, but I laughed at the notion that Joel thought he might swindle me on a business deal. Perhaps Joel could feel the weight of power shifting to me, and he was eager to remind me that he could call some shots. But the truth was, Joel worked for me now, even though he would never quite know it, if I managed things correctly.

I purchased three blue bags for Tara and three black bags for Lynn. Lynn's bags looked more like a laptop case because most of her travel was for work. These days, diaper bags were used interchangeably as laptop bags, purses, beach bags—any kind of bag. The color-coding would help me with sorting bags appropriately; not that the contents changed, but it made sense for me. There would be one bag in Tara's and Lynn's possession at all times, one in mine and Joel's possession, respectively; and one bag circulating. The bags would rotate as each drop occurred.

Joel and I picked a date for the first drop in Newark and Allentown. I found two facilities with lockers large enough to fit the diaper bags in: One was a gym and one was a small entertainment facility with go-karts and miniature golf. Each bag would have a lock in the front pocket, which Tara and Lynn would use to lock the bag inside the locker. They would text me the locker number. I would text Joel; Joel would text his contact; the contact would pick up the bag at the locker. This way, Joel's contacts never met mine. The combination to the locks would always be the same: 33 33 33, for no reason other than I liked the number "three."

Tara started first. I texted her on the prepaid disposable phone that I had given her:

Hey! Playdate tomorrow? Meet me at the playground around 9 am?

She replied:

Sounds great. See you then!

Playdate was code for meeting. *The playground* was code for the shop.

Tara would scoff at having to carry a modest blue diaper bag instead of her $3,000 Saint Laurent bag, but it might help her acclimate to reality, I reasoned.

A similar text to Lynn firmed up our plan to meet later that morning.

Soon, these ladies would be running two bags per week, making $1,000 each, and making me $2,000 dollars per week. Two thousand dollars. A wave of excitement passed through my abdomen. Biscotti's weekly revenue after expenses and taxes averaged $1,500 per week—on a good week. Of course, holidays and special occasions brought in a little more, but for the most part, $1,500 dollars per week is what we could anticipate. I smiled thinking about the red sheet of debt that would soon enough be showing some black, numbers in the positive. Maybe we could even get away as a family, go to the Poconos for the weekend. It had been far too long since we had gone on vacation. No, I couldn't think like that; I was only doing this long enough to get us out of debt. I had to stay focused.

I couldn't help that along with excitement, came an equally prominent wave of anxiety that gnawed at my belly lining. Though I had done my best to ensure our operation would be successful and to protect Tara and Lynn, I couldn't shake this black lining of guilt. Had I really thought through the consequences of this operation? I felt confident that I had. But these qualms didn't matter, now.

This operation was about to begin.

Chapter Twenty-Nine

I put on a scarf and a light jacket before heading to the shop. The Doylestown morning was slightly bitter as the days had shortened and my morning commute remained dark.

I had been up since 4:30 a.m., starting my routine earlier than usual when I realized that getting back to sleep was not an option. I pulled into the shop roughly the same time Eloise and Maribel did, then busied myself with paperwork and prepping duties while they started the morning baking.

I was cleaning the condiment area and refilling the creamer carafes when the door chimed and Joel entered wearing a brown plaid button-up shirt, unbuttoned four buttons down, tucked into his worn jeans with his leather jacket over his shirt. He was carrying two bags: One black, one blue.

I nodded as he walked to the counter and set down the bags by the register. He sat on a stool; his feet dangling like a grade-schooler's.

"Coffee?" I took the bags down from the counter and set them on the floor.

"You're not going to look?" he asked. He seemed a little less jovial than normal; a bit frenzied.

"Look at what?"

"Inside the bags. At the…" he looked around the shop, then continued quietly, "at the baby formula?"

I started his coffee. "No."

This seemed to annoy him further, and though I was keeping my cool, his irritation was pushing my low tolerance for petulance.

"You don't want to see them?" he asked a little louder.

"I trust that they're just what we talked about."

He scoffed in disbelief. "That was a lot of fucking work to get it right. You don't even want to see it?"

"Joel, I'm not trying to insult your effort." I set down his mug and almond biscotti with a heavy thud. "I just don't want to look, alright? I looked once, and once is all I needed."

He could tell by my tone that I wasn't going to budge on the matter.

"Alright," he said resignedly. "They do look good though. Like the real thing." A hint of a pride resonated in his voice.

I smiled curtly. "I never doubted you would make it work."

"It was a really good idea, I have to admit. I wouldn't have come up with it on my own."

"Well, I wouldn't have expected you to," I laughed. "I'm guessing there are not many stroller-wielding moms out there doing what we're doing."

"Or dads," he said. "I look like a dad now, right? I'm all dressed up, carrying diaper bags and shit," he said, as he tugged at his shirt as if to say, "See?"

"You look great, Joel," I grinned, although he still stuck out like a sore thumb.

He sipped his coffee.

"So, everything is set," I said. "I have the locks. I'll put them in the bags' front pockets. My contacts will deliver the bags to the lockers by noon. Your contacts will pick them up."

He nodded.

"I get paid every Friday and Tuesday," I said as more of a question.

He ate his biscotti.

"Joel, I get paid every Friday and Tuesday," I said a little more firmly.

"Yeh, yeh, as long as the bags are delivered, you'll get your money."

"$1,000 per bag," I confirmed.

He nodded again. "Yep."

"Okay, then," I said. "So, now that's out of the way, can we finish our conversation from a couple weeks ago?" I asked softly. I had been anxious to find out more about his relationship with Benoit.

Joel shifted uncomfortably and cleared his throat. "What conversation?" Joel's attempt at ignorance irked me.

"The conversation about Benoit," I pressed. "I want to know if he was involved in this."

He cranked his neck and rolled his shoulders back, then spit air through his teeth as though he was trying to dislodge something from between them. "I don't really want to talk about Benoit."

I stood quietly. Silence always made people talk.

"It's just, I don't know, disrespectful, or whatever," he continued. "If he wanted you to know certain things, he would've told you."

He had a point. But I couldn't help but feel that Benoit would have shared everything with me if our time hadn't been cut short.

"What was your relationship with him? Can you at least tell me that?" I asked. "He always said you were a good friend and that you did things for him. How did you two meet?"

Joel stared at his coffee mug. A smile flashed in his eyes. "We met downtown. At Reading Terminal."

"Reading Terminal," I said thoughtfully. "What, both having lunch or something?"

"Not exactly," he said. He looked down at his hands. "I was real messed up back then. I was using heavy at the time, and he came into the bathroom and found me. I was passed out on the floor. I just," he gestured toward the crook of his arm. "You know, I used too much. I shot up too much is what I'm saying."

I nodded slowly.

"Anyway, Benoit found me and splashed water on my face. Woke me up. I heard him telling someone to get help. Next thing you know, I was in the hospital. I didn't know what had happened or how I got there, but then later that day, Benoit came to check on me. He had brought me a soft pretzel and a root beer. I couldn't keep it down 'cuz my stomach was all messed up, but I remember taking that first salty bite and thinking it was the best thing I'd ever eaten. No one had ever been that nice to me."

I stared at Joel sympathetically. A melancholy sense of loss swept over me as I pictured Benoit visiting a stranger, a junkie, in the hospital and the scarred seam of my heart that held the contents of my love for Benoit tugged; just a little, but just enough to incite a dull ache I hadn't felt in a long time.

"After I left the hospital, Benoit told me he needed someone to help him with things, like errands and shit, and that he'd like to offer me a little bit of money to help him. But I had to stay off the drugs. That was the deal."

I smiled.

"I couldn't take nothin' from him though. Not after what he did for me. And I knew he was just being nice to me. He didn't really need me, but I told him I'd do it, but under one of my own conditions: He couldn't pay me."

"So, that's how you two became friends," I said.

"Well, yeah, I guess. I mean, I never really considered us like buddies, we didn't hang out or anything, but I loved him. I loved him like a brother. I didn't have any family and he…" I thought I detected a change in Joel's tenor, slightly higher than before. He cleared his throat. "He was the only person nice to me. That's all. And I did what I could for him until he…."

He stopped short and took a deep breath in, then he shot the rest of his coffee back with a big gulp and rose. He was visibly agitated, but not in an angry way, more morose.

"Are you leaving? I was enjoying what you were saying. You were saying that you did what you could for him until…? Until he…" I spoke slowly. "Until he died?" I shouldn't have filled in the blank for him; I broke my rule about being silent and had lost the opportunity to know what he might have said.

He looked up sharply and sneered. "Yeh, well, that too." He grabbed the two empty bags I had put out for him earlier. "I gotta go. Are we good now?"

"I guess," I said confused. "But I feel like there's something I'm missing, Joel. You are one of the only links I have from that part of my life, and I never feel like I'm getting the whole story from you."

He stared at the floor and shuffled his feet.

"I know it might not seem important to me anymore, since it has been years since Benoit passed away, and I've moved on and I have a wonderful family now, but it is important. It's important because I am raising a child who has Benoit's blood running through his veins, and I piece together bits and pieces to tell our child all the time. I have details about his childhood from Eloise, of course, but there is the more recent part of his life that never made sense, and that was you, Joel." I never planned to mention Joel to Nathan, but I was hoping that it would get Joel talking a little more.

He didn't look up from his gaze at the floor, but I knew he was listening intently.

"His relationship with you never made sense to me," I said again. "He clearly cared for you. The way he spoke of you was, as you put it, brotherly. Older brotherly, like he was protecting you. I get now that he helped you at a low point in your life, and in turn, you helped him with errands and..." I searched for the word. "Stuff. But there was more to your relationship. I remember when you came into La Castagne and you were stressed out. You had to talk to Benoit about something really important. Remember that?"

He nodded indifferently.

"When Benoit came back to the table he seemed distracted; disturbed. In fact, he always seemed that way after seeing you. But I could tell that something had transpired that day, and now I'm thinking it had something to do with this." I pointed insinuatingly at the bags. "Maybe it matters, and maybe it doesn't, but it is bothering me now. There's a part of me that wants to know. And admittedly, there's a part of me that doesn't want to know. It's like the damn bags: I wish I could be okay not knowing, but I've always been too curious for my own good."

Joel smiled briefly.

"Can you at least tell me this: Was he using drugs?" I asked.

He looked up. "No. No, never. He didn't use."

I sighed in relief.

"Look, I'm sorry," he said. "I know I'm not good at talking and stuff, but I can tell you that he didn't use drugs. He was like you. He liked the business of it."

"So, he was involved?" I asked.

Joel groaned. "Ah fuck, see? This is why I don't like talking. I always say the wrong thing, so I just keep quiet. But yeh, he was involved."

"Did he do what I was doing? Did he move bags?"

"Nah. He was more on the money side of things. I don't want to talk about it, okay?" He shook the bags dejectedly. "I gotta go."

I had gotten as much information out of him as I could get, and it was enough to satisfy me, for now.

"Thanks for that, Joel. I appreciate it."

He shrugged. "See you tomorrow."

Chapter Thirty

My head was reeling, and I desperately wanted to call Kelly and tell her everything that Joel had told me. But for the first time, I couldn't tell Kelly everything, and I resented that. She would have the perfect response; but this time, I'd have to sort through the information I gleaned from Joel by myself.

Some puzzle pieces seemed to fit, such as how the unlikely match of Benoit and Joel had occurred, and why Joel was happy to do Benoit's bidding. Other pieces didn't fit, such as how Benoit got involved in drugs if he made Joel swear them off. Perhaps the most pressing question remained: What was Joel not telling me? He left something unsaid, something that clearly bothered him. I should have let him finish that sentence. I would have to wait for another time to broach the subject; right now, there was work to do.

I put the bags that Joel had left for me filled with diapers and "baby formula" in my office. These days, hardly anyone went into my office besides me, but I still didn't like the way two random bags looked on the floor. I emptied the bottom drawer of the filing cabinet and packed the bags into it, shutting the drawer with a weighty push, then locking it, as I usually did.

While I was slightly tempted to look inside the bags and inspect the quality of the cans, I wasn't interested in facing the reality of my decisions that opening the bags would compel. I would have to trust that they looked like legitimate cans of baby formula to ignore the fact that they were filled with a kilo of cocaine. If I continued to think of the operation as a business, it didn't matter what type of business, as long as it was running smoothly and making money.

I meandered to the shop's front and made myself some green tea. I wished I could make a soy chai latte as well as Jared could. But I had relented that it wasn't my chai-making skills that were lacking all these years; it was that some things just tasted better when other people made them for you. Chai lattes were one of them.

It was about this time that Meg, Blonde ponytail, walked in.

"Hey," she said with a tired southern twang.

"Hi," I said. "It's getting a little cloudy outside, huh? Does it feel like it might rain?" I asked pleasantly. I recognized Meg from the first time she came in with Brown ponytail, but I'd never had a conversation with her.

"Oh, I guess it does. Be honest, I'm not all that used to Pennsylvania weather, yet."

"That's right. You moved here from North Carolina, if I recall correctly?"

She beamed. "That's right! From Raleigh. I loved it there."

"I've never been, but I've heard it's nice down there. What brought you up this way? But first, what can I get started for you?"

She sat down on a bar stool. "Gosh, I wish I remembered what your guy made for me... The cute guy who's here in the afternoons?"

"Jared. He's a doll. And he makes amazing drinks. What did it taste like?"

"It was creamy and had cinnamon in it, maybe?"

Cinnamon roll latte. It was one of Jared's favorite recommendations.

"I think I know what it was. I'll take a stab at it and you can tell me if I got close. How does that sound?"

"Perfect. Y'all are so nice in here," she said.

"So what brought you to Pennsylvania?" I tapped espresso down.

"My husband's job, mostly," Meg said with some reservation.

"Very nice. What does he do?"

"He's in construction. He used to own a company in North Carolina. That's what took us down there to begin with. There's lots of new construction down there."

"And he's expanding up this way?" I asked.

She grimaced. "Well, no. He doesn't have that business anymore. He's working for a different company up here."

I smiled encouragingly. "I'm sure it's a nice change of pace, then."

She shook her head. "Sure, if that's what you wanna call it. Tell the truth, I'm still pretty furious we had to move up this way. I loved Raleigh."

I served her coffee. "Sorry to hear that."

"It's alright," she said. "I'll tell you one thing though. I'm gonna tell my daughters not to marry for looks like I did."

I laughed. "Oh yeah? What will you tell them to marry for?"

"For stability," she said seriously, then laughed a little. "Or at least for a man who doesn't drink, gamble, or sleep around."

I frowned. "Sorry."

"I can handle everything but the gambling. At least running around on me doesn't mean I lose my house."

"Oh geez, I'm sorry." I was beginning to wonder if I should've chosen an occupation as a therapist. People seemed to want to tell me things that I didn't ask about.

"We had it all," she said in a tone like *Voila!* "The big house, the fancy cars. Then the cops show up to seize our properties," she rolled her eyes and laughed, as if she were talking about a time when she forgot to set the right cutlery out for a dinner party.

I raised my eyebrows. "That must have been scary for you."

"It was scary. But now, I'm just mad. My husband gambled all our money away. I had no idea. I thought everything was fine, and meanwhile, he's not paying any of our bills," she shook her head. "Whatever, it's over now. We filed for bankruptcy, and now we're here. Jeff had a buddy who got him a job. It doesn't pay much, and I'm probably gonna have to go back to being a brunette 'cuz I can't afford to stay blonde," she laughed. "But at least I'm closer to my family."

"You have family in Doylestown?"

"No, not Doylestown. I grew up in Harrisburg."

"Harrisburg?" I asked, intrigued. "How often do you go there?"

Chapter Thirty-One

T here are times in your life when you ask yourself: *How did I get here?*

I knew how I got here. But I still marveled at the way a series of choices collectively told a different story than if examined individually. This was how I ended up building a network of women, known simply as *Mothers*: By recruiting one Mother at a time.

In five short weeks, I had recruited 10 women in the Doylestown area, all of whom I knew from different places and circles, and none of whom knew each other.

Tara went to Allentown twice a week to visit her elderly parents.

Lynn went to Newark twice a week for her job.

Meg went to Harrisburg to see family.

Ginny went to Maryland.

Mel went to Atlantic City.

Kate went to Scranton.

Monica went to Delaware.

Mary Ann went to Reading.

Courtney went to Tom's River.

Shelly went to Lancaster.

Each of them had a story that made their recruitment seem natural: I could almost convince myself that I was helping them. Tara could lose her children in an ugly custody battle, her divorce fueled by her massive credit card debt. Lynn needed money for her son's wheelchair lift and husband's PTSD disability. Meg and her husband left North Carolina after filing for bankruptcy, losing their house, and relocating for a job that was barely putting food on the table. Monica's husband lost his job. Mel needed money to support her mother's nursing home abuse lawsuit. Kate was cut off from her trust fund when she told her mother that her stepdad tried to sleep with her. And so on.

So I guess I shouldn't have been surprised when Lynn asked one day, "Can I talk to you a minute?"

"Of course. Can I make your biscotti to stay, then?" I had already made her Americano to go, but she could sit and enjoy a biscotti while we talked.

"Sure, that would be great," she sat down. It was nice to see Lynn settling on a bar stool like she used to do. These days, we had a brief exchange: She would hand me an empty bag; I would hand her a full one with a coffee and biscotti to go. It also was nice to notice Lynn walking with an easier stride these days, a little less weight in each step.

"I had a thought," she started as I set down her biscotti. "I know we are not allowed to talk about our, uh, arrangement to anyone else."

I nodded casually.

"But," she continued. "I have some friends who could, um," she stuttered, then cleared her throat, "who also could move bags to Newark."

My eyebrows shot up in surprise.

"Hear me out. I know you split your portion of the money with me," she said. I had been transparent about the money from the beginning. "And I thought, if I could bring in these couple of women, I would just split my portion with them."

I contemplated her suggestion, but it made me nervous. The Mothers I had recruited, I managed personally. I met with them in person; I could read their body language; I could trust them. Allowing Lynn to recruit a team of her own meant that I lost a bit of control. Unless I came up with strong operational rules beyond the ones that my 10 Mothers abided.

"How many friends do you have in mind?" I asked.

"Four, maybe five. But I could find more, easily," she said.

"I don't know, Lynn…" I apprehended.

"I knew you'd feel a little uncomfortable with the suggestion, Anna, but you have to trust me. I've been managing teams for 20 years. I can manage these women."

"I don't doubt your ability to manage the women," I said. I really did trust Lynn. She was smart, savvy, and certainly knew how to manage people. "But remember, I wasn't planning on doing this for very long. Remember, the deal was only four months. Bringing on more women would extend that."

"I know that, but would it kill us to do it a little longer? I mean, what's six months? I had a contractor out the other day to talk about building a wheelchair-accessible bathroom for Kyle. It would take me a long time to build the bathroom with what I'm making now, but bringing on more women…Shit, I could do it in no time. You have no idea what the stair lift did for him, Anna. He got so excited when he heard me talk to the contractor about the bathroom."

I bit my lip as I stared at the anticipation in Lynn's face. Picturing Kyle using his new bathroom certainly made the offer more alluring. The money five additional women would bring in also was attractive. I had already paid off most of our debt; this would pay it off almost immediately. And there was more than that, if I could admit it to myself, that was bringing me closer to saying, "yes." For the first time in a long time, I felt the rush of business again. The pulse of managing an operation and toggling between spreadsheets and updating numbers, watching them balance out, had fed a part of me I didn't know was hungry. If I was being critically honest with myself, I also should admit that each time Joel handed me an envelope, fatter than the one before, it thrummed my ego a little.

"Okay. But we're going to have to create some rules," I said.

Lynn smiled. "Of course."

The rules were simple, but crucial.

Rule One: Don't ask, don't look. This rule referred to the bag's contents. I had recruited my Mothers under the premise that they were not to ask questions about the contents. It was simply a job, I explained to them, a logistical job that required them to take a bag from one place to the next. Most of them, though a bit skeptical, didn't contest this rule. I made it clear to them that they did not have to do this job, that they could quit at any time. But they couldn't ask questions or look inside the bag. The fail-safe, of course, was that if they got curious enough to look—and I wouldn't put it past them—they would find only diapers and a sealed can of baby formula.

Which made Rule Two the most crucial: The product must be delivered entirely in its original integrity. Otherwise, the woman would not get paid and she'd be eliminated from the operation. No one wanted to risk losing this kind of easy cash, and even more compelling was the fact that nobody really wanted to know what was in the bag. Sometimes ignorance really is bliss, especially if it had a price tag of $500 to $2,500 per week.

Rule Three was for the Mothers only: They could not have more than 10 women in their network, their team. I would stop at having 10 Mothers, too. Managing 10 individuals was a reasonable but maximal number.

Which led to Rule Four: No more layers. My Mothers could create a team of their own, but if their women, who would later become known as, "Moms," wanted to build teams, it was an absolute, unequivocal, *No*. It was imperative that the Mothers made it clear to the Moms that they were not to recruit or suggest any other women.

Rule Five was about association: The women could not know about each other. So far, each of my Mothers didn't know others existed. In fact, each of my Mothers thought that she was my only recruit. I had developed a schedule so that each Mother had a different time slot to pick up her color-coded bags, ensuring my Mothers would never run into each other. As they would start to build their network, Mothers needed to create the same anonymity for each of their Moms. Mothers would have to ensure that the women they recruited didn't run in the same social or other circles; and they were encouraged to choose women from outside of Doylestown. As such, the women wouldn't know about each other; and they sure as hell wouldn't know about me.

Rule Six was similar: Don't tell. These women were not dumb. They had already gauged, like I had, that there was something shady in the bags. Some even may have suspected drugs, but didn't care. Some may have been more naive and had convinced themselves that it was something less offensive. Regardless, no one could talk about her newfound opportunity to anyone else. This was not an operation about which they could blab to their lovers or friends. But because they suspected what they were doing wasn't innocent, it mitigated the natural tendency to share their good fortune (their new stacks of cash) with others. I believed that they would keep the operation secret. So far, my Mothers had.

Final Rule Seven involved communication. Joel and I carried a prepaid disposable cell phone to communicate. As such, each Mother carried one. Each Mother was to supply one to the Moms in her respective networks. In addition, if a phone or text conversation was necessary, they needed to use code names.

PLAYDATE was code for meetings.

Names of parks, such as *CASTLE PARK*, coordinated with drop locations.

Bags would be known as *KIDS*.

The product, the baby formula, would be known as any kind of thing that could be put in a diaper bag: Toys, bottles, pacifiers, etc.

The shop, Biscotti, which was the central location where bags came in and where bags went out, became notorious as *THE PLAYGROUND*.

In essence, a text might look something like:

Hey there! Playdate (meeting) at the playground (shop) on Wednesday? Around 2 p.m.? I'll have my two kids (bags) with me. My son left his pacifier (baby formula can) at your house... Would you mind bringing it?

A few months ago, I wouldn't have believed there were so many women willing to do this job. But soon after Lynn approached me, I also was approached by other Mothers who wanted to recruit Moms of their own. Two things lured these women. First, it was an easy job that didn't cost much more than a little time and some gas money. I provided the diaper bags, and women simply had to show up and go to the places they would normally go.

Second, and most attractive, was the money. Not only did all these women want extra money; most desperately needed it. My Mothers made $500 per bag, half of what I made per bag. Moms made $250 per bag, half of what the Mothers made per bag.

I never wanted to be part of a sales pyramid, but I ended up building a multilevel company, nonetheless. Only I wasn't selling product in a designer bag; I was moving cocaine in a diaper bag. At the operation's height, my pyramid encompassed more than 100 women, 10 Mothers and 100 Moms.

And who was I?

I was Mother Superior.

Chapter Thirty-Two

B usiness continued to run smoothly as winter took hold and Doylestown residents prepared for hibernation. Shop owners exchanged planters full of mums for cone-shaped hollies trimmed with lights, and the smell of the holidays created a pine-filled fog in the town.

My Mothers and Moms reliably were completing their drops, the colored bag system was proving effective, and money was flowing in faster than electricity flows through a wire. Business was so good that I stopped sometimes, waiting for the other shoe to drop.

But it didn't. I had built an operation that ran so smoothly and was so lucrative that the CEO of my old bank would want to take notes. I had paid off our debt, stashed money in savings, and still had piles of cash leftover.

In fact, my only real problem became what to do with all the bags. There were simply too many of them now to manage in the shop. Some Mothers were running bags every day of the week; others two to three times per week. Some Mothers asked if they could build networks in different locations, which I put a hold on for now. I already was feeling overwhelmed by the massive number of bags we were moving.

I'd have to address the storage problem soon. But right now, a new problem was rolling in: Ginny just pulled up in a shiny, black Mercedes Benz.

"New car?" I asked.

"I know!" she crowed. "Isn't it gorgeous?"

Exorbitant spending so quickly was not a problem I had anticipated, but perhaps I should have. My Mothers were making up to $15,000 per week, less after they shared their cut with the Moms; but that kind of cash was not easy to hide. And it easily could become an operational red flag.

"It's certainly beautiful. Why don't you come up front for a cup of coffee, Ginny?"

"Uh, sure," she replied tepidly, as one might when expecting a scolding.

She followed me to the bar and took a seat at the counter.

"Coffee?" I offered.

"Tea. Green tea, if you have it."

"Your car is beautiful, Ginny. But I'm wondering if buying something so lavish will draw the wrong kind of attention." I scooted her green tea, along with a ginger biscotti, across the counter to her.

"You mean, will people ask questions about where I got the money to buy it?" she asked.

"Exactly," I winked.

I had met Ginny months ago in the checkout line of the grocery store. She was ahead of me, holding up the line by passing one coupon after another to the clerk. The beep of the scanning coupons sounded as repetitive as the taps of an old typewriter. When the beeps retired, the clerk looked up lackadaisically. "Your balance is $52.11."

Ginny had sighed and fiddled with a stack of coupons filed neatly in a leather purse. "No, I think you didn't scan the coupons correctly. I-I-just one moment. I must have more coupons. Can you scan them again please?" she had asked.

But the rescanned results by the teenage clerk were the same. I offered to take care of her balance; she accepted sorrowfully, but gratefully. When I had pushed my cart out of the store moments later, Ginny was waiting for me outside.

As with the other Mothers, Ginny's recruitment seemed reasonable; it would certainly ease the financial strain of her husband leaving her and their four kids.

But now she was driving a $60,000 Mercedes coupe.

"Don't worry. I told everyone that Brad had come to his senses and started sending me child support and alimony. Of course, he hasn't," Ginny said in a low voice. "He's still probably in Europe with his mistress…." Ginny's ex-husband was of royal lineage, so it was a plausible assumption that her support payments would be substantial.

"How exactly did you pay for it, though?" I asked attentively.

"With a check," she said.

"That's what I feared," I frowned. "Ginny, people will start asking questions if you are depositing large amounts of cash into the bank. They're technically required to report that type of behavior. We can't afford to have people investigating where your money came from, if you know what I mean."

"I know that," she said. "That's why I created a fake fundraiser. I take my cash to different grocery stores and buy stacks of $100 credit cards. Then I donate to my fundraiser using the credit cards. Once a month, I transfer my fundraising money to my bank."

The surprise on my face would have been the same had she peeled off a mask to reveal she was an alien.

"Holy shit, Ginny. That's really smart." I didn't add the obvious: It also was shameless. Who was I to judge?

"Thanks!" she gloated.

"Alright then, I guess you better get back to work. Do you want another ginger biscotti to-go?" I asked as she licked her fingers and pressed at the crumbs on the plate.

"No way. Can't get crumbs on my new leather!"

I walked Ginny to the door and went back to cleaning the espresso machine while I waited for the next Mother to arrive. As I flushed water into the grouphead, I reflected in awe on my conversation with Ginny. I was curious if the other Mothers had come up with as discerning ways to use their money. I needed to discuss cash management with each Mother to find out. But more importantly, I needed my own cash management plan.

The amount of money the Mothers were pulling in could be judiciously recycled. The amount of money I was making, currently stacked neatly in Tupperware bins marked, "old invoices," could not.

Chapter Thirty-Three

Joel was scheduled to come at 2:00 p.m., as usual.

At 1:55 p.m., I put a "Closed Temporarily for Machine Maintenance" sign on the door and locked up. Joel and I hadn't had much opportunity to sit down and chat for a while. Our transactions were conducted entirely out back between cars, so there was no need for him to come into the shop anymore.

But I was intent on having a discussion with Joel today. I remembered he had mentioned that Benoit liked "the money side of it." I had been wondering what that meant; maybe Joel knew of ways that could help me manage my newfound wealth.

I watched out of my office window, which faced the back of the shop, until Joel's blue BMW with decaled tinted windows and oversized rims rolled up. I shook my head. It was a step up from his maroon Chevy Malibu, but his need to alter an already beautiful car was lost on me. I went out to meet him as he opened his trunk, which was packed with colorful bags; tomorrow's bags.

"Come in for a cup of coffee today, Joel?" We efficiently transferred bags from his car to mine. I glanced around the back of the buildings and locked the car door.

He looked at his Rolex and grimaced. "Don't have much time."

"Come on, just for a minute. I need to ask you about something."

When I used to say that, Joel would flinch and look scared. Now, he just looked irritated. "About what?"

"Business."

He shifted his feet and sniffed, then nodded toward the door in agreement. He sat at the bar in his usual spot. He was jittery, tapping his foot rapidly on the bar ledge and tinkering with a sugar jar.

"I wanted to ask you about the cash coming in." I spooned grinds into the French press.

"Yeah, what about it? You makin' too much of it now?" he smiled sarcastically.

I chuckled lightly. "No, it's not that. But I certainly have enough money to draw attention, and I wanted to know if you could help me with a way to use the cash. An indiscreet way."

Joel stopped tinkering. "I knew it was only a matter of time before you'd be doing what He did."

I tried to seem unfazed. I knew who *he* was. "So, that's what Benoit did. He laundered money?"

He teetered his head sideways back and forth. "Something like that, yeh."

I exhaled inaudibly. Their association was starting to make some sense.

"How did he do it?"

"Lots of ways," he said, as he sniffed and briskly swiped his nose. "You have my coffee, yet?"

I poured his coffee and set an almond biscotti in front of him. I knew I had to stay focused on learning about Benoit's role in the business, but it was hard to resist delving into their personal relationship; I still had so many unanswered questions. "You were saying?"

He took a large gulp of coffee. "I don't know much. I'm not smart with that kind of stuff, but I know that he used a lot of store fronts—La Castagne was one of them—to filter cash. He also had contacts with some kind of banker people, brokers I think is what they're called, who helped. And he took a lot of trips to Paris. I think he did something in Switzerland."

A flashback to a training on money laundering from my banking days reeled in my head: Securities brokers, blending of funds, currency exchanges. Benoit had dual citizenship, he traveled back and forth often; he easily could have made the right connections to hide money.

"So, he would help you with the cash you were making? Is that what he did?"

"No, not me. I didn't do *this* when Benoit was alive. I never got to be with the guys who, you know, dealt big. But I ran around with people who did, and when I heard they was looking for a way to get rid of some cash, I thought Benoit could help. He was smart with that kind of stuff, and it would put me more toward the top if I helped these guys out, if you know what I mean."

"More toward the top of…," I gestured that I didn't know how to finish the sentence. "…of the drug hierarchy? Is that what it's even called?" I felt like a bank clerk who had no idea what it was like to run a bank.

"Yeah, I mean, you gotta understand where I come from. In my

world, there are no fancy executives with college degrees." He emphasized *executives*. "The ones driving around our neighborhood in nice
cars, buying fancy things, they was making money by doing other
things. Things your kind don't talk about."

I nodded. He was right: It was a world unfamiliar to me.

"Benoit was good at moving cash," he continued. "That's all I know.
I don't know exactly how he did it, but…." He shrugged his shoulders
and dipped his biscotti in his coffee.

"So, you moved up the ladder, so to speak, with Benoit's help?
That's how you got to a level where you could do *this*?"

"Well, no. Not at first. I was just the contact between him and the
other guys. Benoit wouldn't let me do anything else."

"What do you mean?"

Joel shifted and rolled his shoulders back, then sniffed and swiped
at his nose again. He always was fidgety, but there was something
different about his demeanor; and I had never noticed the nose-swip-
ing before.

"He wouldn't let me. I don't know. He just wanted me for himself,"
he said spitefully.

"Maybe he wanted to just keep you away from the drugs," I said.
"Surely, you were compensated?"

He looked at me confused.

"Paid. Surely you were paid?" I clarified.

"Uh, yeh. I got a cut from Benoit, but it wasn't much," he said,
then scoffed. "Not nearly as much as he was making."

"You sound resentful about it," I said. "Were things bad between
you guys before he passed away?"

Joel looked up sharply with wide eyes, and that's when I noticed the ratio of blue to black was off; his pupils were heavily dilated. My stomach sunk.

"I wasn't fucking anything before he died," he said loudly. He gulped back the last of his coffee and stood up. "I hate these fucking talks you trap me into."

My mouth dropped open. "I didn't trap you into anything. You mentioned him. I was just asking how to manage all the cash coming in," I said defensively.

He patted his pockets as if he was looking for something. "I gotta go. I don't know what to tell you to do with the fucking cash. Find a way like the rest of us do. Buy a boat or something," he said distractedly. "Where's my fucking keys?" His voice had turned angry.

I needed to calm down Joel. I was alone in the shop with him, and although I was not an expert on drug use, I felt confident Joel was high. And if Joel was using drugs again, he could get dangerous and reckless. God, I hoped I was wrong; I'd have a much larger problem on my hands if I wasn't. Because if Joel became reckless, it wouldn't just ruin my operation; it could ruin my life.

"You're right, I'll find a way. I'm sorry, Joel, I wasn't trying to trap you into anything. I was missing our talks, is all, and I thought you could help." I hoped this would mollify his temper.

He kept patting at his pockets, then finally groaned. "Fuck, that's right. I left the keys in the car."

I stood still.

"You can go out the side door. It's closer to your car," I said timidly. I followed him back to the door, keeping a distance and looking around for things I could grab to protect myself if he did something unexpected.

He stopped with his hand on the doorknob and turned around. "I'm sorry. I didn't mean to get all worked up," he said as he swiped at his nose and sniffed again.

"It's okay, Joel," I smiled, though my pulse raced with fear.

"It's just…" he stopped. "It's just, I don't need another problem when dealing with these guys, okay?"

I nodded.

"Just do your job. Get it done, and there will be no problems."

I stood silent. Was that a threat?

"I gotta go," he said. I followed him out, then closed the door firmly behind him. I wondered what kind of problems there would be if I didn't "get it done." I didn't want to think about it. On top of my storage and cash management problems, I could add that Joel might be doing drugs to the pile.

I just had to do my job, and do my job well.

Chapter Thirty-Four

Marco and I were at Nathan's basketball game, with Lily on my lap and Lucas nestled between us, when Eloise called.

"Hey!" I said cheerily. I thought she was calling to find out where the game was; she usually tried to swing by after work.

"Hey! I was looking for the key to your office. Did you move it?"

My stomach dropped. My storage problem just climbed to a new height: There were nearly 70 bags stuffed in the office.

"Uh, I may have, uh, I think I have it with me," I stuttered. "I must have forgotten to put it back. I was in a hurry to get Nathan to his game." *Lie.* I hadn't kept the key under the succulent plant for months. "What are you looking for?"

"Eh," she grunted. "I needed to pull an old invoice from the filing cabinet. The flour guy is giving me shit about prices again, and I want to pull the last invoice to double check that he hasn't been sneaking in any extra charges."

"Sorry about that, El. I can come back after the game and pull it for you?" I was hoping she would say no. I didn't want to drag the family there, then make an excuse for why I needed to go into the shop alone.

"Nah, that's okay. I'll just get it in the morning."

I quietly sighed in relief. "Okay. You coming to the game?"

"I can't. We have a ton of orders and Jen is waiting for me to do some painting thing tonight. Some bullshit where you take wine and paint a Picasso or something."

I laughed. "Those are fun. They're very popular right now. Have fun, love you."

"Love you, too. Give the kids a kiss from me."

"Will do, 'bye."

I casually wiped the sweat from my hands onto my pants as I hung up. That was too close. I really needed to figure out a better place to store the bags.

"Everything okay?" Marco asked.

"Eloise was just looking for an invoice, but I forgot to leave the key to the office, so she can't get in."

"Do we need to swing by after the game?"

God no!

"No, she's fine. She'll get it in the morning."

"She's still there then? I'm glad business is going so well. It's been nice to see some extra money come in, I have to say!" he gleamed. "Maybe we can get down the Shore this summer. Or Vermont?"

"Definitely," I enthused. "The Shore sounds nice!" We hadn't taken a family vacation in more than a year. I started thinking about how nice of a Shore house we could rent now. Hell, I could *buy* a Shore house. I was getting excited thinking about our vacation, but then another realization hit me: How could I leave my operation for a week? Who would run it for me? Maybe I could set it up so I wouldn't have to be there. No, I could likely get away with that for a day or two, but not a week. I grimaced, then refocused to my much larger problem: Storage.

I needed a place to put all the bags. I also needed a place to put all the money. Aside from using a little here and there, it couldn't sit in the corner of my office in Tupperware bins forever. The recognition that millions of dollars would continue to pile with no real plan itched at me daily, especially when Marco worried about his quarterly sales numbers. I bit my lip and swallowed the taste of blood whenever I wanted to tell Marco, "It's okay, honey. I'll just go grab a stack of cash from the Tupperware bin."

What itched at me more was that I was keeping all this from Marco. What started as "just a few months to get out of debt" had turned into more than seven months, 100 women, and millions of dollars.

Millions of dollars, all dressed up with nowhere to go.

The answer to one of my problems came the following morning.

After spending part of the morning volunteering at the school for the book fair, I saw Dale cleaning out the garage behind the shop as I pulled up. In Doylestown Borough, shops were often connected in the front from side to side, but also connected in the back by an alley, garage, or parking space shared with a store whose face was on the parallel street. This was reminiscent of old commerce towns of the 1800s, where stores were clustered, and space was shared for convenience: Horses could only go so far.

Biscotti shared the space behind the store with the toy store that faced Oakland Street. The space had four small parking spots and two garages that belonged to Dale. Dale owned both buildings; in fact, he owned eight buildings in Doylestown. He was retired now, but he spent his earlier years making smart real estate investments using some of his grandfather's old textile money.

"Good morning, Dale," I said, although it was almost noon.

"Good morning, Anna. It's good to see your pretty face around here. You're easier to look at than Marco, I must say," he said, scanning me up and down with his cataract eyes. Sexist remarks were still okay in Dale's book.

"I would hope so," I laughed. "What are you doing in there?" I nodded toward the garage.

"Cleaning it out. Don't really need it anymore. I was thinking about renting it out."

The only thing that could have addressed my storage dilemma easier would have been if a storage unit fell from the sky and landed in my lap; even then, there would be problems of where to put it.

"How much are you looking to rent it out for?" I asked. "I could always use some extra storage for supplies and whatnot."

"You outgrowing your space already, huh?" He asked in the same tone an adult would ask a child if they were ready to wear big-kid underwear.

"No, the space is great. But you know how it is, things pile up."

"I'm thinking $500 a month, but I can give it to you for less than that. How about $350?"

I would have paid $3,000 for it. "That sounds great, Dale. I'll take it. When will it be ready to use?"

He looked behind him. "Probably day after tomorrow?"

"Perfect."

Two days later, Dale dropped off the key to the garage.

I treated him to a coffee and biscotti, as well as an envelope with a year's worth of garage rental in hundred-dollar bills.

"Whew-y!" he said, as he opened the envelope and thumbed through the bills. "Guess I shouldn't ask where all this cash came from," he winked.

I assumed he was alluding to a common practice that small, cash businesses were known for, in which they avoid ringing up a portion of sales and pocket the cash to avoid taxes. I was doing the opposite: I was trying to find ways to add to my sales, despite the fact that the IRS would get a slice of it.

"It just seemed easier this way, I guess," I smiled.

"You know what this envelope reminds me of?" His wrinkled face leaned in and I could smell his milky breath. "Reminds me of being at my granddad's shop as a boy. He'd take a bill out of a big envelope like this and give it to me and say, 'Now, you save that and invest it wisely, and one day when you're richer than me, you can give me a little bit of the interest you've earned on it.'"

He crunched down on his biscotti. I flinched a little, hoping that his teeth wouldn't break.

"And did you do that for him? Share your interest?" I asked.

He bellowed; a liquid cough followed. "No, I didn't need to. Granddad died a very rich man, far richer than I will die, I'm sorry to say. He left everything to his fourth wife, Regina," he said, shaking his head.

"Yikes. I'm surprised. Often times generational wealth is passed down to grandchildren, but not your luck, huh?"

"Well, he left me and my sister a little bit. I mean, to most it would be a fortune, but—and I'm not saying this to brag—I knew how much money he had, is the thing. I would go into his business and he would have drawers full of cash.

"True story: I remember one time, I was just finishing law school and my granddad showed up at my dorm on a Friday afternoon in his convertible and asked if I wanted to take a ride. Of course, I did, and we drove to the Doylestown airport. He had bought a plane, you see."

I raised my eyebrows. "Wow."

"Yeah. Now, you remember, this was in the '60s. Private jets weren't really a thing yet; he was one of the first people to get the Lear jet. We flew down to St. Kitts. I kept asking, 'Does Ma know I'm flying on an airplane with you?' But he reminded me, 'You're a man now, Dale, Ma's don't need to know everything about a man.'"

I smiled.

"So, we flew down to St. Kitts. I figured we were going to spend a couple days in the sun. But soon as we landed, he told me to help him with some luggage. He and I carried four duffel bags each to a car waiting for us. The car took us to a bank, where I helped him in with the bags again. I was asked to wait outside. It took about an hour, then he came out smiling and said, 'Ready to go?' I was happy to move on to the part of the trip that involved beaches and cocktails. But we just drove back to the plane and flew home. We never talked about it again."

I looked at him quizzically.

He chortled. "Geez, I don't know why I'm telling you this. I kept that trip a secret my whole life. Guess as you get old, you just don't care to keep secrets anymore."

"Are you going to tell me what you went to St. Kitts for? I'm dying to know," I said earnestly.

"Cash. We were there to deposit bags full of cash. See, offshore accounts don't have taxes on interest, and they keep your business private from anyone and everyone. They don't care where the money comes from."

"That's right," I nodded in comprehension.

"Yeah, after he died, I was waiting for his attorney to tell me he had left an offshore account in my name, but he didn't. Guess he only needed me to carry his baggage for him. He wasn't that nice of a man, I came to realize. Only cared about money and women."

"Well, at least you got to ride on one of the first private jets," I said.

"Yes, and I learned how easy it was to offshore cash," he laughed as he clenched his envelope. "You'd need a little more than this for that, though," he joked.

"Oh yes, I'd imagine you'd need a lot more than that." I agreed.

A lot more is what I had.

Chapter Thirty-Five

With my Mothers maxed out of their network of 10 Moms each (and begging for more, which I vehemently declined), I was bringing in well over $100,000 per week. I had so much cash, I almost didn't see it as money anymore. It was like going to the beach for the first time, the sensation of the sand squishing between your toes and sticking to your wet skin: You can't imagine ever tiring of the wonder of it, but not long after, you don't even notice the sand, and later, you may even resent it.

Handling abundant cash weekly naturally brought me back to the problem of where to put it all. I was pleased to learn that most of my Mothers had thought of responsible and creative ways to use and store their cash.

But they made far less than I did. I had moved my Tupperware bins to the garage alongside the bags, figuring the best hiding spot was in plain sight. But this wasn't a long-term solution. I might have to find a way down to St. Kitts.

At the moment, though, I had an even bigger problem to manage:

For the first time, one of my Moms didn't show up for her drop today, and Joel was not going to be happy about it.

Joel pulled up and got out of his car, closing the door heavily. He wore jeans, T-shirt, and his leather jacket, even though it was nearly 90°F. Joel didn't dress up for Doylestown today.

"Did you hear?" he asked with his hands on his hips, feet shuffling. Joel looked around before leaning in, "Mussert didn't show up." *MUSSERT* was the code name for one of the Lancaster drops. His eyes were steely blue, and I could see the vein in his shaved head pulsing.

"Yes," I said. "I know. Let's finish putting the bags in the garage and we can go inside and talk about it."

I already knew from Shelly, my Lancaster Mother, that one of her Moms hadn't made it to the drop. I grimaced; Shelly was my most streetwise Mother. She built her network quicker than any of the other Mothers, and had each Mom running one bag per day, the most bags of any of the networks. She liked the taste of money the same way a shark liked the taste of blood, so I knew she was just as distraught about the missed drop as I was. Although, she didn't have to deal with Joel.

He snorted, then threw his hands up in a "might as well" fashion. We unloaded quickly, then I locked the garage and led him inside through the side door.

"Someone got sick, according to my Lancaster contact." I reached for the French press.

His nose flared. "Got sick? My people don't give a flying fuck if your contacts got sick or got hit by a car. They're expected to show up, dead or alive."

"Trust me, my contact is well aware of her responsibilities. It won't

happen again. I'll figure out a backup plan to avoid it in the future."
I defended.

"Do you know what happens to me if things go wrong? If drops
get missed? The people I deal with, they're not nice people, Anna. I
know you live up here in la-la-land, but where I come from, I don't
just lose my paycheck, I could lose my fucking fingers. Or worse."

There was a knot in my stomach. Sometimes I forgot—or maybe
I just chose not to think about— who was on the other end of these
bags. There was a whole world of people who didn't do this for a couple
months to make extra money. This was their life, and they took it
seriously. Dead seriously.

"I'm sorry, Joel," I said resignedly.

He inhaled sharply. "Just make sure they get it there tomorrow.
They'll have to take two bags."

I looked surprised. "You always said one bag per person, or it
gets suspicious."

His nose flared again. "Well, we have to change the fucking rules
a little!" he said forcefully, his eyes still dilated. The tone of Joel's voice
made the hairs on my arm stand up; like having a sweet dog your
whole life who one day bites your hand.

"I'll make tomorrow happen, two bags, even if I have to do it
myself," I said timorously.

As if he became aware of his temper, he moderated it with a loud
exhale, then more gently, "Thank you."

I stared at him blankly; I had never seen this side of Joel, and for
the first time, I felt genuine fear. The last time he raised his tone, I felt
cautious of him, but not fearful. I was certain now that he was using

drugs again, which meant I couldn't trust him. And if I couldn't trust him, I had a problem. I had a lot of problems.

"I gotta go," he said, swiping at his nose furiously.

"You don't want any coffee?"

"Nah, I got shit to do."

I nodded and placed a "Be Right Back!" plaque on the counter. "I'll follow you out. Use the side door."

He pushed away from the counter and hastily walked toward the door. He swung the door open to leave and nearly collided with Eloise, who was coming in at the same time.

"Oh shit, sorry!" Eloise said breathlessly.

"Uh, yeh, it's okay," Joel said nervously with his eyes down. "See ya," he nodded to me.

"See ya," Eloise said skeptically as he swiftly left toward his car.

Eloise turned to me. "Who was that?"

I froze. I was not prepared for her question, and my heart was already pumping more blood than my body could handle.

"An old acquaintance," I said.

"That guy is an old acquaintance? From where?" she asked incredulously.

"I used to know him in Philly. We worked at Kahn & Hague together," I lied.

"Why was he using the side door? And was that his car out back?"

Shit, shit, shit, *think*.

"Yeah, I ran into him a while ago. He moved to Doylestown. He comes in once in a while." My sentences were staccato-like. "He couldn't find parking today, so he parked out back. He asked me if it was okay. I told him not usually, but I'll let it slide this time," I laughed nervously.

Eloise nodded slowly.

"I let him leave through the side door since he had already broken every other rule," I chuckled.

Eloise barely smiled. "He looked familiar. Do I know him?"

My mouth was dry.

"I don't think so," I said. "He worked down in the mail room at Kahn & Hague. I don't know if Benoit knew him."

Lie, lie, lie.

She looked at me thoughtfully with her hand on her waist.

"What are you doing here, anyway?" I asked. Eloise never came in between shifts.

She moved her weight from one foot to another. "I forgot my phone. I didn't realize it until I reached for it to set a wakeup alarm from a nap. There went my nap."

"Join me for a cup of coffee, then?"

She stared for half a second longer than normal. "Wish I could, but I have to run a couple errands before coming back."

"Rain check, then," I said.

"Sure, yeah, rain check."

We stood in awkward silence for a second.

"I'm gonna grab my phone. I'll see you later." Eloise headed toward the dough table.

"Yep, see you later, El."

I could tell Eloise didn't believe my explanation, and it was the first time in our relationship that I had lied to her. We had experienced many things together over the years: Death, birth, marriage, family, business. But I had never lied to her. And lying to Eloise didn't feel good; it felt as heavy as the bags were getting.

Chapter Thirty-Six

As summer continued to heat up, dousing the days with an uncomfortable film, so too, did I have a fever I couldn't shake. Though we had only the one missed drop, Joel's demeanor persisted as grungy and stand-offish. We hadn't had any more heated conversations, but I remained leery that Joel may be back to being an addict, and I knew I'd have to address that sooner than later. Eloise and I had moved to a state of pleasantries, avoiding real conversation. I could tell she felt some way about me, but she didn't say it. Marco and I never did take the kids to the Shore. His sales pipeline finally started pouring in deals, and he was busier than ever, sometimes not home until late into the night. He would creep into bed and cradle me from behind. "Sorry I'm late, honey. I love you."

I'd mumble a sweet reply and we'd go to sleep, connected, but not connected.

Money piled in faster than I could keep track of it. I got into the habit of lazily throwing it into one of the bins, envelope and all. Far gone were the days that I used to count and stack it neatly.

I droned on throughout my days, shuffling bags and piling money that I couldn't spend; transporting the kids to the pool, making dinner, and dropping into bed exhausted—only to do it again in the morning. Such was the typical hum-drum of two, busy working parents, I supposed (minus the piling stacks of cash). But w*hat was it all for?* Though the bins were full, I felt empty. Guilt had become something that felt normal to wear; like one gets used to wearing braces or a cast.

This would be the cloud that hung over me as summer turned to fall, and I wondered just how better off I really was.

The bartender presented our order of oysters, six raw and six baked.

Marco and I clinked our first two oysters together and exclaimed "Cheers!" before shooting them back with a smooth gulp.

"You okay tonight, hon? You seem distracted." Marco prepared his next oyster.

"I'm fine," I said cheerily. "Just busy. You know how it is when the weather turns colder; people swarm in for coffee and warm drinks. Just a lot to manage, is all."

So far, I hadn't actually lied to Marco about anything. My answers were truthful, if not the whole truth. But I hadn't lied to him. This was imperative to me.

"Anything I can do to help?" he asked sincerely.

"It's nothing that won't pass," I said unconvincingly.

"I'm sorry I haven't been around as much lately. I feel like I've left you on your own, at home, and with the kids. I never thought I'd be a weekend dad," he said sadly.

"You're not a weekend dad. You're still home early enough to read them a book sometimes and take them to football."

It was football season again; where had the time had gone?

I smiled tenderly. "You're still happy at work?"

"Yeah, it's fine. Hey, we should go away," he said. "When was the last time you and I got away for a weekend?"

"It has been a while," I replied.

"When I get my commission check, we're going away. You and me. Pick a place, but don't go crazy," he laughed. "Maybe a couple of nights in Bedford Springs?"

Or a couple of nights in St. Kitts, I thought. If only I could tell him that there were millions of dollars stacked in the garage behind Biscotti that would allow us to take a private jet to a secluded island where a mansion filled with butlers and masseuses and champagne would await us. There was a little pang in my chest that we had gotten to a place of keeping secrets from each other; or rather, I, keeping secrets from him.

"I would love that! Bedford Springs is so beautiful in the fall," I smiled.

"Let's make it happen then. We have not taken much time lately to focus on us."

"I know. We have been busier than usual."

We used to have this perfect predictability to our conversations. Lately, it felt more laborious to keep the exchange lively. It felt more like we were catching up on what's been happening in his world and my world, which were worlds apart.

"I've missed you," Marco said.

I looked up, concerned. "What do you mean? I've been right here."

"Yeah, I know," he said.

The pang in my chest intensified. "Marco, did I do something wrong? I thought we were good. Are you unhappy?"

"No, no, I'm not unhappy." He grabbed my hand and squeezed it. "I just... sometimes I just miss the way things used to be. Before both of us were working so much. I know that's wrong of me to say because I screwed up Biscotti. I got us into the position that made you go back to work, and I know that. But I miss how we used to be. You know, we used to have this rhythm that just stayed steady. Now it seems," he shrugged. "Uneven."

"Uneven? How?" I asked. I knew why it felt uneven to me, but I was curious how it felt uneven to him.

"I guess, you're just not as, I don't know, available?"

I looked at him intensely. "Available? Available for what?"

He could sense my defensiveness and tried to backtrack. "I was so used to you being around and, I don't know..."

"Just home?" I asked scornfully.

He exhaled. "No. Listen, I didn't mean it like that. I miss you, is all. I feel a little disconnected, is all I was saying."

Of course, we were not as connected as usual. I had felt it too, but I couldn't believe Marco was suggesting that maybe it was because *I* was working so much. I had been running around like a lunatic, doing illegal things, trying to keep our lives together.

I was the one who gave up my career five years ago to raise the kids and gladly used our savings to fulfill his dream of having a biscotti shop.

I was the one who didn't complain when my days turned from

upscale banking lunches to wiping snotty noses while he shot the shit with Eloise and perfected biscotti and latte recipes.

I was the one who swooped in like Superwoman to save our business because he had run it to near-dissolution. And I did it while still coordinating childcare, rides for the kids to activities, school functions, and stocking the house with milk and toilet paper.

And I was the one who entered the dirty world of drugs to dig Biscotti out of a well of debt and to pay for football equipment, vet bills, and new water heaters.

And I never complained.

Yet here Marco sat complaining that our rhythm was off.

I took a full breath as my eyes filled with tears. "Do you have any idea what I do on a daily basis? The number of things I have to manage? Do you have any idea?"

I swiped at a tear as it started to fall.

Marco sat up alarmed. "Of course I do, babe. I'm sorry, I wasn't complaining about you. You're amazing. I'm sorry. I know I'm just as responsible."

"Do you? Just as responsible for what? You ask if you can help with things around the house, but do you even know what that means? Do you know who the kids' dentist is and when their next checkup is scheduled? When the kids wake up with a fever, do you automatically assume you're the one who will skip work that day and start planning for coverage? Do you keep track of the emails we get from the schools about upcoming events? You don't. You assume I will; otherwise, you would have known that Lily's preschool bake sale is tomorrow. Are you going to stay home from work for that?"

"I would if you had asked. I could have put in for time off, if I had notice," he said.

"Right, if you had notice. Should I submit an official request for your time off? Complete with dates and instructions? It's more work for me to ask you to do it than it is for me just to do it myself."

"It's my fault that you don't ask?"

"I shouldn't even have to ask, is my point!" My tears retracted to form an angry gloss over my eyes. "Nobody has to ask me to work full-time, plus pack lunches, do laundry, run to schools, and coordinate dinner! I don't have some magic life coordinator telling me what to do next! God, it's so fucked up the way it is for mothers. We have to do everything, the obvious jobs and all the invisible ones that add up to *two* full-time jobs. And we have to take care of our husbands and their needs too. Like when they don't feel connected."

He sighed. "That's not fair, Anna. I am sorry you feel so over-whelmed, but you are taking this in a really bad direction. I don't even want to talk about this anymore."

"You don't want to talk about this anymore? Why? Because I didn't say, 'I'm sorry, Marco, that you feel so uneven, so disconnected: Let me fix that, too?'"

He stared at me, then gathered his napkin and threw it on the bar. "What the fuck does that mean? Fix it, too? Do you feel like you're the only one trying here?

"I'm busting my ass to get back into a career I swore off five years ago," his voice a decibel louder. "And I gotta be honest, it sucks most days. I feel like a failure for what happened with Biscotti, and I force a smile on my face as I watch you run it better than I ever could. I wake up every morning trying to figure out how to get my dignity back,

Anna; and I'm sorry that I miss bake sales and dentist appointments in the meantime, but I'm trying. And I'm trying to be a good husband and a good dad, and apparently, I'm failing at that, too."

My anger turned to resentment; resentment for myself. I knew most of my reaction was misplaced anger. As exhilarating as my operation was at one point, it mostly was now a burden I didn't know how to lift.

"I'm sorry," I said tearfully. "I'm sorry."

I turned my face from the bar to hide the tears coming down my cheeks.

Marco exhaled loudly, then rubbed my leg. "It's okay. I'm sorry, too. Hey, don't cry, babe. I'll do better."

"You don't have to do better. You're already perfect. It's me. I need to...I need to re-prioritize."

"I think maybe we both do." He lifted my chin and gazed sweetly at my tear-streaked face. "When Biscotti started going downhill, I should have come to you. We could have solved it together. Instead, I hid it from you, and I ran to fix things in another direction, leaving you with my mess. I'm sorry. I'm sorry I did that to you."

"No, don't be sorry. I'm sorry. You didn't do anything wrong," I sniffled.

"No, I did. I broke our rule: Us First, right? We have never failed when we've done things as a team, and I went solo. I shouldn't have gone solo."

My heart ached with guilt. It was I who had gone solo. I had gone so low. Too low. I needed to bring myself back up to the surface of the water to breathe again.

"Us First," I smiled lamentably.

Marco kissed my cheek. "Us First."

Chapter Thirty-Seven

I woke up the next morning with a hangover of guilt.

My eyes didn't flutter open like a butterfly's wings flapping softly while sucking nectar of a flower. Rather, they sprung open like a swinging saloon door, forcing my eyes to stare intently at the ceiling while Marco slept next to me.

Last night's conversation weighed heavily on my conscience and reminded me of how drastically our lives had changed in the past year. It was easy to say the changes weren't drastic; people started new jobs all the time. But the result of the changes, nonetheless, had been significant. For the first time in our marriage, Marco and I were off balance. And the worst part was that he thought it was his fault.

The guilt tightened around my chest like a boa constrictor squeezing its prey every time I thought of him blaming himself for my distracted behavior. In reality, it was my reckless secret life that was pulling my energy from the people and things that mattered most.

The morning lulled on while the question circulated in my head, reverberated down my body, and ended back where it started: *Where do I go from here?*

I started this operation with a four-month expiry but had quickly found myself running an operation with no real end. I had negotiated terms and pricing. I had created rules, routes, and fail-safes. I had coordinated a network of 110 women who had collectively made millions of dollars, and I had created an operation that was more efficient than any business I had ever been part of before.

What I hadn't done, what every sound business plan has, was develop an exit plan. And there was the not-so-small detail about my business that didn't apply to most businesses: The viability of a reasonable exit.

By the time I saw Joel's car park in front of the garage, I still hadn't come to a resolution about what to do next to get back to a life of normalcy.

Joel barely grunted a hello as he opened the trunk of his car, holding onto the oversized spoiler as it sprung up. He usually waited for me to open the garage, then backed in a little to transfer the bags, but he seemed in an agitated rush today. He was wearing a different leather jacket, the one from the day he shoveled the snow outside my apartment after my first date with Benoit. Joel placed two bags on the ground next to my feet while he reached for two others.

I picked up the bags. "Whoa, hold up."

He stopped with two bags in his hands.

"What's with the bags?" I lifted the bags, gauging their weight. "They're heavier."

He shrugged and put two more bags by my feet, then turned to fetch two more.

"Joel," I said forcefully. "Hold up."

He stopped and sighed exasperatingly.

I lifted the bags up and down slowly. "Why are the bags heavier?"

I looked around to make sure no one was watching. An occasional smoker sometimes loitered in the back of the shops on a smoke break. Now, though, we were alone.

Joel lifted both bags slightly. "So what? I don't know."

"You don't know?" I asked incredulously. "Joel, I've been lifting these bags nearly every day for the past year and I know what they feel like. And these bags, these bags are heavier."

"I told you, I don't know."

I glared at him, my heavy breath creating swirly clouds in the thick, cold air as I spoke. "I think you do know," I said calmly. "And you can either tell me, or I can open the bags to find out myself."

Please don't make me open the bags.

He shuffled his feet, then kicked a rock, which went skipping along the pavement before thunking into a wall. He dropped the bags onto the ground next to him and gestured his hands pleadingly. "Look, can we just do our fucking job, Anna?" he asked agitated. "I don't have time for this. Do you want the bags, or not?"

Do I want the bags? As if I had a choice, I thought. Or do I?

"I want the truth first, Joel. The bags are heavier, and I want to know why."

"Maybe there's more in them, I don't know." He confirmed my suspicion.

"More formula?" I asked. "How much more?"

By the weight of it, I guessed double.

"There might be an extra can in there. So what?"

I sighed loudly at the thought of an extra kilo of cocaine in each diaper bag. Not that it changed the bag dramatically, but it meant that Joel was getting reckless.

"*So what?*" My mouth gaped open and my brow furled. "Why didn't you ask me beforehand? You can't make changes without talking to me first." I shook my head, then said in an obstinate tone. "Frankly, I don't know if I'm comfortable with having an extra can in each bag."

"You don't know if you're *comfortable* with it?" Joel sneered. "Jesus, look who acts like a princess these days."

"I'm not being a princess, Joel," I said incredulously.

"What difference does it make? The bag's the bag," Joel said with a slightly higher tenor to his voice.

"It makes a big difference," I said. "What we do requires a certain amount of trust. How can I trust you when you're sneaking in extra cans and hoping I won't notice?"

"It shouldn't matter, Anna. A bag's a bag."

"No, it's not. It's not to me. Extra cans mean extra risk."

Joel rolled his eyes and ran his hand over his marred head.

"And extra risk means extra pay," I said boldly. I didn't plan to say that, but his attempt to trick me annoyed the shit out of me, and I wanted to make him pay for it, literally.

His eyes shot wide open. "Fuck that!"

I jumped imperceptibly at his sudden outburst.

"You're out of your mind, Anna!" he snorted. "Extra pay," he laughed mockingly.

"What's so fucking funny, Joel?"

He lunged toward me and stuck his finger in my face. "What's so fucking funny, Anna, is that you think you can start getting greedy on me." Joel's spit showered my face and I took a sharp breath in as he continued to shout. "You think you call the shots? Huh, Anna?" He slammed the palm of his hand against the garage door, making a thunderous boom that caused me to jump.

"You think you're the one running this whole thing? Well, you're not! I fucking am! I'm running this operation. Without me, you have nothing! You are nothing!" He stepped back and laughed sickeningly. He picked up the two bags by his feet. "Are you going to open the fucking garage or not?"

"I will not." I held an unyielding gaze. My body language displayed that I was ready for the fight, but inside I was choking with fear.

He laughed dubiously. "No? You're not going to open the garage? Then I'll just leave the bags here outside the garage and let you take them all in yourself."

"I wouldn't do that," I said.

"No? And why not, Anna? What are you going to do?"

"Nothing. That's what I'll do. I'll do nothing with the bags and when your contacts find out none of their deliveries were made, you'll be the one making up reasons why the bags are sitting outside a garage with nowhere to go and no one to take them. I, on the other hand, will be sipping my latte, staring at the bags from inside."

He narrowed his eyes. "Fuck you. You wouldn't do that."

"Mmm, you sure about that?"

He exhaled incredulously. "I knew I shouldn't have trusted you for this long. You got too baked."

"Too baked?" I asked.

"Yeh. It's when people forget their place and they start getting greedy. It's not a good place to be, I can tell you that," he sneered with a noxious look. "The temperature can get too hot for people who get baked. Just ask…" he snickered. "Never mind."

Something told me that he meant that as a threat.

"Just ask who, Joel?" I asked in an irritated voice.

He stared in the distance, then pierced his dilated gaze straight through me. "No one. No one you can ask anymore, at least."

Benoit. A shiver sped up my spine and slapped the back of my neck like a stick hitting me. He did mean it as a threat. I wanted to ask more, but I didn't want to give into his game. He clearly was trying to scare me, and I couldn't let him think he had succeeded.

I rolled my eyes. "No, Joel, I'm not baked. I'm exactly who you started doing business with. You, on the other hand, are not. You've become erratic, showing up and taking off with this irritated, agitated sort of quickness, and now you're adding more formula than we agreed on. You're the one who has changed. You're the one who seems baked."

He shook his head, then said a softer tone. "Open the fucking garage, Anna. I don't have all day."

I knew then that I had struck a chord. He had to get these deliveries made or, like he said before, he could lose a couple of fingers, or worse. He needed me more than I needed him.

"Double pay," I steeled.

He stared at the wall of the adjacent building, then with an irritated reluctance: "Fine. Just open the garage."

I nodded and unlocked the garage, lifting the metal door with a loud swoosh.

We loaded the bags into the garage with silent efficiency. I had to hurry; we had taken twice as long as usual and there might be a customer waiting inside for me.

We finished and I locked up.

"See you tomorrow, then," I said cautiously.

He grunted. "Yeh, see you tomorrow."

Joel turned around to walk to his car, pausing to light a cigarette, and that's when I saw it. On the back of his leather jacket, toward the bottom, was a leather strap that buttoned onto the bodice. There was a space for two buttons, but one was missing.

The remaining button was silver with a panther head embossed on it.

Chapter Thirty-Eight

M y mind flicked back to six years earlier when I sat in a cold white room, wrapped in a cardigan, hours after Benoit was found dead in his hotel room while Officer Long held up a plastic bag with a silver button inside whose face bore the insignia of a panther's head.

"Do you recognize this button?" Officer Long had asked me.

I had shaken my head.

I hadn't recognized that button. But today, I saw its twin; I was sure of it.

I slowly made my way back into the shop where I leaned on the mixer with both hands, steadying my queasy body.

My mind wanted to play tricks on me. Perhaps it was coincidence that Joel had a jacket with the same button as Officer Long had showed me, I tried to convince myself. It was a long time ago, and my memory might be fuzzy, my mind also said. But a jacket with a missing button? A missing button with a panther head on it? I exhaled a disbelieving sigh. I was as convinced as a mother whose child was taken at birth:

It was the same button, and somehow that button was involved in Benoit's death.

The question was: *How?*

As I contemplated that, other pieces of the interview with Officers Long and Harley flitted behind my eyelids and echoed in my ears.

"Do you know of any friends or contacts of Mr. Massenet's that would have been known simply as, 'B.P.'?" Officer Long had asked.

B.P. I rolled the initials around in my mind as my eyes blindly searched the room for a correlation of B.P. and Joel. Obviously, not his initials. I hadn't heard of him having a nickname. *B.P.*...I came up empty. Maybe the button and the initials were not related.

The button. Where had the officers found the button? I had assumed it was somewhere in Benoit's hotel room; that they had found it when investigating the scene. So how did Joel's leather jacket button show up in Benoit's hotel room? I never had known Joel to come to the hotel. That's not to say he didn't go when I wasn't there, but with the amount of time I spent at Benoit's place before his death, I would have bumped into him at least once.

I put my shaky hand on my head, which pulsed loudly in my ears. I felt bile lift out of my stomach toward my throat and I ran to the bathroom to vomit. I vomited angrily at first, emptying the feelings of rage that had set in at the newfound realization that Benoit's death was not an accident. It was not Sudden Cardiac death. I had felt that all along. Now, I knew it after seeing Joel's button.

I vomited again, this time out of fear. I was doing business with a murderer, and not just a murderer, but the person who killed the man I once loved and the father of my son.

Finally, the vomiting relented. I sat on the floor and sobbed, the porcelain of the toilet bowl cold on my back as I leaned against it. I sobbed for the loss of Benoit, not an achy-heart sob, but an ache for all the secrets that came to light so many years after I had made peace with his death. I sobbed for the reality of what I had gotten into. And I sobbed for the reality of what it might take to get out of it.

"Aaagh!" I moaned softly, but aggressively. What would I do with Joel, now that I knew he was involved in Benoit's death? If he hurt Benoit, he could hurt me too. Exiting was going to be harder than I thought.

"B-ding!" The door to the shop chimed open.

I jolted alert just as the bathroom door swung open and Eloise stood in front of me. "I got it." She stared at me with a mixture of disgust and apathy.

Chapter Thirty-Nine

Ten minutes after Eloise walked thickly toward the front of the store, mumbled a pleasantry, and made an espresso for a customer, she was back in front of me with both hands on her hips.

"I didn't know you knew how to make espresso," I said quietly. By then I had peeled myself from the bathroom floor and sat on a stool near the dough table. Eloise took the stool on the other side.

"Spill it, Anna." Her voice was calm, but authoritative; the way a shop owner tells a kid to release the stolen candy bar from his hand.

I inhaled sharply and my lip began to quiver. "Why are you here, Eloise?"

"What do you mean 'Why am I here?' I'm here to check on you, Anna."

"Check on me? Why?"

"Because you need checking on, that's why. I know you probably haven't noticed, but you've been acting different lately. You've been acting different for a while, to be honest. At first, it was a good different, like someone who's on supercharge. I thought it was the shop that was giving you a boost of energy or confidence. But then, it changed into a more quiet and calculated type of energy; like you had a million to-dos in your head at all times."

"You watched me?" I asked incredulously.

"Yeah, I watched you, and I'm not ashamed to say it," she said defensively. "I initially thought maybe you were running around on Marco. I figured I'd catch you at some point with another guy, maybe sneaking off in the afternoons when no one was around, and I was going to catch you both and squeeze his balls until they popped like water balloons. Then I was going to drag your sorry ass somewhere and remind you how Marco is the best damn human being in the world and you must stop this shit before you ruin your marriage and your life."

I managed a slight chuckle at the image, which was entirely believable.

"The weird thing is that I did catch you with another guy." She had a sour look on her face. "That afternoon when I ran into your 'old friend?' It only took me a millisecond to realize you weren't involved with *him*. In that way, at least." She said *him* with vehemence.

I shuddered and let out a disgusted groan.

"But the interaction left me feeling creepy, and I knew he wasn't an old friend dropping in to say, 'Hi.' So, I watched you for a while, especially in the mornings when you'd creep off for a minute, and instead of catching you with another man, I caught you with a bunch of women, hanging by that garage out back. Open, shut, open, shut. Bags in, bags out."

My mouth dropped open and my heart sank through the bottom of my torso. I thought I might vomit again. Eloise had been watching me for how long? I thought I was invincible. I thought I had covered all my bases. Yet, I was caught like a snowshoe hare face-to-face with a hungry lynx.

"I couldn't figure out what was going on back there, you ladies always were so quick," she said. "I've wanted to talk to you for a while, but I didn't know how to approach you about it. So, I decided that today I would stop in during the afternoon lull and have a coffee with you. Then I find you on the bathroom floor crying? It's time for you to talk, Anna. And let's start with what's in the garage."

I rubbed above my brow as I tried to think of what to tell Eloise. How to tell Eloise. She wasn't going to take any bullshit answers, and truthfully, I was running out of the will to give her any.

"You want to know what's in the garage?" I asked meekly.

"Anna, you know I don't have patience for dumb," she said.

"No, I wasn't playing dumb, Eloise," I said with a languid snort of laughter. "I'm just saying the words out loud. The garage. The guy. Joel, is his name. The women. Over 100 women, if you want the truth. The bags. The bags, Eloise," I scoffed in disgusted bemusement. "The bags are full of cocaine."

There, I said it.

Eloise gaped, and she pushed back from the table and stood up. "*What?*"

I nodded my head slowly and said in a tired voice, "Yes, El. The bags are full of cocaine. Two kilos each," I said with a shameful pride.

She stood with her hands on her hips. I could see contemplation spinning behind her eyes. Then she rubbed her lower lip, dragged her palm against the back of her neck, and sat back down.

"So, now what?" she asked.

I looked up at her. "What do you mean?"

"Well, you've obviously gotten yourself into trouble, Anna. Drugs? Really? Never in a million years did I see that coming."

I nodded slowly. "Neither did I."

"So, how did you…how did you get started in all this? Who's the guy then, Joel? Is he your dealer? Who are the women? God, I have so many questions."

I told her about Joel and how I'd met him when I was with Benoit; how Joel was his friend who "helped him with things." How I ran into Joel at the restaurant equipment store and his timing was just perfect enough to have me agree to hold a bag. I told her how at first, I didn't know the bags had drugs in them, but once I became aware, I made a choice. A choice to continue for the money because we needed it. I told her how I had planned to hold bags for just a few months, but then I met other women, mostly moms, who desperately needed extra money; and somehow it had turned into a large and still-growing operation.

I told her about Lynn, who was not only able to put in a chairlift for her disabled son, as she originally planned; but as one of my head Mothers, was able to make her house entirely handicap-accessible; let her husband work in the garden all day and see a better therapist about his PTSD. All this while Lynn cut down on her work hours to join art classes with her seriously neglected daughter, whom she has taken to Paris twice now to the Louvre and once to Amsterdam to see the Rembrandts at the Rijksmuseum.

I told her about Tara, who was able to pay off her credit card debt and afford a life coach and therapist who helped her address her insecurity issues that stemmed from her mother's constant reminders of her not being *enough;* not smart enough, not pretty enough, not worth enough. How Tara also had hired a personal chef to teach her the art of cooking (while her husband was at work) and how she had rekindled the fire in her marriage by cooking for her husband nearly every night, enjoying a bottle of wine together, and acting like the carefree Tara her husband fell in love with on their post-college European backpacking trip.

I told her about Meg, whose husband gambled their lives away and sat most nights at a bar, leaving with other women while Meg tucked in their three blonde-haired daughters. I explained how Meg felt helpless without a high school diploma—relying instead on a pretty face and a fake blonde ponytail—until she started making her own money. The money Meg made from the bags helped her become certified in Pilates and helped her open a studio where she filtered her bag money to buy a modest townhouse next to a playground for herself and her three daughters, minus the drunk, gambling husband.

I had stories for days, I told Eloise. I had convinced myself I was doing something good: I employed 110 women and changed their lives. That was the positive side of this operation that helped me forget the dark side. Of course, the dark side could put me and all these women in prison and leave them with nothing, which was worse than when I met them.

Eloise's eyebrows were in a fixed state of raised shock.

"But it has gone bad, El," I said.

"Shit, Anna, don't tell me they're on to you."

"What? Who? No, no one's onto me. At least I don't think so. I thought no one knew what I was doing, but then you showed up this afternoon and burst that bubble for me."

"So, the Government isn't watching you?"

"Not as far as I know."

"What's the problem then? I mean, aside from the obvious, that you're dealing drugs," she said sarcastically.

"I kinda hate when you put it like that," I said with humility.

"Distributing? Muling? What's the problem?"

I took a breath. "The guy, Joel, my contact…"

She nodded impatiently. "Did he hurt you?"

"No! I mean, he's never laid a hand on me. But I think he's doing drugs. He did them before knowing your brother. It was Benoit who got him clean and helped him stay that way. Anyway, now he's back doing them, and he's turned aggressive."

"So, you are afraid he will hurt you?" she asked.

"I don't know. But that's not really the problem. Not today, at least. I…I think he may have had something to do with Benoit's death."

Eloise sat up straight and inhaled sharply.

I told her about Benoit and Joel's relationship before he died, how Benoit was laundering money for Joel's network, and how Joel inferred that Benoit had gotten "baked."

Then, I told her about the button.

Tears formed in her eyes. "Bastard."

Just then the door chimed.

"Dammit," Eloise said. "I got this. You're still a mess. I'm chasing whoever is here out of the shop and closing up until Jared gets here."

I could hear Eloise talking to a young man, explaining the machine just broke, but offering free biscotti for the inconvenience. Then she followed him out, locked the door, and turned the "Open" sign to "Closed." She switched off the front lights as she walked back. She brought two cold bottles of water with her and set one in front of me.

"I have something to tell you, too," she said. "Something that has bothered me for years, but now makes sense."

I looked up, surprised.

"When Benoit died, his attorney reached out to me as the beneficiary. Benoit had an account in Switzerland with more than $4 million in it."

My mouth fell open. "What?"

She nodded. "He also had a safety deposit box with a note that said if I were ever reading that note to be careful about using the money. That it didn't come from his day job, but that it belonged to me and I should contact someone named B.P. if I needed help using it. He left a phone number."

B.P. A wave of anxiety pulsed through me. "Eloise, do you have that note, still?"

"Yes."

"El, I think Joel might be B.P.," I said excitedly.

"You think he still has that phone number? After all these years?"

"Joel always carries two phones. One is his personal phone, which I've never had the number to, and one is a disposable. He gets a new one every week. I do, too. We all do. That's how we run our operation; using text codes on prepaid phones. Anyway, that's not important. What is important is if that phone number on Benoit's note is Joel's personal phone number, we'll know who B.P. is. And when I was being questioned by the police after Benoit's death, they kept asking me if I knew of any contacts of Benoit's who had those initials. They didn't tell me why, but you don't have to be a detective to figure that it was because B.P. must have been a person of interest."

"They asked me, too," Eloise said.

"Why didn't you circle back with them after reading the note?" I asked.

"I don't know. I figured if Benoit trusted this person enough to direct me to him, or her, then I should keep it secret."

I nodded. "So, what did you do with the money?"

She narrowed her eyes. "You first."

I snorted. "It's in the garage."

"What? You have all that cash in the garage? How much?"

I shook my head. "I don't know for sure. Millions."

She slapped both hands on the table. "Good God, Anna!"

"I know. That's another problem. I don't know what to do with all of it, but I have an idea. I need to fly it to St. Kitts."

"You're gonna need help to do that," she said.

"I don't need it. But yes, help would be nice. Your turn. What did you do with the money Benoit left you?"

"It's still sitting there," Eloise said. "I thought I'll give it to Nathan one day. If Benoit had known he had a son, he would've left it to him."

The bulge in my throat fattened. "You didn't have to do that. You know that, right?"

"I know that, but what the hell else would I do with it? You're my family. I would have shared it with you all, anyway."

I laughed, pitifully at first, then louder.

"What's so funny?" she asked.

"I should learn to open up about my problems sooner. If I had come to you at the beginning about our financial problems, I never might have gotten into this mess. I would've just taken your millions, had I known you had it!" I kicked her lightly under the table while laughing.

She laughed heartily. "Maybe you would have. But something tells me you've enjoyed building this business of yours, just a little."

I grimaced. "I hate to admit it, but I did, at first. I always hated that it was cocaine, but running the operation was exhilarating and challenging. I loved the rush of it, but of course now, the honeymoon is over. And it turns out, I'm married to a murderer."

She nodded gravely. "Speaking of marriage, you have another problem, too," she said.

My stomach dropped. "I know."

"When are you going to tell him?"

"I don't know," I said. "It's been eating me up inside."

"You've never kept a secret from Marco. How have you been able to manage keeping all of this from him?"

I rubbed under my eyes as tears welled up again. "I guess at first, it seemed like a temporary way to make a few extra bucks. I didn't want to hurt his pride. He already felt so bad about our struggles and going back to his old job. I figured if I could quietly take care of things, it would be a relief; and it would be over before anyone needed to know about it."

A fat tear slowly twisted down my face, dodging left and right like a slalom skier avoiding the obstacles down a hill.

"Then, it just snowballed," I continued. "I enjoyed watching these women turn from frail and broken to confident and controlling. I enjoyed every stack of cash I placed in those bins. Each dollar reminded me of what I had built, and that there was still a sharp businesswoman inside of me. I even enjoyed the anonymity of it, having a secret that kept me above everyone else.

"But the feelings of enjoying it turned to shame every time I looked into my kids' eyes, every time I kissed Marco goodnight. I've laid in bed for hours while shame robbed me of sleep. But I didn't know how to stop, and truthfully, up until these last couple of months, I didn't want to stop. But now I do, and I don't know where to start."

Eloise came over and wrapped her arms around my shoulders from behind. We cried softly together, like many times before.

Finally, she said, "Do you remember what you said to me after Benoit died? When I collapsed in your arms crying?"

I shook my head; I truly couldn't recall.

"You said, 'You're going to be alright, Eloise.' And I asked, 'How do you know?' And you said, 'Because I'm going to be with you, and I'll make sure of it.'"

I nodded and closed my eyes at the memory, tears blooming behind my eyelids.

"And I'm with you now, and it's going to be okay," she said. "And the even better news is that we aren't alone anymore. We have Marco."

"He'll never look at me the same again. I've lied to him for almost a year." Tears sprung harder. The thought of disappointing Marco was crushing to me. I couldn't picture the inevitable revulsion in his face without crying more.

"You don't have a choice, Anna. You have to tell him."

"I know I do," I sobbed an achy pout. "Do you think he'll still love me?"

She smiled. "I know he will."

Chapter Forty

M arco walked in from work and I stood up from the kitchen counter, where a half-empty glass of wine stood idly. It was quiet in the house. He leaned over and kissed me on the cheek. "Hi, beautiful! Where is everyone?"

"Eloise has them. She took them to dinner," I replied.

He looked confused. "That was nice of her! What's the occasion?"

I smiled humbly. "An impromptu date night."

Marco raised his eyebrows and put his hands out. "That's great! Where are we going? Should we try something new? Maybe that new BYO tapas place? Share a bottle of wine? Loosen up a little? Let our inhibitions go?" He grabbed onto both my hips and wiggled them slightly.

I laughed quietly. "I have somewhere else in mind. Can I drive?"

"Of course, you can. Hey, are you okay?"

"Yeah, I'm okay."

He held me loosely and looked at my face. "I can tell something's bothering you. What is it? I hate seeing you sad. Let me see that beautiful smile."

I couldn't break right now; I couldn't, yet. I wanted to stay in that moment and freeze the gentleness on Marco's face and the love in his eyes, put it in a bottle, close the lid, and never let it go. I wanted to know that things wouldn't change between us; that I hadn't screwed up everything.

I conjured some bravery. "I'm good, babe. Come on, let me take you on an adventure."

"Anywhere with you, my love." He followed me out the door.

We drove toward town and I pulled up behind Biscotti to park, right next to the garage.

"Did you forget something in the shop?" Marco asked.

"Not exactly," I replied. "Come in for a minute."

I unlocked the side door and we went inside. Jared had just closed 30 minutes prior, so it still smelled of coffee and dough.

Marco followed me to the front where I had prepared a semi-picnic on the counter with Jared's help. White linen was draped over the counter; atop of it lay a low-cut bouquet of flowers, bottle of wine and two glasses, candlesticks ready to light, a large board of cheeses and meats, and a fresh-cut loaf of bread.

"Wow, this is nice! The whole place to ourselves?" Marco beamed.

I gestured for him to sit down as I lit the candles and poured us each a glass of wine. Marco picked up a piece of soppresata and popped it in his mouth, making an appetizing groan as he chewed. We lifted our glasses.

He started to toast, but I interrupted him. "Actually, I have a toast tonight, if you don't mind."

He nodded merrily and grabbed another piece of meat with one hand and wrapped it around a chunk of pecorino. I smiled as I watched him. Everything about Marco was authentic—from the way he smiled to the way he couldn't resist grabbing a bite while I mulled over my toast.

"I'd like to toast to the greatest man I know and will ever know," I started.

Marco stopped. "Your dad? Don't say your dad. Say me, please say me," he teased.

I rolled my eyes. "Yes, you, honey. You are the greatest man I've ever known."

He let out an exaggerated sigh of relief while prepping another morsel of meat and cheese with one hand.

"I say that because you wake up every day with the goal of making me and the kids happy, at whatever cost to you. You never complain, you don't ask for anything, and you're perpetually happy."

"What's there not to be happy about?" he asked. "I have the hottest wife, and three healthy children, and a plate full of meat and cheese in front of me!"

I laughed.

"Are we good? Can we toast? I need both hands to get some bread," he laughed pleadingly.

"Almost."

He pouted.

"You also have a way of fixing things and making me feel like it was okay that I broke them. Like that time I backed my car out and hit your truck with it, despite having 900 cameras and beeping noises telling me a 5-ton truck was behind me?"

"It wasn't parked in its usual spot," he shrugged playfully.

"Well, I appreciate you. I appreciate all of you. Every moment you spend trying to make me smile. And I love you. I love you so much, Marco." My lip started quivering. "I just want you to know that. I love you most."

"Cheers my love. Thank you. I love you, too. And I love your smile, so don't start crying now! Let's eat and drink. Salud."

"Salud," I choked back the knot in my throat that held my tears at bay.

We ate and talked about the kids and I swallowed down the impending doom with gulps of wine, each swallow heavier than the last.

Finally: "Marco, I have to tell you something."

"Okay," he looked at me skeptically while taking a swig of wine.

I took a deep breath. "You know how you said I've seemed disconnected lately?"

"Oh, forget about that. I shouldn't have said that."

"No, you were right. I haven't been fully present. I've been distracted."

He nodded while chewing.

"And there's a reason for it." My voice quivered. "And I'm scared to tell you the reason because you're not going to like it. And worse than that, I'm afraid you'll never look at me with the same amount of love you are looking at me right now with."

He stopped chewing. "What's going on, Anna?" he asked in a serious tone.

I looked down and shook my head. "What I'm about to say is going to shock you, so before you react, just promise me you'll hear me out...."

"Anna, just tell me," he said impatiently.

"A few months ago…well, a year really, shortly after taking Biscotti over, I ran into an old acquaintance," I started.

His face dropped. "You're seeing someone else?"

"No! God no, Marco, no. Please babe, never. I swear, I would never even think about cheating on you. I can barely even say the words. No, not that."

He sighed relief, but stared at me skeptically, one hand frozen on a pepperoni wrapped cube of provolone. "What then?"

I cleared my throat. "So, I ran into an old acquaintance from when I lived in Philly and, long story short, he approached me with an opportunity to make a little bit of extra money…."

Marco's face twisted with a mixture of disgust and disbelief.

I grabbed his free hand with my sweaty palms. "Please just hear me out before coming to any conclusions."

"I'm trying, Anna. But so far, this story is not starting off well."

"I know." I wanted to go back to five minutes ago when we were laughing together and to avoid this conversation altogether. If I believed I could keep a secret from him for the rest of our lives without having it ruin our marriage from within like a slow-growth tumor, I just might have.

"I'm just going to say this quickly and let you ask me questions after," I said.

"Please."

"Okay. So, he asked me to hold a bag, and if I kept this bag safe for one night until someone picked it up, he would give me $500," I winced at the sound of it out loud.

Marco's eyes bulged and his eyebrows raised. "Fuck, Anna, a bag? You held a bag of drugs for someone?" he asked incredulously.

I gasped. "How'd you know it had drugs in it?"

"Are you fucking kidding me?" He pulled his hand away. "You know where I grew up, right? In South Philly if you were holding a bag, it wasn't filled with groceries. It's dangerous, Anna. When you start moving drugs for these people, you enter a world you can't get out of. Are you still doing it? Tell me you're not still doing it."

My stomach had filled with rocks, sinking it to the bottom of the ocean floor. "Yes," I said meekly. "It gets worse."

Marco dropped his food with a tiny clang and stood up and ran his hands through his thick black hair. "Oh my God, babe. Tell me how deep you are."

"About 110 bags deep," I said.

His face fell to meet my stomach.

"What?!" he said exasperatingly. "You've moved 110 bags of drugs? What drug? As if it matters. But what is it? Pot? Coke?"

"Cocaine. And it's not 110 bags in total. It's 110 bags twice a week, sometimes more."

He let out a guttural moan. "Oh no, babe, oh my God. What have you gotten yourself into? Do you have any idea what kind of danger you've put yourself in—put us in—by doing this?" Both hands were on his shaking head as he seemed to stare at swirling, blank thoughts of questions with no answers.

As ludicrous as it seemed, until this moment, until Marco asked that question, I *hadn't* fully grasped the consequential gravity of my actions. Of course, I knew there was danger, but the only person I had talked about the matter with was Joel, who was far from pointing north on a moral compass. The women in my network didn't know they were running cocaine, though surely some—maybe most—suspected it was something illegal. But as long as I protected them, they didn't ask questions and took their paychecks weekly with a smile. But Marco asking me that question, asking if I really understood the danger I was in, that *we* were in, made me feel, for the first time, foolish and reckless. I felt like a child whose mother walked in on her dipping lollipops in a toilet bowl then eating them, awareness of the filth negated by the humor in the game and the sweet reward in the end. The weight of the realization was heavy, and I felt small under it.

"Can I ask just one question?" he said in a soft voice.

I nodded with my eyes down, afraid to ask him how he didn't have more than one question.

"*Why*? Why did you do it in the first place?"

I looked up and tears filled my eyes, but I held them back. I didn't have the right to cry. "I guess I thought at first it was an easy way to make a couple of extra dollars, like watching someone's dog for a week. I didn't know that there were drugs in the bag the first few times: I swear I didn't. We didn't run bags of cocaine in St. George, Utah," I said hesitantly. "I honestly didn't know."

He shook his head and snorted softly in thought.

"After a bag or two, it seemed so easy. I just would put a bag behind the counter for one day, and voila, I had an extra $500. We were in really bad shape at the shop—worse shape than you probably knew—and I knew this would climb us out of the debt. And it did. It made a huge difference in our expenses. But also, it helped pay for the little things that we didn't have money for. I know it seems stupid, honey, but I was stressing about how to pay for things around the house and for the kids." I shrugged. "The boys needed football uniforms. That's how it started, and then it just grew from there."

He sighed and sat back down on the stool. "I don't know what to think right now, Anna." He didn't look directly at me.

I grabbed his hand pleadingly. He didn't reciprocate my touch, but he didn't pull his hand away either, "I know. You have every right to be angry…." I paused. "To be basically anything with me. I deserve it."

We sat in silence. The refrigerator hum and dim interior nighttime lighting made the walls feel closed in. I hadn't told him everything, but the worse was over. I'd hoped.

Finally, he sighed and looked at me. I felt a spark of hope catch in my chest.

"I'm pissed. I don't want you to think that I'm not," he said.

I nodded.

"But I don't think there's much time for that now. Tell me every-thing. *Everything*," he emphasized. Then, with more melancholy, "so we can find a way out of this."

The spark of hope turned into the tiniest of flames. He said *we*.

Where to begin? "Well. I told you I was holding bags at first, just one at a time. Then I met a couple of women who needed extra money…"

He gasped. "Other women?"

I blinked slowly. "Yes. I know you'll have a million questions about this, but let me just spill everything out at once and you can judge me, question me, hate me, or whatever afterward."

He nodded in frustrated agreement.

"I met other women around town; everywhere, really: School, the gym, here at the shop. I even met one woman in line at the grocery store. I'll explain in time how each one of them ended up, for lack of better word, working for me. But the gist of it is the same: They all needed extra money and I had a way of making that happen pretty easily. Once I found out the bags held drugs, I negotiated a higher rate—$1,000 per bag—which I would split with these women. Eventually, these women found other women to split their portion. It just got so big, so fast. I honestly never could have imagined there were that many women willing to do a random job without understanding what they were really doing."

"Wait," Marco interrupted. "They didn't know that they were running coke?"

"No. Only I knew. I disguised it."

"How?"

I sighed. "I changed the bags to diaper bags and made Joel—that's my contact's name—package the kilos in canisters of baby formula."

He snorted in shock. "In *baby formula* cans? Oh my God, that's insane! And they never opened the cans to look inside?"

"They couldn't. They were sealed. I bought a can sealer. Actually, I made Joel buy the can sealer, but that's beside the point."

"Holy shit, babe. That's the craziest thing I've ever heard." He chuckled. "You thought of all this? I don't know whether to fear you or admire you! It's brilliant, really." His face had the look of someone who just won a race he was favored to lose; a look of shock, disbelief, and a little bit of pride.

The flame emboldened.

"Yeah, well, I guess....It worked, at least. So far, no one has opened any cans, and everything has run smoothly."

"So, you have how many women carrying these bags for you?"

"110 women. But I only have contact with 10 of them. My 10 women each have 10 women."

"And they each take a bag a week?"

"Two to three bags a week. Some take bags every day," I winced.

"At $500 per bag?"

"They get $500; I get $500."

He quickly did a rough calculation and his eyes bulged. "Wait, you get $500 per bag on hundreds of bags per week?"

"Well, technically, as of today, I get $1,000 per bag. But I just negotiated that this morning. So, yes. For all intents and purposes, I've been getting $500 a bag."

"Anna, that's more than $100,000 a week." His hands were back in his hair, holding fistfuls of it mercilessly.

I nodded.

"Babe. How much money have you made in total?"

I sighed. "I think nearly $5 million. I don't know for sure."

He stood up so quickly his stool fell over. "Holy shit! Holy shit! Holy shit! Holy shit!" He was bouncing back and forth as he chanted.

I couldn't tell if the flame had just ignited into a fire, or if the "holy shits" were about to pinch the wick.

Finally, he asked, "Where is it?"

"It's out back in the garage."

"In a *garage*? You've kept $5 million in a *garage*?"

"I didn't know where else to keep it. You can't simply deposit that kind of money in the bank, and I certainly couldn't bring it home. I started putting it there, and, well, it's still there."

He looked at me blankly, then a smile broke through. "Can I see it?"

The flame ignited.

Chapter Forty-One

After spending two hours in the garage, counting $100s and binding them in stacks of $10,000 with rubber bands, Marco and I looked at each other with exhausted exhilaration.

"Five million, two hundred and ninety-two thousand dollars," he said slowly.

I let out a loud sigh of disbelief. "Holy shit." I smiled a little. I couldn't help it. I had stashed away more than $5 million in one year of an operation I ran flawlessly. When the ethical nature of the business was set aside, the sheer efficiency and profitability of it were nothing short of impressive.

"We can't keep it here," Marco said.

"I know. I have a plan for it. I was trying to figure out how to execute it, but now that you know everything, it will make it easier to accomplish."

He gestured his hand up. "What is it?"

"I want to rent a plane. A private plane to St. Kitts. I can open an account there and deposit all of the cash, untaxed, unquestioned. I have to get it there quietly, and a private plane is the best way to do that." I looked around at the mountains of cash.

He raised his eyebrows. "I don't see why that wouldn't work."

I nodded.

"And after that?"

I inhaled sharply and exhaled out a breathy sigh. "I don't know."

"We have to find a way out of this. You can't continue. It has to stop," he said seriously.

"I know that. I have an idea, but I haven't thought it all the way through. I need a little more time."

"How much time?"

"A week maybe. Two? I don't know. I need to focus on getting the money out first."

"I'll help. We'll do it together."

I smiled, and he smiled back with a tired wink.

I crawled over to him, stacks of cash shuffling beneath my knees, and I straddled him. "Are you still mad at me?" I slowly unbuttoned his shirt.

"A little, but you sitting on top of me, and me sitting on top of $5 million, lessens the sting a bit." He took hold of both my thighs and shifted me powerfully closer to him.

"I'm sorry I didn't tell you earlier. I'm sorry about all of it. But I love you for helping me now, and for loving me still."

He pressed me further down into his lap. "I could never stop loving you."

"So, you forgive me?" I undulated slowly.

"I'm starting to…."

"What else can I do?" I whispered in his ear before biting his lobe.

He moaned, picked me up, and laid me on my back on the bed of cash, making love to me with a million-ton force.

A 5 million-ton force.

It was hurricane season in St. Kitts, which seemed fitting given my personal turmoil.

Marco and I rented a private plane out of the Lehigh Valley airport—better that no one recognized us in Doylestown—for a weekend trip to St. Kitts. The plane would take us back home in two days, so I'd be back by Monday to continue with the operation. Last year at this time, I dreamed about going away for a weekend with Marco; I certainly didn't have one in mind that involved two large suitcases glutted with cash.

Although I was excited to be spending quality time with Marco, time we desperately needed to reconnect, a twinge of guilt pressed on me about using the money for a personal reason. To this point, I hadn't used any of the money for me. I only had used it pay bills at Biscotti; bills at home; and pay for items for the kids. Sometimes, when I could think of a reasonable way to do it, I had sent money to my Mom and Dad, too. But as we boarded the private jet, bypassing commercial security and lines, being handed a glass of champagne as we stepped up the jet's staircase, it wasn't without remembering the cost of getting here.

But hey, we were here now, and my marriage was far more important than worrying about how we got here. I was excited to be with Marco, and I intended to make the most of this weekend.

"Holy shit," Marco said when we boarded the luxury private jet. "Did you ever think you'd be on one of these?" He smiled the way a kid smiles on his first trip to Disney World.

"No. Oh my God! Look at this!" I pointed to a beautiful spread of berries and cheese, crackers and caviar, and the remainder of the bottle of champagne sitting in an ice bucket.

Marco smiled. "I did that. I told them I wanted this trip to be special. 'Spare no expense!' I told them. Seriously, babe: How many times in your life have you been able to say that?"

I laughed. "Never. I can honestly say Never."

He picked up a strawberry and walked closer to me. He held it up to my mouth. I winced as I slowly bit at the berry seductively. We both laughed at the cliché moment that, after five years of marriage, didn't have the same effect as in the first five months of dating; but it still stoked a flame that had been contained in embers.

"Now, baby," he said, grabbing me around the waist and pulling me in close. "We are going to forget our problems–just for two days–and we're going to forget about all the shit we've dealt with this past year, and we are going to enjoy this fucking vacation. Just you and me."

I kissed Marco longingly. "I love you. Have I told you that lately?" I said, laughing.

"It's so good to hear you laugh again." Marco stared at my face intently.

"I've missed you so much. I've missed us." Then I paused and said what I really had missed the most. "I've missed me, too."

We kissed again and settled into our cushy white leather seats, enjoying our fancy spread, while something else started to spread: Hope.

Chapter Forty-Two

The kids were already in bed when Marco and I walked through the door Sunday night.

St. Kitts was everything we had hoped it would be. Not only had Marco and I reconnected, spending steamy nights in a villa overlooking the moonlit Caribbean; we also had deposited $5.2 million into a newly established bank account.

Eloise was sitting on the couch with a glass of scotch playing Sudoku from today's paper. A fire roared loudly behind her as she looked up apprehensively.

"So?" she asked.

I sighed tiredly. "Everything went well."

She let out a long, puff-cheeked breath. "Good."

She poured two more glasses of scotch and handed one to me and one to Marco as he came in from unloading the car.

"Can you believe this woman, El?" Marco sat down.

"It's always the ones you wouldn't expect, isn't it?" She half-laughed. "If I had to pin this kind of thing on any of the three of us, I'd have put my money on the street kid from South Philly," she said, pointing her glass at Marco. "Second bet would've gone on the orphaned lesbian raised by a drunk father and a barely adult brother. Third place bet would have been anyone else *but* Anna from Utah. That's for fucking sure!"

We all laughed and clinked scotch glasses. "To people surprising you."

There was a quiet moment while sipping our scotch in which I felt we shared the same combination of emotions—adrenaline, fear, pride, repugnance—but mostly, that we should have felt worse about the situation than we did. At this point, we were focused on finding a way out.

"Let's talk about the inevitable: What to do next. How to get out," Marco said seriously.

I nodded.

"Joel doesn't know any of the women in your network?" Marco asked me.

"No. He's never met any of them. Most of the women have never met each other, not through me, at least."

"And you haven't dealt with anyone other than Joel? You've never met his contacts or anyone on his side?"

"No. Well, there was Panda," I said.

"Panda?" Marco asked warily.

"He was the first guy who picked up bags from the shop, but I only met him a few times. He went to upstate New York, I think. Joel said he had disappeared, whatever that means."

Marco grimaced.

"I'm not worried about Panda," I assured him. "Even if he could be tracked down, I'm a nobody to him. He doesn't even know my name."

"So, if we take Joel out, there's no trail to you," Eloise stated with authority.

I winced. "Take Joel out? Jesus, you make it sound like we're in a Mafia movie, El."

"I'm just saying that Joel needs to go," she said defensively. "I don't know what that means exactly. But we have to make sure he can't resurface."

"How do we accomplish that without calling Don Corleone?" Marco asked sarcastically.

I laughed pathetically. "I think there's only two ways to get rid of Joel. Death, which we're not going to entertain," I glared at Eloise. "Or blackmail. And luckily, we have ammo. We could use the evidence we have about Benoit's death against him. I could make him believe that I would go to the cops if he didn't let me break away."

They both nodded unconvincingly.

"But what would be his incentive to admit that? And what would prevent him from turning you in if you gave him up to the police? He could tell the police everything about your operation," Marco said.

"He could, but there would be no evidence to support it. We've only ever communicated on prepaid phones. He's never met any person in my network, so he couldn't provide witnesses. And by the time the cops would come around, the money and all the evidence would be gone. If he pointed to the garage, it would be empty with no trace of cocaine because the canisters came to me tightly sealed. I rented the garage with cash and nothing more than a handshake with Dale, so there's no paper trail to me. And trust me, Dale would cover for me if I asked him to: He has nothing to lose in his old age.

"In the end, it would be Joel's word against mine. And I could say that he was bitter that we had uncovered his identity through the note in Eloise's safety deposit box, and that he was making up stories in revenge. Who do you think the cops would believe?"

Marco sighed. "I guess it could work. But it's risky. If Joel doesn't let you walk away, and you have to turn him in, the cops could dig deep enough to find something on you, I'm sure. Video footage out by the garage? Something."

"There are no cameras out there. You don't think I've checked 1,000 times? The only logical building to have one would be us or the toy store, both owned by Dale; and he's too cheap to invest in security cameras," I countered.

"I still don't like it. I can't imagine dealing with the legal nightmare if he were to turn you in and the risk of you going to jail," he stopped. "Fuck. I can't even think about that."

"Well, it's all we've got. You have to remember: These types of people don't go to the cops for help: They're terrified of the cops. If Joel went to them to rat me out, he'd be investigated for 10 other things. I know Joel; and he won't go to the cops. Especially if I offer him another way to continue his operation—not with my network of women—but by giving him a transition period while he creates new contacts. I think he'd be okay if I did that. I hope. I'll offer to forego my pay during the transition period."

"And what if that doesn't work and he freaks out and gets violent?" Eloise asked. "You said that he punched the garage the last time you saw him, and that you think he's using drugs again. What makes you so sure he won't hurt you?"

"He can't hurt me, or his operation is gone."

They both looked skeptical.

"Look, guys, it's always about money for these people. They don't care who does what, or how it gets done, as long as everyone gets paid. So, if I can convince Joel that I can help him continue his operation with his own new people, he'll be okay."

"I still don't see him walking away with a 'Thanks Anna' fist bump," Eloise said with mocking seriousness.

"No, of course not. But he'll have no choice. He'll know that I could go to the police with my discovery of his involvement in Benoit's death. Then he'll lose his operation for certain, plus have the cops after him for a murder."

"It could work, but we'll need to keep working on details. Also, you'll need protection. I'll go with you," Marco said.

"He'll never talk if you're with me, Marco. But don't worry, I have protection."

They looked at me confusedly as I scratched the back of Polo's ears.

Chapter Forty-Three

The water rushed swiftly beneath me; the full moon illuminated off the icy peaks, creating a light show as the water galloped over rocks and crashed against the shoreline.

I had been standing on the bridge for 20 minutes. It took me and Marco nearly 30 minutes to haul the cans to the middle of the bridge with our daughter's red canvas wagon; its weight created a hollow clink as the wheels rolled slowly over the rough bridge floor. The narrow bridge, known to locals as Suicide Bridge, no longer allowed cars to pass over it. It connected two wooded areas and towered high above the river where the current swelled over jagged boulders. These days, the bridge mainly was used as part of a popular weekend walking trail.

Marco, Eloise, and I had spent the better part of the day unpacking each diaper bag with gloved hands and pulling baby formula cans out in preparation for tonight.

"Damn, these look legitimate," Marco had admired.

It was the first time I had seen the baby formula cans, and I had to admit, they did look legitimate. None would be the wiser to assume it wasn't a diaper bag full of what it was supposed to be full of: Diapers and perfectly sealed cans of baby formula.

After packing the car with the bags, I sent a text to Joel:

Playdate.

Not meeting at the playground.

Dropping pin for location.

Come ASAP.

We can share a bottle of Pinot.

I pictured Joel mouthing, "What the fuck?" with a bobbing cigarette between his lips as he read the text. *Bottle of Pinot* was code for emergency.

There was a five-minute pause before Joel replied:

I'll be there.

Marco had driven me to the location on the pin, a bridge near a small, old merchant town. Together, we had lugged a day's worth of cocaine, intended for drops by the Mothers the next morning, to the middle of the bridge. More than $4 million of cocaine sat in neatly piled rows in the wagon, held together with loose netting. Two smaller piles sat idly on the floor next to the wagon near the bridge's edge.

"You sure you're going to be okay?" Marco asked hesitantly. I had never known Marco to be as uneasy as he was these past couple of weeks that we had spent formulating our plan. The fear that something would happen to me had worn him so thin that I was afraid he might snap and crumble.

I kissed him lightly. "I'll be okay."

"And you're sure he won't hurt you?"

"He won't dare." I looked down at Polo, who was shifting from one paw to the other with a small whimper. "It's okay, boy. I know it's

cold. We won't be here for long," I assured him. He wagged his tail
warily and gazed at me with unrelenting loyalty.

"Polo, you take care of her, you hear?" Marco patted his head.
"Anna, please, don't take any chances. If you feel unsafe at any point,
just wave the signal, and I'll come running. I'll be just behind that
tree line."

"I will." He kissed my forehead and we embraced for a moment.
Then he pulled away, a gloss glazed over his eyes.

"He'll be here soon. You'd better go."

He walked away, our arms extending with locked fingertips until
he walked far enough for our fingers to break. When he was almost
out of sight, he turned around. I blew a kiss to him. He winked back
and ducked into the darkness.

I watched my breath create an icy fog that seemed to linger longer
than usual, as if it, too, had no idea what would happen to it next.
I remembered the day I agreed to hold a bag, just one bag. Joel had
entered the shop so nonchalantly, as if he was there by accident. Yet, the
deliberateness of his presence was nothing resembling a coincidence.

I looked at my watch. It was 11:15 p.m. He should be here any
moment. I fumbled with the video recording function of my phone;
rehearsing where to hold it for maximum visual and audio. Then I
checked that the backup high-end audiotape recorder that hung from
a cord around my neck was ready for execution.

I saw two headlights approach and the blood in my body turned as
cold as the water beneath me. The car stopped just short of the bridge
with a graveled taper. The headlights retired as the engine stopped,
and Joel climbed out of the driver's seat; his frame disproportionate

to the vehicle. He slammed the door and walked briskly toward me. His steps reverberated against the metal bridge floor.

I hit the red record button on both devices, making sure the cans were out of the camera's line of sight.

Polo growled as Joel approached, and the hair on his nape stood straight up. Joel's gait slowed when he saw Polo and he raised both hands. "Whoa, Anna. What the fuck?"

Polo bucked slightly and I tugged him back with a quiet "easy" command.

"Stop there," I said when Joel reached a 10-foot distance from me.

"What the hell is going on?" he asked breathlessly. His posture had lost its aggravated edge and his gaze nervously darted from me to Polo, then to the pyramid of cans sitting in the wagon behind me. Panic struck his face when he saw the cans. "Holy shit, what are those doing here?"

"You owe me some answers," I said calmly.

"I owe you what? You dragged me to a bridge for answers? You're fucking kidding me. You couldn't have waited until tomorrow to ask me whatever you need to ask me? I mean, what can be so goddamned important?" He looked cautiously at Polo, who was standing rigidly on all four legs, a low groan humming out of him.

"I want to know what happened to Benoit."

"How would I know what happened to him? He had a heart attack or something. Isn't that what they said?"

"I think you know it wasn't a heart attack that killed him," I said. "I know you were in his hotel room when he died."

He let out a snort. "What are you talking about? I wasn't in his hotel room."

"You were, and I know you were because of that." I pointed to the bottom of his jacket.

He looked down. "What? My pants?"

"No, your jacket. The button in the back, or rather, the missing button, toward the bottom."

He crooked his neck around to see the one remaining button that was fastened next a nub of thread where another button once rested.

"My button? So what?"

"That missing button was found in Benoit's hotel room the day he died."

He stuttered. "So…," Then, he scratched his head and said loudly, "How do you know it was my button? Who cares, anyway?"

"I know it was your button because it had a panther head on it identical to the one that's on your jacket. How many buttons are out there that look like that? And how many of those would have ended up in Benoit's hotel room?"

"This is fucking stupid, Anna!" he said boorishly. "So, there was a button that looked like mine in Benoit's hotel room. Who cares? He's dead. Why does it matter?"

It was clear I was going to have to spell this out for Joel. "Because I want to know why you were there. I know you had something to do with his death, Joel. You said that he got baked. And then you end up in his hotel room the day he died? Why were you there?"

"I already told you, I wasn't there," he said impatiently.

Without turning around, I kicked behind me, and a small stack of cans went tumbling over the side of the bridge. They landed in the water with a quiet clink as they hit the rocky current below.

"What are you doing?! Do you know what happens to me if those cans don't get delivered?!" Joel screamed and took a step toward me. Polo bucked forward and growled loudly, and Joel jumped back. "You'd better keep that fucking thing away from me," he pointed frightfully at Polo.

"Like I told you when we first met, he'll be okay as long as I'm okay," I said.

"What do you want, Anna? You want the truth?" he shrieked.

"Precisely. And the next lie you tell me will cost you another pile. As you can see, you get only two more chances."

"Fuck!" he screamed, and he ran his hands over his shaved head. He settled his hands on his hips. "Fine, I was there the day Benoit died. Is that what you want to know?"

I gasped quietly. "Why? Why were you there?"

"Because I needed to talk him out of something."

"Talk him out of what?"

He paused and shuffled his feet. "He wanted out."

My heart dug into my ribcage. "He wanted out of his business with you? And you wouldn't let him go?"

He threw up his hands. "It wasn't really up to me, Anna. He had become a liability to the people I worked for. He knew too much about their business, and they couldn't let him walk away that easily."

I trembled as Joel confirmed my fears. "Why did he want out?"

He looked at me pathetically, "You know why. Because he wanted to start fresh with you."

A sharp pang swelled as my heart throbbed.

"And you couldn't let him go, so you killed him."

"I didn't kill him!" he shouted defensively.

I kicked behind me, and another pile of cans tumbled over the bridge's edge. Only the massive pile in the wagon remained.

"Oh my God! Stop! No more, no more, okay. I killed him. Ahhhh!" he wailed an anguished moan and danced around in agitation. Polo growled and flounced his paws wildly at Joel's reaction. Joel quickly quieted. "Okay. Shit. Okay. Sorry," he said toward Polo, though he didn't dare directly address him.

"How?" A nauseous feeling rose from my belly. "How did you kill him, Joel?" I wanted him to hear the words that he killed Benoit. He didn't "take care of it," or "handle it," or however else he likely reported to his people. He killed a man. He killed his friend who had saved him from dying in a dirty, public bathroom. I wanted him to relive every moment of it.

He looked up at the sky and sighed loudly. "With insulin."

"You injected him with insulin?"

He remained quiet.

"Joel?" I pressed.

He looked at me resignedly. "Yeah. Some sort of high concentrated insulin called u500."

That would explain the sudden cardiac arrest. And because Benoit was diabetic, insulin wouldn't have been conspicuous on a toxicology report, if it had shown up at all. My head was reeling with as much agitation as my heart.

"Joel, why?" I pleaded. "Why would you do that? Why would you kill Benoit? He was your friend. He took care of you."

He stared at the moon on the horizon with a deflated posture. If I could have seen him clearer, I might have seen a look of regret and grief. I had hoped that, at least.

Again: "Joel, tell me why? What did you gain by killing him?"

He inhaled sharply, then looked at me with a deadpan stare. "I got a promotion."

The blood in my body turned from liquid to fire as the callousness of Joel's explanation raged through my veins. He killed his friend, the father of my child, for a promotion.

"For a promotion? You're fucking pathetic, Joel! Do you know that? You're a joke. Your loyalty lies with people who make you a drug dealer and a murderer? And you killed the one person in your life who truly cared about you, who literally scraped you up off the floor? And for what? A promotion to what? To be one small step higher on the lackey ladder?" I scoffed. "Pathetic. You're pathetic, always have been and always will be, Joel. And I want nothing to do with you. I'm out," I said emphatically.

"That's what this is really about," he jeered. "I knew it. You want out." A sickening laugh escaped him. "Sorry to tell you, but I can't let you out either, Anna. You also have become too valuable." Joel had turned instantly cold and his words tumbled out like ice.

"And how do you plan to stop me? You can't kill me. Your operation would be lost. And you've worked so hard to make it where you are," I said caustically.

He snorted and shook his head agitatedly. "I can find new people for your routes. You're not that irreplaceable."

"That's good. In fact, that's exactly what I wanted to hear, Joel. You will find new people for the routes and you'll never bother me again."

He sneered. "Right. Okay."

"I'm serious. And I want to make this crystal clear: After tonight, I will never see you again. You will not come by the shop. You will not contact or threaten me in any way. And if you do, or if anything happens to me, a copy of this videotape…" I nodded toward the recorders, "with your confession to Benoit's murder, will go directly to the police. Along with how and where to find you and all your stupid fucking bosses you protect so valiantly."

He laughed mockingly. "You wouldn't know where to find me."

"No? You sure about that? They couldn't reach you at your phone number that ends in 4423?"

His mouth dropped open a little. "How do you have that number?"

"I know a lot of things, Joel. Or should I call you *Black Panther*?" From a hotel lobby phone, Eloise and I had called the number left in Benoit's safety deposit box: Joel's voicemail said that we had reached Black Panther, aka *B.P.*

"What?" he asked flustered. "How do you know that?" Joel wasn't smart enough to act casual through shocking revelations.

"Like I said, I know a lot of things: Where you live, where you hang out, and who you work with. Do you really think I wouldn't have done my homework on you?" I lied. I didn't know anything past his phone number.

"What the fuck? You've followed me? How do you know all that stuff?"

"Doesn't matter. What matters is that you will leave me alone, or you might as well put the gun to your own head at the same time as you point it at mine. Because you will *never* survive coming after me."

"Fuck!" he screamed. Polo growled.

"There's nothing more to say, Joel. It's time for you to go."

"What about that?" he whined, pointing to the wagon.

"That's collateral damage," I said indifferently.

"What? No, c'mon, Anna. Let me take it. I'll get killed if it doesn't get delivered."

"Not my problem, Joel. Truth be told, I was going to let you take it. I set out tonight willing to offer you a transition period to make new contacts in my operation. But that all changed when I realized what a cold and hopeless person you were. I figured out that you killed Benoit, but I hoped that it was at least to save your own life. Turns out it was for a promotion," I shook my head. "And then you threaten *me*? Uh-uh, Joel," I said with a mocking laugh. "Not tonight. Not fucking ever. Now, you walk away with nothing."

"Anna, please, I'm begging you. Let me take the cans."

"Time for you to go, Joel."

"No, no, no, wait," he stuttered. "Don't do this. Just let me take the cans. You're not going to do anything with them, anyway. Even if they get delivered, you won't get paid for them. Just let me take the cans, please, Anna." He pleaded with both hands up, glancing worriedly at the wagon.

My blood poached any sympathy out of my body. "I won't say it again, Joel: Get in your car and leave."

"Please, please, wait. I'll give you money now. I have money in my car."

"I don't want another dollar from you."

"What do you want then? Anything. Name it."

"I already did. I want you to leave me alone."

"Done. I will. I swear."

"And I want you to suffer for killing Benoit," I said icily.

"Aw, come on. I will suffer. You've already kicked enough coke over the bridge to make me suffer, and when I have to tell my boss that I need a few weeks to get the routes back, I'll be lucky to stay alive to do it. But if I show up without the cans, Anna, they'll kill me."

"Again, not my problem, Joel." I had had enough. I took a deep breath in as Joel scraped his panicked hands over his head, and then I stepped back and pushed the wagon with a nudge from my hip and it jolted toward the edge with a slow, heavy roll.

"No!" Joel screamed, as he lunged toward the wagon and draped himself over it just as the front wheels tipped off the bridge's edge.

The commotion made Polo thrust forward with a ferocious growl toward Joel, and in a flashing instant, Joel turned toward Polo, lost his footing, and propelled the wagon, with Joel on top of it, straight over the edge.

I gasped and pulled back Polo from jumping off after Joel. "Oh my God!" I covered my mouth with a violently shaking hand as a deafening crash broke beneath us in the fast-moving current.

"Oh my God," I cried again. I stood paralyzed, the numbness of shock taking over my body. Polo whinnied next to me.

I felt fast footsteps approaching, shaking the metal bridge grates beneath my feet, and I turned to see Marco running toward me. He grabbed me frantically and pulled me in tight, breathing heavily into my hair. I sobbed. "What just happened? Oh my God, what just happened, Marco?"

Marco turned off my recording devices. "We have to get out of here."

I nodded weakly. "Is he dead? Do we go down to see if he… survived?"

"There's no surviving that fall, Anna. You know that. Come on, we have to go now." He led me swiftly down the trail toward the woods where our rented car was parked. Polo followed excitedly behind.

The frigid air felt like a thermal blanket as it wrapped around our ice-cold bodies.

Chapter Forty-Four

When Marco and I returned that night, Eloise hugged us both with violent relief. She and Marco exchanged a look, and he nodded.

"So, you did it?" She asked him.

"Didn't have to," he said.

"He's still a liability?" She asked with concern.

"No, he's not. The job is done," he assured her.

I watched in confusion; they had always had a secret language I couldn't figure out. Turned out that Marco and Eloise had a backup plan: Marco had never intended to let Joel leave that night.

"You were going to kill Joel?" I asked Marco in disbelief.

"I couldn't let that scumbag, that scumbag who had taken advantage of my wife and put my family in danger, walk away. I just couldn't sleep at night knowing he was out there."

"I was going to kill him if he didn't," Eloise chimed in. "He killed my brother, and would have killed my sister," she said, gesturing toward me.

"I can't believe it. I almost made you both kill someone? I'm so sorry." I sunk down dejectedly on the couch and cried. The gravity of what did happen, and what could have happened, submerged me further into a hazy denial. Marco put a blanket around my shoulders. I looked up at him gratefully, though I didn't feel like I deserved kind gestures.

"You didn't almost 'make us' do anything. But it's not worth mentioning ever again. It's done," Marco said.

"Do you think they'll tie us to his death?" I asked meekly.

"How could they?" Marco answered. "He'll wash up downstream somewhere. By the time they find his car back at the bridge, there will be no tracks to find. It's starting to rain now, and it's supposed to rain all night. Any tracks will be washed away."

"But when it hits the news, my Mothers, the women, they'll recognize the bags. Someone might talk," I said with concern.

"You're going to have to get to them first," Eloise said. "Remember, these women trust you, Anna. And although they might not have known there was cocaine in the bags, they knew something was fishy. They're not looking to get themselves in trouble. Can you imagine the cops saying to any of them, 'It's okay that you carried these bags of unknown content for a year without asking. Thanks for telling us now?'" Eloise scoffed incredulously.

I nodded. "You're right. I have to tell them in the morning that the operation is dead." My stomach turned when I said the word dead, thinking of Joel lunging over the bridge and the thud that followed. Repulsion throbbed through me.

"Then, you need to get out of town for a few days," Marco said. "Go to Utah with the kids."

"I'm not going to leave right now. Not without you," I said incredulously.

"No, things need to look normal, Anna. I'll go to work, El will run the shop. Just until things clear."

I acquiesced. "Okay. After I talk to the Mothers tomorrow, I'll leave for a few days."

We sat in silence, thoughts and fears racing through our heads.

"I think I'm gonna go home," Eloise said. "And I'm going to sleep until June."

I smiled weakly. "Love you, El."

She hugged us and left briskly, as if staying was too much to handle, too much to process. After she left, I looked at Marco. "I'm so sorry, Marco."

"No need for that now, babe. I know you're sorry, but you don't have to feel so responsible."

"I do. I was so mad at you for leaving me in the dark when things got bad at the shop, then I went and left you in the dark about this."

"I guess we're even, then?" he shrugged.

"Let's promise to never do that again—leave each other out of our problems. Us First. Always. No matter how bad it is," I begged.

He set his glass down and pulled me in tight. "Us First."

"Marco?" I asked.

"Yeah, honey?"

"I want a crowded bed tonight; I need it. I need to feel crowded."

"Me too."

We crept upstairs and plucked each child from his bed, then laid them gently into ours. Marco and I crawled in, sandwiching their sleepy little bodies, while Polo slept deeply on the floor beside us, his heavy breaths a reminder of how hard he had worked tonight.

I reached my hand over our three kids, their sighs creating the sweetest lullaby, and touched the tips of Marco's fingers. He reciprocated and clenched my fingertips, rubbing my thumb with his. I wished we could stay in this bed forever, the kids sleeping between us, our fingers interlocked. It felt so safe here.

A tear filled with sadness and joy, fear and contentment, chilled but warm, fell sideways over the bridge of my nose to meet the tear in the other eye, and they dripped in tandem onto the pillow.

I went to work the next day as automatically as a car shifts gears. I was numb with fear, but I knew that I had to take care of some business before leaving for Utah.

My Mothers would be picking up their bags soon, though no bags would be awaiting them. I had texted each of them:

Change in plans.

Meet me at the playground at our normal time but tell your friends that today's playdate is cancelled.

Lynn was the first to arrive. I met her out back and motioned for her to come in for coffee.

"No bags?" she asked.

I shook my head. "Not today. Come in."

She was confused, but followed me in through the side door where I had an Americano and a French press cup of coffee waiting on the counter.

"Biscotti?" I asked with a tired smile.

"Sure. What's going on, Anna?"

I inhaled, then exhaled. "It's over, Lynn. The job is over. There will be no more bags."

She stayed quiet, sipping her Americano, then asked, "Why not?"

"Because I can't get any more bags," I answered. I didn't elaborate on why I couldn't get them anymore. That the supply and the supplier were floating in a river, literally.

She nodded thoughtfully, still confused.

"But, also, because it's just time," I said. "This was never meant to be a forever job. It was meant to serve a purpose, to get us both a little bit of money for our families, and I think we've both made enough by now." I had made $5.2 million, which meant each of my mothers had made just over $500,000 each.

She smiled. "Yeah, we've made a lot of money."

We sat in silence for a moment before Lynn continued. "I have to admit, even though I hate to see it end, I tend to agree. It's time to stop. I'm ready for a vacation," she laughed. "Although, I have to tell you, some of my Moms are going to be pretty disappointed. This money has really changed their lives."

I shrugged.

"No, really, Anna, I don't think you understand how much this money has meant to some of the women. You only know how much you've helped me. But that's not all."

Lynn still thought she was the only Mother I dealt with; they all thought that.

"One of my Moms, Claire, rode the train with me in the mornings," she said. "We had gotten close over the years, as will happen when riding the train with someone." I smiled; I had married the man I became close to on a train.

"She's a single mom. Her husband died."

"Ah," I grimaced.

"Yeah. She was gone from the train for a week or so, and when she came back, her husband had passed away. He died in a car accident."

"Oh my God. That's awful."

"It is awful, but even more awful is that she was back to work a week later because she was broke. No life insurance, no savings, and now a funeral to pay for. That's when I asked her if she'd be interested in carrying some bags. I knew she needed the money."

I nodded.

"So, she paid for the funeral. But that's not all. She has two boys, one was supposed to go to college, but figured he couldn't go after his dad died. Lo and behold, he still went to college. Because of the bags. And the bags are because of you."

I felt touched, but not proud. Yes, I had helped these women with an opportunity to make money that impacted their lives dramatically. But I also had put these women in danger, and I wondered if they even knew it.

"It's not what you might think, Lynn," I said.

"Yes, it is," she said matter-of-factly.

"No, it's not. I'm no hero. If you knew everything, you might come to think a lot less of me," I said.

She shook her head. "You think we didn't know what was in those bags, Anna?"

I looked at her, stupefied.

"Come on. We didn't know for certain because those cans were sealed up nice and pretty, but we knew we weren't taking bags of baby formula from place to place. You'd have to be a fucking idiot to think that," she laughed. I always did like Lynn.

"You opened the bag," I choked in surprise.

"Of course I did. We probably all did. But it didn't matter because we all had bigger problems than what was in a goddamned bag, Anna. We had families to feed, houses to save, kids to put through college…. Hell, I even have one Mom who went to college herself! Finished her degree all these years later. She was so proud."

A tear streaked down my face.

"There are a lot of ways to help people, Anna. Not all of them are glorious or things you'd brag about. But I truly believe you helped us because you wanted to. If I had to guess, you didn't use much of the money you made on you. I never saw you in here with new clothes or shoes."

I shook my head. "No. I only used it once for me," I agreed, thinking about the St. Kitts trip with Marco.

"See?"

"Listen, Lynn, you might see some stuff in the paper or on the news. I need you to keep your composure, and tell your Moms the same thing."

She nodded.

"I don't know why I'm telling you this, but just know that I never planned on this job ending this way," I said resignedly.

"There's never a good way to quit a job, Anna. Everything will be okay. It has been great working with you." She got up to leave. "See you around?"

"You're still going to come in for coffee, aren't you? Maybe we can find another business to do together," I winked.

"No doubt," she winked back and walked out, taking with her just a little bit of the guilt that had squeezed my chest the past year.

The conversations with the other Mothers went similarly, except for my conversation with Shelly. Shelly always was my most lucrative Mother. By running more bags than any other Mother, Shelly had made closer to $700,000, and she loved every dollar of it.

"Why?" she asked, concerned. "We were just getting started."

"Honestly, Shell, we had gone further than I originally planned. It never was meant to be a long-term job. It's time to end it."

She nodded with a sigh. "Alright. But if you ever need anyone for another job, of *any kind,*" she emphasized, "call me. I'll work with you every day of the week and twice on Saturday," she said.

"I'll keep that in mind, Shelly. Stay well."

And in one single morning, an operation that employed 110 women – 111 if you included me – and that had collectively made more than $10 million in one year, was finally bagged.

Chapter Forty-Five

I t had been over two years since I had seen my parents, and even longer since I had seen the red rock mountains of St. George, Utah.

I winced inside with heartache when I saw my father and hugged him as tightly as I dared. "Hi, Dad," I said sweetly. He was thin and frail; his muscles had deteriorated in his wheelchair, but he grinned and put his arms around me with vigor. Then, he reached out to the kids.

"There are my favorite grandkids!" He said that to all of his grandkids, I laughed. At least his spirit was well.

My mother greeted us with an earnest hug. For once, I felt as tired as my mother looked, and it made me smile with sympathy for her; sympathy I had lacked until now. Sympathy I couldn't have had until I was a mother who had to make sacrifices I never imagined.

"I have some cookies inside." She knelt down to the kids. She rose. "Hi, honey," she smiled at me and rubbed my arm.

"Hi, mom," I said. Her voice felt like a warm blanket.

I had taken a flight to Utah the day after I met with the Mothers. Before leaving that morning, Marco walked in, flustered. "The paper," he said out of breath.

I was lining up our suitcases to load in the car. "What?"

"The front page of the paper," he said, passing it to me.

On the front page was a picture of washed up cans of baby formula floating on the pebbly shore of the Delaware River. My heart sunk through the floor.

"Oh my God," I panted.

"Read the article," Marco said.

The headline read: "Drug Deal Goes *Splash*! Man's Body Washes Ashore with $4M of Cocaine."

The article went on to explain how Joel's body was found, along with cans of baby formula that upon opening, each contained a kilo of cocaine. The victim's car was found near a bridge six miles upstream. It appeared the victim fell over the bridge as there were broken wooden railings, but it was unclear as to whether the victim jumped willingly or if there was foul play. Police could not comment, but said that it appeared to be a drug deal gone bad. The police had no leads and were awaiting an autopsy report of the victim's body.

Marco and I looked at each other with dread. "Now, what?" I asked.

"Now, we wait."

I nodded and loaded the kids into the car. A cloud of dread and fear followed me 2,000 miles across the country. I struggled to stay present with the kids, nodding absently as they broke all rules about how much candy to eat or soda to drink. "Whatever you want," I repeated. I couldn't stop thinking about the newspaper article, and trembled as I mentally reviewed ways the police could connect Joel's death to me. Marco and I had talked endlessly about potential links or holes that might lead the police back to me. In the end, we kept coming up with a fair conclusion that the police wouldn't find anything: We just had to stay quiet and let the tide roll away.

Now I was in Utah, and though I didn't want to leave Marco, it felt good to be back in my hometown, and even better to be back in my home.

I sat next to my mom on the porch swing. Though it was cold in Doylestown, it was still a very warm day in my desert hometown. I looked out at the layers of reds and pinks that made up the landscape here for miles, their bright contrast against the cloudless sky. A side-blotched lizard scattered quickly across the patio, then darted into brush.

"Mom?" I looked at her reverently. She seemed so peaceful sitting there with her rheumatic hands crossed. I realized I had never heard my mom complain about her snarled knuckles.

"Mmm-hmm?" she replied pleasantly.

"I'm so sorry," I said, tears filling my eyes.

She kept rocking. "Why on earth are you sorry, honey?"

"Because," I choked on a sob. "Because I didn't know how hard it was." I started crying.

My mom scooted over to me and put her arm around my shoulder. "Oh, honey, don't cry. It's okay. What's really wrong, sweetheart?"

I put my head on her shoulder, an unnatural thing for me to do; today it was exactly what I needed. "No, I didn't know; I didn't realize," I sobbed.

"Realize what, baby?" She was concerned: The last time I cried to my mother, my age still had a single digit.

"I didn't understand how hard it was to be a mom. I didn't understand the sacrifices you'd make as a mother; the things you'd do for your family. I resented watching you work all those jobs, coming home tired all the time. But I just didn't know." My voice cracked between sobs. "I just didn't know because I wasn't a mom."

"Ah, it's alright honey. You couldn't have known. You can't know until you're a mother how strong you can be," she said softly. "Motherhood changes a woman. You do things as a mother that you didn't think you could ever do."

If only she knew. I desperately wanted to tell my mom everything, but I couldn't. I never could burden her with the weight of knowing what I had done.

"I know that now, Mom," I said sincerely. "I now know how hard it is, and what you'll do to protect your family."

She choked a tearful inhale.

"I can see how strong you truly are, Mom. And you're much stronger than I am. After Dad's accident, you worked every day, tirelessly, without complaint. I don't know how you did it; I really don't. But I want you to know that I see you now. I see you for who you are; for the strong woman you are. And I thank you for being so strong."

Her shoulders shook and we sat in silence. It was as if two planets circling the same sun finally harmonized in orbit.

"I don't know what problems you've been dealing with lately, but I do know that you will get through them," she said resolutely. "Since the day you were born, I always knew you were different. You've always thought differently, acted differently. You're unique, Anna. You can do things other people can't do. So, whatever problem you're having, it'll be okay. It always has been okay for you. You always find a way through your problems, and if you can't go through it, you go around it, or under it. But you don't get stuck behind it, that's for sure. Not ever. Not since the day you were born."

"I hope so, Mom. I'm afraid for the first time in my life that I've screwed up in a big way," I whimpered.

"Nah, you just have to find a way through it," she said.

I sat up and sniffled, wiped my eyes with my sleeve. "Thanks, Mom. I love you."

"I love you, too." She swiped her fingers under her eyes.

"Hey," I sniffled. "Your birthday is coming up?"

She smiled. "Yes."

"I have a gift for you." I handed her an envelope.

She looked at me confused. "You didn't have to buy me anything, honey. Oh, geez." She opened the envelope and pulled out the paper inside, unfolding it carefully. She squinted to see the words, then looked up, surprised.

I nodded, tears restricting my words.

"You bought my house?" she choked.

"Yes. I bought your house for you. It's paid off." My parents had remortgaged it twice since Dad's accident. Though their house didn't cost much, they still couldn't have paid it off in their lifetimes.

"Oh Anna! Oh my gosh."

"The house is yours, forever. The insurance is paid for, too. And I have a contractor coming tomorrow to do some repairs on the house, on everything. You can redo anything you'd like. He'll send me the bills."

"What?!" she shrieked between tears. "Are you serious? But how?"

I smiled. "By finding a way through, I guess."

She shook her head, staring at the title to the house. "I can't believe it. Thank you, Anna."

Though I still couldn't sleep at night for worry about my fate and the fate of my family, I hoped that at least my mother would sleep better at night knowing that the house was theirs, no one could take that from them. It felt good to be able to give her that sense of security, and it made me think of all the other women who might have slept better at night because of the money they made from my operation.

As Lynn said, there were a lot of ways to help people, and not all of them were ways to brag about. But in the end, I hoped this operation made more of a positive impact than a negative one.

Now, I needed to focus on a way to get over, around, and through this operation's closure so that maybe I could get some sleep, too.

Chapter Forty-Six

T he next 10 days played out in slow motion, every hour longer than the last.

Marco and I spoke several times a day. He said everything was quiet and to sit tight until further news appeared.

I took the kids to the spots I played at as a kid. We pranced in the creek where I used to catch pollywogs and crawdads; we hiked the hills and mountains that left our white sneakers stained red; we lay on blankets at night, gazing at a cloudless sky filled with millions of stars, stars that felt so close you could gather them into a glittery bouquet to keep forever.

I soaked up every second with my children, cherishing their innocence; and I vowed to protect them, no matter the cost. I would fight for them always, and if they ever found themselves in the same position I was in, I would protect them then, as well. Hell, I'd fight alongside them: That's what mothers do.

One morning, Marco called. "Honey, I think it's time for you to come home."

I exhaled relief. "Really? You sure?"

"Yeah, come home. There's a flight that leaves in the morning."

"How do you know? How do you know that it's the right time to come home?"

"I just know. Come home. I miss my family."

Chapter Forty-Seven

The kids and I flew back to Pennsylvania the next morning. Marco picked us up from the Philadelphia airport. The paper was sitting on the passenger seat when I got into the car.

"Page A8," Marco said.

I nodded, surprised that the news had been demoted from front page to Page A8.

The headline read: "River Victim With $4 Million In Cocaine Still Unidentified." The article cited that police could not find a single trace of the victim's existence: No fingerprints, no DNA, no valid car registration; nothing. Police couldn't even release a photo because the victim's face was so marred and bloated from the fall into the river. For now, they had no leads to follow, unless further evidence appeared. They asked the public to come forward if it had any information that would help with the investigation.

Tears of relief filled my eyes. "It's over? You think that's it? You think no one will come forward?"

"Who would come forward? There's no one to provide further evidence," Marco glanced back at the kids, who were fighting over the lollipops he proffered when we landed. "We both know the women you worked with will not say anything, if they even noticed the article at all," he said in a quieter voice. "And your old contact's *friends*," he indicated, "are certainly not coming forward. Trust me, no one cares about a junkie."

I nodded.

"And the formula, or anything else they would have found at the river would have been carefully handled. There would not have been any fingerprints to find, nothing to trace back."

I nodded again. We had used gloves and wiped everything carefully before hauling those cans of baby formula to the bridge, knowing that some of the product would end up in the river. I had collected all the bags and phones from the Mothers and Moms, respectively; and Marco had disposed of them, burned them, probably. The garage was swept clean, and Marco and Eloise had spent the last 10 days filling it with true storage items. Turns out, we actually did need the space.

It seemed as though it really might be over.

I leaned my head back on the seat and looked out the window; tears stung my eyes. Marco squeezed my hand.

That night, Eloise and Jen came over. We ordered pizza and played board games, then we tucked the kids into bed. Marco and I went to sleep, tangled together and bound by a deeper love than ever.

And for the first time in more than a year, I slept.

Epilogue: One Year Later

I sat at my desk in my new office, two doors down from Biscotti, as I consulted with a young woman applying for a grant to enroll at Delaware Valley Community College.

Georgia signed her name at the bottom of the application, then looked up with a hopeful smile, her teeth browned from years of Meth use. "I can't believe I might be going to college," she beamed.

I gathered her paperwork and placed it in a folder. "I'm really happy for you. It will take a couple of weeks to hear back from the college and arrange for the funds, but you should be enrolled by the next semester."

She put her hand to her chest and giggled. "I don't know even what I'm gonna be yet. Do you think that matters?"

"Nah. You have some basic courses to take before you have to figure that out. But you'll know pretty quickly, I think. And the school will help you."

"Thank you, Anna. Thank you so much. I never dreamed of going to college. Not after everything I've done." She was referring to the years of drug use and prostitution before rehabilitating in a women's prison, hoping to build a better life for herself after release.

"You're fulfilling my dream as much as I'm fulfilling yours," I said sincerely. "I love helping women, especially deserving women." *This time, I was doing it legally,* I reflected.

"I guess I'll wait to hear back from you!" she said, with an excited slap on her knees.

I followed her to the door and extended my hand. Georgia inhaled proudly as she shook it, then left with an extra step in her stride. I swelled with hope for her.

The Massenet Foundation opened its doors six months ago with an anonymous donation of $8 million, funded from Switzerland and St. Kitts bank accounts. The nonprofit foundation granted scholarships to women recovering from drug use. It also helped with expenses that kept the women from going back to drugs: Child care, medical costs, housing, food—basically, anything that slipped through the government funding's cracks. Sadly, that was plentiful.

In the six short months the foundation was established, it had granted more than 20 scholarships and promoted placement of another 23 women into steady employment. Marco quit working with Gary and ran the donation campaigns while Eloise managed Biscotti.

"Mommy!" The door rung open. This door had a Liberty Bell hanging from its knob.

"Hi!" I gleamed, as Marco and the kids lopped in, Lily running to sit on my lap. Marco leaned over and placed a tender kiss on my head.

"Mom, you ready?" asked Nathan.

"Yeah, Mommy. Let's go!" Lucas begged.

I laughed. "Yes, I'm ready."

They all cheered.

"Let's go to the playground."

Acknowledgements

I want to start by thanking first and foremost, and forever, my husband, Rocco. Without your support, this book would have been much harder to write, this life would be much harder to live, and my heart would be much harder in general. I love you the most.

My children – Mason, Rose, and Luca – were my biggest cheerleaders while writing my first novel. Thank you for reminding me every day just how awesome being a mom is and for teaching me what unconditional love means.

To my editor, Lisa Horst, who I am proud to call a dear friend first, and a colleague second. Thank you for soaring my words to new heights, all the while telling me you believe in me. I needed that. Thank you with all my heart.

To my mom, Bonnie, who not only read every draft but sent many encouraging texts and phone calls and told me I had written the best book in the world. You said what a mother should say about my first novel, and I love you and everything you represent.

I want to thank each person who suffered through the long, unedited first draft of my book and offered sound feedback and praise. You know who you are, and you're fantastic.

Thank you to all my friends, my "girls," for the constant encouragement with this book (and with life). It took over two decades to realize how much I needed girlfriends, and geez, I'm glad I figured that one out. Love you all dearly.

And finally, thank you to every woman I've met for inspiring, intriguing, and sometimes downright shocking me with your stories, examples, and strength. I feel fortunate when you confide in me and share your experiences, which sometimes make it into my books, but always make it into my heart. I see you; I see how strong you are. You keep going, girl.

About the Author

Michelle Lee lives in Bucks County, PA with her husband, three kids, two dogs, and fifteen chickens.

She finds that most people have a story to tell if you're interesting enough for them to share it with, patient enough to listen, and humble enough not to judge it.

The Playground is Michelle Lee's debut novel and the first in the *Secret Lives of Moms* series.

Be on the lookout for the second novel in the *Secret Lives of Moms* series, *The Clinic*.